'It's strange; this is a ha

'Ravenscar?'

'Yes, and Hawkshead itself. People seem, well, suspicious!' Ellie seemed surprised by her choice of words.

Laura laughed. 'I know what you mean.' Had she not been brought up in Yorkshire before she went away to train and then practise in London, she would have seen some truth in the old stereotype that harsh country ways breed a peculiar mix of thrift, taciturnity and quarrelsomeness amongst members of the old farming communities. 'Don't worry, I still have patients who refuse to accept female doctors. I was considered an oddity. A year and a bit later, they're just getting used to me.'

She nodded. 'Why did you come here?' Laura's answer seemed important.

'Yes, why?' The big question. Why Ravensdale rather than Camden?

Looking out at the tarn, seeing how the wind had slanted the trees, noticing the wide open horizon, she found the answer.

'For the peace and quiet.'

Kate Fielding was born in Yorkshire and read English at University. She has published crime fiction, family sagas and had stories published in magazines such as *Bella*, *Woman & Home* and *Cosmopolitan*, as well as writing books for young adults. *A Winter in Ravensdale* is her second *Ravensdale* novel. Kate Fielding lives in Ilkley with her two daughters.

*By the same author*

Ravensdale

# A WINTER IN RAVENSDALE

*Kate Fielding*

ORION

An Orion Paperback
First published in Great Britain by Orion in 1997
as *A Secret Place*
This paperback edition published in 1998 by
Orion Books Ltd,
Orion House, 5 Upper St Martin's Lane,
London WC2H 9EA

A CIP catalogue record for this book
is available from the British Library.

Printed and bound in Great Britain by
Clays Ltd, St Ives plc

*For Mary and Gill*

# CHAPTER ONE

Laura Grant woke to the pure white beauty of Ravensdale in winter. The wind had carved the overnight snow into drifts like cresting waves. Sunlight threw one side of the valley into sparkling, mysterious mounds, criss-crossed by half-submerged walls, the other into deep shadow. Even the river was thinly iced over, and the tracery in the windows of the ruined abbey opposite showed like old lace against the morning sky.

Not that she had long to let the sight sink in. The phone rang. At this time, just after first light on a Thursday in mid-January, it was bound to be a patient needing a home visit. Suddenly the snow seemed less impressive, more of an obstacle. How would the roads be, she wondered, as she hurried to pick up the receiver.

'Dr Grant? Jim Blackwood here from Ravenscar Hall. Sorry to bother you.'

She recognised the businesslike tone; responded in kind. 'That's OK. How can I help?' Downstairs in the kitchen, flicking on the kettle as she wedged the phone under her chin, she talked and listened. Once more she glanced out at the white world. Ravenscar, the great limestone escarpment, rose unblemished, its skyline sharp as a blade's edge, tinged with pink.

'Nothing too serious. One of our orienteers managed to get himself lost. He fell and sprained his ankle.'

'Last night?' Laura made herself coffee. Though Jim gave the impression that he had everything under control, the incident sounded serious enough to warrant a call. The visitors to his outdoor pursuits centre at Ravenscar Hall were all youngsters from Yorkshire schools, sent there on residential courses. Losing a pupil in rugged country during a snowstorm, in the dark, all alone, could create the sort of publicity that the new centre could well do without. 'I'll be up as soon as I can.'

'Bring your shovel.'

'Is the road that bad?'

'It depends. What are you driving?'

She described the sturdy, off-road type of vehicle that she'd chosen to invest in before the winter had taken hold. Here in the dale, it was a necessity.

'You'll be OK in that. I'll send Paul out with the snow plough. He'll meet you half way.'

Forewarned, she forearmed herself with shovel, heavy boots, jacket and thick gloves. She rang the surgery and left a message that she would miss the eight hundred; Gerald Scott's early morning meeting before the routine business of the day began. She said she hoped to make it back before surgery.

Setting out down the lane towards Hawkshead village, Laura was still new enough to the area – this was only her second winter here – to pride herself on being intrepid. In places, the snow had drifted to wall height on either side of the narrow road, blown by arctic winds and still lifting in powdery white flurries. The scale and force of the natural phenomenon struck her after a decade of sheltered city living. In London, two inches of snow snarled up traffic and frustrated the commuter; here she was coping with two feet or more, and a transformed landscape.

The chugging approach of Dick Metcalfe's battered, open-topped Land Rover put her in her place, however. Well into his seventies, still running his farm on Hawk Fell single-handed, and now out taking feed to his needy flock of matted, stoical Swaledales, the old farmer cast a baleful eye as she struggled out of the valley towards Ravenscar. He had no need to say it; he reckoned nowt to her foreign car. He pulled in to watch as she skidded and ground to a halt.

Laura jumped down to survey her predicament. Despite traction from all four wheels, her back end had skewed sideways into a hidden ditch. She was a mile or so out of town, but still a further mile from the Hall at the top of the fell. 'What's the road like up ahead?' she asked Dick, taking her shovel from the back.

'Road? Nay, road's right enough.' He leaned out to criticise her digging technique, giving her to understand that this snowfall was nothing compared to the winter of '79, let alone those of the forties and fifties, when a blanket of snow settled for months, from November through till March. 'In those days it came and kept on coming, a real lap-up. Anyhow, where are you headed?'

'Ravenscar Hall.' She dug and grew hot beneath her jacket, scarf and hat. Then she flung the shovel into the car and jumped back in. It was a point of honour to get out by herself. Not that Dick was offering to help. She felt the weight of his prejudices, carefully revved the engine, selected her gear. To her relief, she eased forward out of the ditch.

'Hmm,' Dick grunted. 'That's another half-baked idea if you ask me.' He offered no comment on her success.

'What is?' Laura noticed that he wasn't wearing a scarf to protect his wheezy chest; only his regulation cap, moulded to the shape of his head, an open-necked shirt and an out-at-elbow jacket.

'That outdoor adventure place, or what have you.'

3

'Not your cup of tea?' She edged past him, wing-mirrors touching.

'Nay, I give it six months,' he chuntered. A pregnant ewe in the back of his Land Rover clattered her hooves and reared up. 'If that. Daft as brushes, they are.'

Concentrating on the road once more, Laura edged up the hill. She was glad to see the Hall's yellow tractor, complete with snow plough, crawling towards her. Soon they would meet and her path to the tarn would be relatively clear. The plough heaved banks of snow into rough piles, leaving a smooth, packed surface to drive over. Within fifteen minutes she should reach her destination.

Paul Miller greeted her from his tractor cab. He was one of the partners at Ravenscar, along with Jim and Gabriella Blackwood, responsible for the 'half-baked' scheme to open up the old hall as a going concern. Now he backed into a gateway and swung the great metal plough clear of the track to let her through.

'Morning.' Laura manoeuvred past. 'How's the patient?'

'Good.' He jumped down and ran to accept her offer of a lift back to the Hall.

'You mean you got me here under false pretences?' A good-looking New Zealander, Paul was a born optimist, a team player, a man of action and few words. This was how he struck Laura, with his stocky physique, his deep, emphatic voice. Life meant running with the ball, expecting a tackle, going down and rolling out of trouble. To him, the spectacular snowfall was a challenge to be met head on.

'No, the kid's crook all right. It's his leg. We had to bring you in to be on the safe side.'

'I was joking. Will you have to send him home?'

Paul shrugged and gazed out across the icy tarn as they drew near the house. 'We leave that to the teacher in charge.'

4

'Who found him?' She braked in the yard, then reached for her bag.

'I did. He'd gone off-course and lost the others. But he did the right thing, took shelter in the trees by the tarn. He was late back, so I went out after him, no problem.'

Laura paused to glance up at the stark outline of Ravenscar Hall. The L-shaped building still kept the feel of its church ancestry. Once part of the vast Hawkshead estate, taken over from the monks of Ravensdale Abbey during the dissolution of the monasteries, in the eighteenth century it had fallen into the hands of a Quaker sect. It must have suited them, being plainly built with narrow windows and tall chimneys.

Its setting on the exposed moortop between Ravensdale and Swiredale demanded strength to withstand relentless winds, though there was some shelter in one direction from the scree slope to the north. In summer its view over the peaty, brackish lake across the limestone pavement on to Black Gill brought many visitors to soak up its isolated beauty. Today, in the strangely altered snowscape, the house seemed inhospitable, with its bricked-in windows, casualties of an ancient government tax, its heavy closed doors and low, snow-laden roof.

Inside, however, the stern impression was reversed. Recent renovation meant light, bright rooms with central heating, a modern kitchen to cater for groups of forty, and upstairs a series of small dormitories, six beds to a room, new bathrooms, the buzz of teenagers getting ready for another day of communal living.

Breakfast TV, loud music, glimpses of bright T-shirts, the hiss of showers took Laura back to her own school trips. Now, though, she sympathised more with the worried teacher who came down the corridor to meet her than with the raucous competition to be first, last, quickest, slowest in whatever pre-breakfast activity was demanded of the young visitors.

'I must be getting old,' she said to the teacher, following her to a room at the end of the corridor.

The woman showed her in and introduced her. 'Sam, this is Dr Grant. She wants to check the damage.'

The door closed and Laura rolled back the bedcover to manipulate the injured leg, check reflexes and look for signs of swelling in the ankle joint. 'That seems fine,' she reassured the embarrassed boy. 'Any other problems?'

'Stiff fingers and toes,' he admitted.

'Still?' She tested for loss of sensation.

'A bit.'

'You didn't black out?'

He shook his head. 'I told myself to stay awake.'

'Good. Well, I'm not worried about hypothermia. Your temperature would have had to drop well below ninety-six degrees for there to be a real problem. And you were well wrapped up?' Laura understood that Sam had been rightly scared, but that Paul Miller's prompt action had saved the day.

'I got straight inside my bivvy bag after I fell. I decided to stay put. And I had an emergency flare so I set that off and just waited.'

Laura stood back from the bed. 'You'll live. No frostbite, no broken bones. The sprained ankle needs a rest, that's all. You won't be charging across the moor for the rest of your stay.'

He jerked his head in reluctant agreement.

'You were lucky,' she reminded him. 'Last night was the coldest on record for five years.' She reached the door, turned to see him crestfallen. 'And pretty sensible too. You didn't panic. That took some nerve.'

'Tell that to the others.' He glanced sideways from under flopping dark brown hair. 'I'm the nerd who got lost in the blizzard, remember.'

Laura smiled and left him to his crisis of confidence. 'No

long-term effects,' she promised the teacher, then went downstairs to look for Paul or Jim. Instead, she found Jim's wife, Gabriella, waiting for her.

'I hear he's OK?' She came forward, looking scarcely older than the teenagers she supervised; a slight, eager figure with a pretty face and light brown hair swept back. 'Thanks for coming anyway.'

'That's fine.' Kids were going noisily about breakfast, dressed in big jumpers and trousers. There was a youth hostel style of self-service, followed by chores, directed in a laid-back fashion by Paul. 'This looks great.'

'I don't know. It's a bit chaotic.'

'Well, chaos makes them feel that it's not like school. More independence.'

'In theory. Coming here is supposed to encourage self-sufficiency.' Gabriella walked Laura to the door.

Laura appreciated the Blackwoods' and Paul Miller's level-headed response to a potentially serious situation. 'There won't be any repercussions for you after last night?'

'Let's hope not.' She shrugged. 'Jim's on the phone to the parents right now.'

'I envy you moving in here. It's so nice and peaceful.' Laura drew comparisons between Gabriella Blackwood's situation and her own. They were of a similar age, both new to the area, and probably seeking similar respite from the stresses of city life. And she liked her modest air and practicality. She put down her youthful appearance to the fact that she was an ex-athlete; a runner still occasionally to be seen training on Hawk Fell.

Gabriella tilted her head sideways. Inside the house doors banged, voices laughed, crockery and cutlery rattled into metal sinks. 'Call this peaceful?'

'At least you brought the place back to life.'

'Thanks. Drop in for a coffee some time.'

'I'd love to.' A new friendship was an appealing prospect. Laura braced herself for the drive and slide across the moor down into the village.

In Hawkshead she was, it had to be admitted, short of friends of her own age. She liked and admired the Dot Wilsons of the dale. Dot had been her landlady when she first arrived, before she moved into Abbey Grange. She was an astute, plain-speaking, rock-solid ally with a ferocious reputation as a cook, housekeeper and oral historian, but Dot belonged firmly to the old school. Gabriella, it seemed, could be more on Laura's own wavelength. Before too long, she would contact her and make a firm date.

'Two of your patients rang to cancel because of the weather.' Sheila Knox greeted Laura in Reception with the good news. 'The bad news is, we've had to arrange four more home visits already.'

She'd hardly set foot inside the modern, one-storey building by the river before her day ran out of control. Four more visits on top of the three she already knew she had to make, one as far out as Askby by the Lower Falls.

'And Matthew rang to say he's snowed in in York. He won't get back before lunch, so don't bother struggling over to his place as arranged.' Sheila lowered her voice to pass on the private message, as Laura kicked off her snowy boots and changed into indoor shoes in the small cloakroom behind the Reception area.

Laura hid her sinking feeling at the mention of Matthew being in York. This meant he must have dropped Sophie and Tim at his ex-wife's house and been stranded overnight. She tried not to imagine what this might have entailed.

'Did Gerald grumble about me missing the eight hundred?' She studied her list of appointments and smiled at the patients sitting quietly in the waiting area.

'He hummed and hahed, as per usual.'

'Did he twiddle his glasses?'

'Twice.'

Laura smiled. 'Nought out of ten, Dr Grant!' As senior partner, Gerald Scott placed a heavy emphasis on attendance at their daily case conference. So did Laura; the best communication about their patients was still face to face, in liaison with their third partner, Philip Maskell, and with Joy Hartley, the practice nurse. But she didn't go along with Gerald's autocratic style, whereby non-attendance met with a definite frown of disapproval and a coded system of tell-tale fiddles with his steel-rimmed glasses; the more he twiddled, the worse his temper. Now she crossed the waiting area and poked her head around his door before she went into her own room and began consultations. 'Sorry I couldn't make the meeting, Gerald. Did I miss anything important?'

He glanced over the top of his glasses at her. 'Laura? Oh yes, we got your message. Two referrals to Low Royds, one case of confirmed meningococcal meningitis; school informed.' His vagueness and off-hand manner had the intended effect of putting her in her place. 'What held you up?'

He knew very well, but she went through the rigmarole of telling him.

'Hmm. That's their third call-out in a week, isn't it?' Gerald indicated agreement with the Dick Metcalfe school of thought that the scheme to run Ravenscar in its present guise was a half-baked one that would make too many demands on their precious resources. 'Can't they get themselves down here to the health centre once in a while?'

'Not if there's a suspected fracture.'

'And was there a fracture?'

'No.' Laura withdrew before Gerald had the chance to jump in with anything else and retreated to her own room. One to one with patients, dealing with glandular fever and glaucoma,

9

abscesses and swollen adenoids, she recovered her equilibrium. There was satisfaction in making a correct diagnosis, in listening sympathetically and earning the respect of the wide variety of people who came through her door. Alert to unspoken signals, unearthing hidden symptoms, she would soon get things moving. After eighteen months in the far-flung practice, she'd had direct contact with most of the patients on her list and felt she was building a good rapport.

The last patient of the morning made his exit; a member of the Braithwaite clan from Swiredale, undeterred by deep drifts and biting winds. 'It's blowing a bit thin over the top,' he admitted, on hearing that Laura herself had already been up to Ravenscar. He conceded she must be a hardy type, despite her city past. 'And they've forecast worse to come.' He went off cheerfully with a prescription to ease his angina, predicting blizzards before the day was through.

'But there's not a cloud in sight.' Laura joined Philip for a coffee break.

'Was that Harry Braithwaite?' Philip caught sight of the sturdy back stooping into the old Rover car. 'He's famous for his forecasts up and down the dale.' He handed her a mug, keeping to neutral territory. He'd caught the edge of Gerald's criticism of Laura before Surgery.

'. . . This lot up at Ravenscar,' Gerald began as he too joined them for coffee. It was as if they'd never left off the subject. 'Are they properly trained and insured to run that sort of place?' He stirred his sugar with undue vigour. 'They're not just some cowboy outfit, are they?'

Philip sank into a chair and stretched his legs. 'Wasn't Jim Blackwood some sort of expedition leader before they came to Ravenscar?'

'He's a mountaineer,' Laura confirmed. 'One of the best in his day, apparently.'

'That doesn't mean he's qualified to organise dangerous

activities for youths unused to rushes of adrenaline brought about by unwonted physical exercise,' Gerald pointed out. 'Any fool can climb a mountain. It takes skill of a different order to plan it for others. And what about the other chap, the Australian?'

'Paul Miller. He's a New Zealander.'

'Some kind of rugby player, isn't he?'

'Ex-international. He's the one who went out and brought the boy back last night.' Laura defended him.

'Yes, but what are his qualifications?'

Philip drained his mug and stood up. 'I'm sure they're properly licensed, if that's what you're getting at. Personally, I hope they make a go of it.'

'They'll have us up and down there like yo-yos if we don't watch out,' Gerald muttered, shaking his head. 'Before long we'll find ourselves unwittingly involved in an unsavoury incident. Is it a mixed place; boys and girls?'

Philip laughed. 'Yes, shocking, isn't it?'

But Gerald refused to lighten up. 'Asking for trouble,' he insisted.

'Better than a massive stone quarry.' Laura knew that she was pushing her luck. Gerald had remained touchy about the failed plans to take rock from Ravenscar and it had caused difficulties between them during her first few months in the practice.

Philip sighed and left her to her fate.

Gerald watched him leave through narrowed eyes. 'That's funny; it's not like Philip to walk out on a lively debate.'

Laura took his mug and as a concession rinsed it through. 'Only this once,' she warned. 'You're wicked, Gerald. You know exactly what you're doing when you wind us up.'

In Reception, Sheila looked up from her correspondence and gave Laura a helpless shrug.

\*

11

That night, starlight reflected off the crisp white snow. No blizzard, Laura noted. It was scarcely dark when Matthew finally turned up at Abbey Grange after seven o'clock. She heard his car, resisted the urge to complain about his lateness and went to the door to greet him.

Weary, his face strained after the difficult journey through Wingate and Merton, then on deep into the dale, he put his arms around her.

She kissed him and drew him indoors, shutting out the unnaturally bright evening light. The house was warm, as plainly furnished as it had been when she took it over from Lilian Rigg, an ex-patient and one of her first friends in Ravensdale. Its white walls were alive with flickering shadows from the open fire.

Matthew sighed and dropped into a chair. 'Thanks, Laura.'

'For what?' She fixed him a drink and sat on the rug beside him.

'For not giving me a hard time.'

She'd schooled herself not to nag about the complex situation with Matthew's ex-wife and children. This was, however, the first time he'd stayed in York overnight. Noble restraint came with a high price-tag, she felt. A band of pain tightened around her forehead. 'How was the journey back?'

'A slow crawl all the way. The roads were clear by lunchtime, but nothing really got moving until much later.' He didn't want to talk about the weather. Instead, he rested his head back and closed his eyes. 'Sorry about lunch.'

'Don't be. I made sure to give Maisie a ring to see she had everything she needed.' Though no doubt stranded at Hawksworth Hall, Matthew's mother was not the sort to be worried by the snowfall.

'I know. I just stopped off at home. She's invited a couple of friends around for the evening, cosy as anything. She says this

12

snow reminds her of the good old New England winters. She's come over all nostalgic; out with the family album.'

Laura rested her arms across his lap. 'Do you want to talk?'

Matthew looked down at her, her face in shadow, firelight creating a haze of fine-spun, wavy hair down to her shoulders. 'Not now.' He bent to kiss her. 'Later.'

What was she to do with this flux of emotion between them? Where was the still, calm centre?

Sometimes she found it when she was out walking with him on Ravenscar, with not a soul around. Sometimes in bed, like that night, for a time after they'd made love and she lay beside him, staring out of the window at the stars.

But not in the fractured, stuttering interchange that came later, when he wanted, *needed* to talk through his problem with Abigail. It was after midnight when she felt him sit up in bed.

'Laura?'

'I'm awake.'

'She asked me to sleep with her.'

'Abigail? Did you?'

'No.'

'Did you want to?'

'No.'

Laura felt sick at heart. Abigail had left Matthew long before Laura came on the scene, and for a time had been dismissively scornful of their relationship. Then, when her own affair with David Worthing had come to an end, she'd turned her attention back to Matthew. Not in obvious ways at first, but she used their two children to tether him to her whims, complaining about lack of money, the lack of time that he was prepared to give them. Why did Laura always have to be around when they came to stay with him at Hawkshead? Didn't Sophie and Tim deserve some exclusive time? It was a deadly card to deal to someone as prone to guilt as Matthew.

'Abigail's in a state,' he began again.

'What do you want to do about it?' She knew she sounded detached and cool.

He swung his legs over the side of the bed. 'What I want doesn't seem important sometimes. It's the kids I'm worried about.'

'She's blackmailing you, Matthew. She's using them.' But Laura knew that pointing it out was a long way from him seeing it and sorting it out for himself. She felt a hollow helplessness as she saw him sitting hunched, gripping the edge of the mattress.

'You're sure you don't want to throw me out after what I just told you?'

She raised herself and put an arm around his shoulder. 'Listen, I'd much rather know what Abigail's up to. And you said you didn't want to take up her offer.' But Laura couldn't convey the black emptiness she faced as she pictured Abigail, small and determined, imposing a long history of shared commitment on Matthew's conscience. Laura had no illusions; his ex-wife wanted him back.

# CHAPTER TWO

For the first day, maybe two, the snow lay pure white. Whipped by the wind, it clung to black tree trunks and hung heavy on their branches, until sun melted the ice on the river and the boughs sloughed off their snow. It froze again at night into giant, jagged icicles hanging from outcrops, from the roofs of barns and houses. By day, the snow would lose its grip, slide and thud in avalanches on to recently cleared paths. By night, ice would take hold once more.

Philip and Juliet Maskell drove from their home at Bridge House into Hawkshead on the fourth morning of the freeze, noticing the marred beauty. Patches of earth had begun to show through on the sunnier slopes, as if the snow blanket grew threadbare. Sheep trailed narrow paths across fields to their mangers, while ploughs had cleared drifts from every lane and farm track, heaping up rough mountains which would linger, dirty and debris-laden, long after the thaw.

Philip sighed at the familiar rhythm. Days lengthened; but it would be the end of February before they felt the benefits of lighter evenings. He counted up. It would be his twenty-first spring working as a GP in Hawkshead, Laura's second, Gerald's thirtieth.

'Drop me here,' Juliet suggested as they drove through the main square. She pointed to the bus stop outside the Falcon, preferring while the snow lasted to use public transport to reach her job as a dental receptionist in Merton. She gave him a kiss on the cheek, reminded him to post a couple of letters, then got out of the car. She glanced up at the pub and turned back. 'When's Alison's baby due?' The landlord, Brian Lawson, and his wife expected it to be any day now. 'I must buy a card.'

Philip saw her off before he drove the final few hundred yards to the health centre, built on a flat stretch of land beyond the playing fields, backing on to Ravenscar. Was it his imagination, or was Juliet still finding it difficult to cope?

It had all started with his affair with Mary Mercer the previous summer; a one-off, mad, middle-aged lapse, he told himself. But Juliet had gone into herself, talked less, made fewer plans. He'd fancied that Christmas had brought about an improvement; having the three boys at home with their various girlfriends, living in a full house again. She'd made the holiday special as she always did, with that knack of making everyone feel welcome, and pulling out the stops over food and entertainment.

But afterwards, when Simon, Jim and Ian had gone back to jobs and university, she'd lapsed into that semi-detached manner of not asking him when he would be home in the evening, of failing to tell him about her own day. Often, she would drift off to bed without letting him know.

He accepted it. He deserved worse, if anything. The affair with Mary had come out of the blue, had flung him off a plateau of genial reliability into the dizzying depths of doubt and confusion, fuelled by desire. Mary, Mary; so unlike Juliet, almost young enough to be his daughter, deeply sexy, deeply dramatic. She had said from the start that it would never work out. She warned him not to get involved and had tried to protect herself from falling in love with him, had moved out of Bridge House where she'd arrived as a lodger, had done everything to discourage him.

16

But Mary had become his summer obsession, with her dark, painted eyes, her pale skin. She churned up his sleeping discontent, roused him from complacency. If he could love this other woman as he did, what then was his marriage worth? If he could lie and deceive in order to have Mary, ought he not to make a clean break with his old life, his preconceptions? These questions could have plagued him for months, for years even, if Mary hadn't put a sudden end to it by chucking her job in Hawkshead and going to work more than a hundred miles away. Now he never saw her, except in his mind's eye; disturbing sexual images of her, or tender memories of their time together.

And Juliet had made no fuss. She'd known all along, said she'd been waiting for him to tell her. He'd expected recrimination, a battle towards a new understanding. Instead, he experienced his wife's withdrawal. In the autumn they'd entered a sort of limbo from which they'd never emerged.

'Morning, Philip.' Sheila handed him his mail as he walked into Reception. He sifted through it: results of biopsies, an update on the meningitis situation throughout the county, assorted fliers from drugs companies. 'Gerald left a message; can you run the eight hundred for him? He's been called out to Ginnersby. Old Tom Sutcliffe.'

'His asthma?'

'No, he woke up this morning with a painful swollen leg. Gerald went straight off.'

'Hmm.' Laura joined them. 'Pity I don't have any glasses to twiddle.'

They went into a huddle in Philip's room, he, Laura and Joy Hartley, to discuss a referral for a case of worsening dementia in one of Laura's patients, and for Joy to check in with news from her ante-natal clinic of the previous day.

'I was a bit worried about Alison Lawson's blood pressure,'

17

she told them. 'No signs of foetal distress, but we're still waiting for the baby to turn himself round.'

'Breech presentation?' Philip checked the notes. Alison and Brian had waited a long time for this first baby. They'd been ready to embark on infertility treatment just before the pregnancy happened spontaneously. He'd kept a close eye on Alison throughout the past nine months, and was anxious lest anything go wrong now. 'What did you say to her?'

'I told her to take it easy.' Joy indicated that Alison wasn't likely to heed the advice. Running the Falcon was a hectic business, and Alison tended to push herself to the limit.

'Perhaps we should get her an ante-natal bed in Wingate?' The b.p. chart wasn't all that alarming, however; not high enough to indicate pre-eclampsia. He doubted that the hospital would free a bed for her on this basis. 'I think I'll call in later and suggest complete bed-rest.'

'How will Brian manage?' They were coming up to the weekend, the busiest time at the pub.

'He'll have to phone relief staff. Did she show signs of oedema?'

'In her ankles.' Joy nodded, then moved on. By eight-twenty they were ready to go their separate ways and meet their first patients of the morning.

Philip had Jim Blackwood at the top of his list, for a regular check on a diabetic condition that the owner of Ravenscar Hall was determined to keep under strict control. He admired the fact that Blackwood's diabetes hadn't held him back from leading the active life of mountaineer, expeditioner and now organiser of the centre. Visits to Philip were an essential monitoring exercise. He liked to keep his appointments early and short.

He came in now, exuding tough good health. Dressed in up-to-the-minute trekking gear – fleece jacket, running-trousers, high-quality boots – with his taut features and short grey hair, determination in the movement of every muscle, he looked distinctly out of place in a doctor's surgery, and he wasted no time. 'Can you give me something to clear up a couple of ulcers on my foot?' He took off his boot to display a common side-effect of the disease.

Philip looked, then wrote out a prescription. 'How are your hands and feet in this cold weather? Are they numb?'

Jim shook his head. 'And no disturbed vision either. I stick to my diet.'

'Eating little and often?'

'Yes. No faintness, no sweats.'

'It sounds as if you're doing pretty well.' Philip took out the blood pressure cuff and strapped it around his patient's muscular arm. 'No breathlessness?'

'No.'

'Sure?' The reading was high. Unlikely as it seemed from Jim's rugged lifestyle, there could be a future heart problem.

'Sure,' he insisted.

Philip put away the instrument. 'No point telling you not to overdo it, I suppose?'

'I'm not going to sit in an office all day, if that's what you mean.' He rolled down his sleeve. 'No, I'll keep on doing what I can, which is most things so long as I manage the damned condition properly.'

'Well, we may be able to take your hypodermic away from you before too long, and put you on sugar-reducing tablets instead.' Philip explained that some mature diabetics did begin to produce small amounts of their own insulin. Jim was forty-two; a candidate for this option.

'I've thought about it but I'm not sure it would give me the same freedom to lead a normal life. We're coming up to our first busy period at the Hall.' Jim was on his feet, ready to leave. 'And we're down one member of staff.'

Philip recalled that the Blackwoods had arrived at Ravenscar as part of a foursome; themselves, Paul Miller and his wife, Marianne. But Paul's wife hadn't stayed the course. In fact, she was gone by Christmas, back to Leeds. Rumour had it that she wasn't cut out for the outdoor life, nor the isolation.

'I'm glad business looks good,' Philip said.

'Well, it was a risk, but we knew that. Ravenscar's an ideal area for geological studies, and most schools have to send their kids on residentials as part of their geography courses. We combine that with outdoor pursuits. It seems to be paying off.' Jim was upbeat and determined as he headed for the door.

'I'm glad you're here.' Brian Lawson met Philip as he stepped inside the bar. 'Alison's not feeling too good. I made her go upstairs and put her feet up.'

Philip turned down his offer of a drink before he went up. The Falcon was his local, with its quirky display of old sporting paraphernalia; rowers' caps and blades, cricket bats, fishing-rods. Faded team photos lined the walls. 'That was going to be my advice too; bed-rest until the birth.' His interest in Alison's welfare was more than professional. He'd become good friends with her and Brian since they'd taken over the pub four years earlier.

'She won't like that.' Brian came out from behind the bar. 'There's nothing wrong, is there?'

When Philip went into the bedroom, he found Alison lying fully-clothed, her feet propped up on two pillows.

'Look at these,' she complained, pointing to her swollen ankles.

He pressed the swellings and watched the depressions made by his fingertips slowly fill up. He noticed her wince with pain. 'Have you been getting twinges?'

'Not really. Well, a few.' She wouldn't look him in the eye.

'Since when?'

'Since first thing this morning. I didn't want to say anything because I knew Brian would rush me off to hospital straight away.'

Philip turned his attention to his patient's abdomen. To his surprise, he found that the baby had turned and that its head was engaged. The cervix too was already partly dilated.

'Is this it?' Alison tried to sit up.

'It sure is. You've been in labour for a good few hours.'

He leaned over to listen to the baby's heart. As he feared, the baby, starved of oxygen, was giving an irregular heartbeat. 'We need to get you to hospital right away,' he said quictly. He glanced round to see Brian hovering by the door. 'We need an ambulance.'

The worried husband went off quickly to the phone.

'When we get you in we'll be able to monitor Junior's heartbeat. Don't worry, you'll be in good hands.'

'Will I need a caesarian section?' Alsion sounded frightened. She gave sharp gasp of pain.

'Let's hope not.' He waited for her to recover.

Brian soon reappeared with news of the ambulance. 'It has to drive over from Wingate. They'll be as quick as they can.' He sat by the bed and held his wife's hand.

'Awkward little sod, isn't he?' Alison tried to smile. 'I don't think this baby's going to wait for any ambulance.'

'What do we do?' Brian appealed to Philip.

'Sit tight. There's still time.' Philip kept his fingers crossed. It was rare these days for a GP to be involved in a delivery and a long time since he'd attended one as potentially complicated as this.

'I'm sorry. It's my fault. I kept putting off saying something!'

'How do you feel now?' Brian gripped Alison's hand more tightly as Philip moved in again to check the foetal heartbeat.

'Keep calm,' Brian pleaded.

21

The more he panicked, the steadier Alison became. 'Who's having this baby, you or me?' she reminded him.

Philip stooped to listen again. This time the heartbeat was stronger. 'OK, you're doing well now. And so is Junior.'

By the time the ambulance did arrive, blue light flashing, with all its paraphernalia, Philip was instructing her to push. Meanwhile, all the signs were that this was going to be a normal delivery after all.

He worked hard, encouraging Alison, then telling her to stop at the critical moment. At last the baby emerged. 'There. You've done it. You've got a girl.'

'A girl?' Brian looked at Alison as though Philip had said 'alien'.

The baby breathed after thirty seconds. He cut the cord, heard the lungs expand, and the first cry as he handed Alison her daughter.

Too late, the busy ambulance crew brought in resuscitation equipment while Philip watched the dark, bedraggled head of the baby girl against her mother's breast.

Brian cried, the baby bawled. When they weighed and tested her, they found the muscle tone was good and the scores high; no apparent damage had been done by her rushed passage into the world.

Celebrations in the Falcon were well underway before Philip left.

'News travels fast.' Brian glowed with pleasure from his station behind the bar. 'You'll help us to wet the baby's head, Philip?'

He relaxed into one of the best times a GP could have; an occasion that helped him realise what kept him in general practice year after year.

Brian re-told the story to anyone who would listen.

'How often do you get that sort of service on the NHS these days?' he crowed.

'Alison's the star of this show.' Philip was pleased nonetheless. It felt good to know that a mother and baby were upstairs doing well, instead of anxiously wired up to a monitor in a hospital ward. Alison's blood pressure had returned to normal straight after the birth, and he'd brought Joy over from the health centre to provide nursing care. Gerald and Laura had covered his afternoon appointments; now there was nothing to do but share in the general congratulations.

'Impatient little beggar couldn't wait,' Brian told Dot Wilson after he'd offered her a celebratory sherry. Dot was one of those people who made up the backbone of Hawkshead. He'd fixed up for her to put in some extra cleaning hours to help keep things straight in the upstairs rooms for as long as Alison was laid up after the birth. She'd been glad to accept.

Dot insisted on knowing every detail: baby's weight, hair and eye colour. 'I expect you wanted a boy to join your cricket team?'

He declared he was over the moon, didn't mind a bit. 'Anyhow, girls can play cricket, can't they?'

'Yes, and you'll have a bat in the poor little mite's hands before she can even walk, knowing you.' Dot didn't give way to sentimentality. As a grandma, she didn't believe in parents being over-ambitious for their offspring. 'What's she going to be called? Nothing too fancy, I hope.'

'Emma.'

This seemed to be within reasonable bounds. Dot nodded and drank up, spry as ever; her routine of setting out from Town Head each day to clean at Bridge House and keep an eye on community affairs uninterrupted by the severe weather. She simply put on her dead husband's thick socks and wellingtons, an extra cardigan underneath her coat, and waded out into the snowy streets.

She'd been passing through the village square when the ambulance arrived, on the scene at the Falcon when the baby's birth was announced. 'Here's wishing her health and happiness.' She put her glass on the bar, collected her shopping bag and went on her way.

Philip was leaving in her wake, saying his goodbyes and heading for the door, when he bumped into Abigail Drummond, Matthew Aire's ex-wife. She recognised him and hauled him back in for another drink.

'Or is your dinner already burned to a cinder?' She explained that she'd just dropped Sophie and Tim at their father's place for a long weekend.

'How's Juliet?' Abigail was good at the civilities, but she usually worked her way quickly on to more interesting territory. 'Did the boys come home for Christmas? I expect you were pleased. It was my second Christmas in York. I never thought I'd hear myself admitting this, but I did miss Hawkshead. I was nostalgic for the old carol service at St Michael's and the get-together at your place on Boxing Day.'

Philip nodded in the right places and let her run on. He found himself unexpectedly warming to the conversation. Abigail was an attractive, boyishly slim woman with short blonde hair. She ran her own successful conservatory business and had not taken the Aire name when she married Matthew. Though she must be in her late thirties, she looked younger and had a technique of drawing people into confidences in a flattering way. In fact, he hadn't seen her since the separation.

'Tell me, Philip, how do you think Matthew looks?'

'Fine, when I last saw him about a week ago.'

'He didn't look tired or stressed?'

'Not especially. Why?'

'Oh, I don't know. I find him so hard to talk to these days. He seems unhappy.' She paused. 'Not just about Sophie and

Tim. He's bound to miss them. But he's on edge and that's not like him.'

Philip looked steadily at her. 'How long have you known me, Abigail?'

'Eleven, twelve years. Oh God, is it really that long? It's OK, Philip, I didn't really expect you to spill the beans. You can't blame me for trying, though.' She glanced round the bar at the regulars, mixed with one or two strange faces. 'Who are they?'

'The new people from Ravenscar.' Gabriella Blackwood and Paul Miller sat down with another couple, presumably teachers in charge of a school party.

'Things are changing round here.' Abigail sounded surprised. Then she saw Dick Metcalfe arrive with Kit Braithwaite and a couple of other cronies. They tramped trodden snow into the carpet, wheezed and coughed. 'Then again . . .'

They finished their drinks, then parted with friendly smiles.

'Love to Juliet,' she reminded him. 'Tell her I'll pop in and see her some time.'

Juliet received the message impassively. She was glad, though, about the Lawsons' baby. 'They must be thrilled.' The evening meal was on the table, they sat and faced each other.

'What about you? How was your day?' The routine questions swathed whatever raw emotions still existed between them, burying them deeper from view. He expected the normal reply: 'The same as usual, no news.'

'I went to see Luke Altham at Bootham & Wood's.'

They were solicitors in Merton High Street, well known locally. In fact, Philip and Juliet had got to know Luke personally during the quarry debate. 'When?'

'Today, in my lunch hour.'

'What for?'

Juliet put down her knife and fork and looked straight at

him. 'I needed to find out what would happen if we were to separate.'

Still he couldn't make contact. 'Who's talking about separating?'

'I am. At least I think I am. I want to find out what happens to the house; who stays here and so on.'

'Just like that?' Fear darted through him, then a burst of anger.

'No, not just like that. It's taken me seven months to get as far as Luke's office.'

'Why? Why, in God's name, couldn't you talk to me about it?' He got up from the table and strode to the window.

'Because I would have weakened. I would have listened to you, Philip. You would have given me all the reasons why I should stay.'

He expelled air from his lungs like a boxer taking a body blow.

'And I know them inside-out. I should stay because of the children. I should stay because this is my home, because it wasn't me who had the affair.' She cast a hand this way and that. Her normally open expression was creased with pain.

'Because we've been together half a lifetime!' Philip couldn't stop himself from adding. They were middle-aged, they hadn't built alternatives into their vision of the future.

'I know that,' she said quietly.

'So, we have to talk about it. Let's try to work it out.' He couldn't believe that Juliet's visit to the solicitor was a final move. Perhaps it was a warning, meant to jolt him into action instead of treading carefully around her hurt feelings.

'You know how sorry I am. Even at the time I couldn't believe that I was doing it to you.' He moved towards her across the carpet they'd chosen together last autumn, within the four walls that had contained most of their married life.

She pushed him away. 'What am I supposed to do now? Be

26

charitable, accept your apology? Philip, for heaven's sake! I don't need your guilt. It weighs me down.'

'Right then, I'm not sorry!' He couldn't win, he knew. 'No, that's a lie. I hate what I did to you.'

At this twist into angry frustration, she rounded on him. 'You traded me in, like a lot of men your age. You turned me into a victim. I despise that.' She had been an independent woman. Staying with him since last summer had altered the balance. Now she was a wronged wife sticking by her man. She was shouting, hurling words across the room. 'I never thought it could happen to me!'

'Me neither. It wasn't meant to.'

'But it did. *You* did.' The anger dropped away. She covered her eyes with her hand. 'And I find I can't deal with it. Some days I think, yes I can. I can come to terms eventually with you loving someone else. Other women do. But I can't bear it. I won't.' She left the room dry-eyed, dissolving his world as she went.

# CHAPTER THREE

'I'm going to see Laura on my way to school.' Aimee Scott explained to her mother why she was leaving the house early and going into work with her father.

'Dr Grant,' Gerald insisted, waiting for the car windows to de-mist. 'If it's professional, it's Dr Grant.'

Janet Scott came out of the tall Edwardian house on to the drive.

'Don't worry, it's a regular appointment.' Aimee felt the cold wind slice through her black denim jacket. The weekend had brough fresh snowfall, but style could make no concession to climate. She persisted in wearing her skinny black sweater, her tight trousers and heavy boots, which, though chunky, were pathetically non-waterproof. She visited Laura's surgery once a month for treatment for her anorexia; a deal she'd made to get herself out of hospital after her accident the year before. Without counselling for her eating disorder, there would be no release from the Wingate Archipelago.

Anyway, Aimee found she could talk to Laura. It would have been pointless, in contrast, to try to explain to Philip Maskell, or anyone else who'd known her since she was born, why it was that controlling her weight was so crucial. He would have jumped to conclusions, stuck up for Gerald's role in the family's problems, judged her.

Her mother stood and watched her get into the car. 'Good luck.'

'It's not an exam.' Not yet. A-levels loomed, but didn't start until summer.

Janet pursed her lips. 'Do you want me to phone school to tell them you'll be late?'

'No. I won't miss any lessons. I've got private study first thing. Thanks.' She made herself meet her mother's gaze. Whenever she felt her fuss, Aimee's impulse was to snap back and hurt. She wanted to be left alone.

'Say hello to Laura from me.' The pain came through in small frown lines between Janet Scott's light grey eyes.

'Dr Grant!' Aimee made fun, hoping to lift the mood. 'Don't worry, I haven't lost any weight this month.' She hadn't gained any either. Christmas had been a careful exercise in fooling the family into thinking she was tucking into the mince pies and pud.

'Ready?' Gerald looked at his watch.

Sideways on, Aimee thought he looked like an eagle; beady-eyed, sharp-nosed. All her life he'd waited to swoop and pounce.

Janet closed Aimee's door, covering her anxiety with a smile. 'What time will you be back?' she asked Gerald.

'Late. I've got a fundholders' meeting in Wingate.' The prospect made his temper shorter than usual.

But Aimee put his bad mood partly down to the fact that she was seeing Laura. It unsettled him to know that she talked through her problems with his new colleague. He called it washing their dirty linen. But the accident had shaken him out of his prejudices; he'd agreed that Aimee should get help after months of denying there was anything wrong. And now he had to live with the consequences. At least he didn't actively interfere; she gave him that much.

'We don't often talk about you, you know,' Aimee told him

as the big red car slid down the drive. 'So you needn't be so vain as to think we do.'

'Don't tell me, I don't want to know.' He edged too far out on to the road. A passing van had to swerve out across the central white line.

'I bet you don't care much either. You think this therapy lark is a load of . . .'

'Thank you!' He shot out into a gap in the traffic. 'Wipe that window, will you?' Handing her a cloth, he concentrated on the road.

Aimee sighed. Forget the eagle. These days her father reminded her more of a farmyard hen, scratting and pecking his way around. He grew flustered easily and went over the top in his reactions. She was still occasionally scared of him, but more often scared *for* him instead.

'Look at that idiot!' He fumed about a driver who overtook them as they approached the Old Bridge. A hump made it impossible to see oncoming traffic. He wiped the already clear windscreen with the back of his hand, checked switches and levers, worried about black ice.

Meanwhile Aimee gazed out at the steep hills; a patchwork of small fields rising to open expanses of moorland still under a deep covering of snow. The car swished along gritted roads through the town to the health centre, where they pulled in and Gerald waited for her to get out with her schoolbag so that he could lock up and prepare for his morning meeting.

'Hi, Aimee.' Joy Hartley stopped on her way in to ask her if she would babysit the following Friday.

Aimee liked Joy's three kids. They said funny things with serious faces. She would read them stories and let them stay up after their official bedtime.

They made the arrangement, then Joy hurried into the meeting. Aimee found an out-of-the-way corner in the waiting area and flicked through a magazine until the eight hundred was over.

By the time she went in to see Laura she was bored. She'd studied the posters about asthma, healthy pregnancy and heart disease. She'd read and scoffed at the society pages and rejected her own horoscope.

Waiting rooms were designed to deaden your awareness of your symptoms, she decided. It was a cunning ploy. By the time you got into the doctor's room, you couldn't give a damn about your headache and your acne, your insomnia or your chest pains. 'Just give me a prescription and let me out. Oh, and by the way, I had a small heart attack this morning, but I know you're much too busy to bother with that.' There would still be a queue of people waiting outside with bandages and rashes, looking as dazed as you felt.

This morning Laura looked up from her desk when Aimee walked in, her welcome warm and genuine. 'How are you?' She overrode Aimee's own stony expression.

'I'm OK.' She pulled the frayed cuffs of her jacket, took a bite at her thumb nail.

'How's school?'

'Fine.' Boring actually. She was working hard, though, to prove that she could get the grades that her brother Nick had got; three straight As. Two hours' work per subject per night. Keep a grip.

'Shall we take a look at your weight then?' Laura stood up and led her through to Joy's room, where they weighed her with scientific precision. 'Down almost a kilogram.' She made a note.

Aimee shrugged. 'I am eating, honestly.'

'Come on, back to my room. A couple of pounds doesn't worry me. Just don't let it slip too low.' She noted the girl's painfully thin arms and legs. 'You're not vomiting it back, are you?'

She denied it, then admitted that Christmas dinner had been too much for her. 'I didn't want to make a scene. Nick was home with his girlfriend, Fran. I had to eat most of the stuff, but I couldn't cope afterwards. I made an excuse and went to the bathroom.'

'Just once?'

'Twice.' Aimee wasn't a good liar. How could Laura know how bad it felt to have that disgusting swollen feeling, the horror of being fat? Laura was one of those tall, naturally slim women without hang-ups. Aimee pushed her long black hair behind her ears and studied the carpet two feet in front of her.

'OK, that's still not too bad. You're better now that it's all over and you can cook and choose for yourself?'

The girl nodded. 'But now I've got this weird thing that if I eat too much I'll fail all my exams.' It sounded stupid even as she said it. 'I mean, I know there isn't really a connection, it's just that I'm sort of superstitious. Like, if I eat a Kit-Kat I'll fail Sociology Paper One. If I eat a Mars bar, I kiss goodbye to all my Drama papers.'

'You won't,' Laura assured her, half amused.

'I know it's not logical.'

'It's a control thing,' Laura explained. 'In one way it is perfectly logical. You think that if you can control your calorie intake, in other words, if you can dictate the shape of your body, which is a pretty basic, fundamental form of control, then all your other worries like exams are relatively simple. Kit-Kat: hard. Sociology: dead easy. And so on.'

'I must be mad.'

'No, but you sound unhappy.' Laura looked at her waiting for more.

'The thing is, how can I prove I exist?' Aimee said after a long pause.

Laura continued to listen to the striking girl with her glossy dark hair, her ornate silver rings, her dramatic dark clothes.

32

'I'm disappearing, you know. Sometimes I don't mind. In fact, I'd like to vanish. When Nick's girlfriend is nice to me and gives me a present, I wish the ground would swallow me up. Other times, like when Dad offers her a drink, I'm screaming inside, "What about me?"' She paused. If she cried now she would be really angry with herself. She swallowed hard, and felt herself begin to shake. 'Most of the time I don't mind. I'm thinking, "leave me alone". Mum asks me what I want to eat. Just leave it, why can't she? My teacher wants me to read out part of my essay so he can pull it to pieces in front of the others. I'm choking. My voice is all weird, until he gives up and moves on to someone else. He thinks I'm pathetic, but I'll prove him wrong.'

'You'll get your grade A?'

Aimee nodded. 'You must think I'm really weird.'

Laura tried to defuse the tension. Anorexic patients often lacked a perspective that would help them find a comfortable place in society. She recognised Aimee's desperate lack of self-esteem.

Her pale face flushed pink. 'Am I going on too much? I never really talk about it unless I come here. It's not as if I want to bore everyone else stupid.'

'You're not boring me. I'm thinking.'

'I am being good about the food part, except for Christmas.'

'You're still well below your target weight, but I'm not too worried. How are things at home?' This was where Aimee usually clammed up.

'Fine – ish.'

'You all survived the festive season?' A testing time for families.

'Sort of.'

'Meaning?'

'There isn't a lot to say. No one's beating each other up, we're all dead civilised in our house.'

33

'But something's worrying you?'

'Dad is, a bit.' She shook her head. 'Anyway, it's got nothing to do with me counting calories, has it?'

'I don't know, has it?'

'He's working too hard.' And that was all she was prepared to say. They discussed practical ways of coping with the stress of exams, of building up mental and physical resilience. By the end of the session Aimee felt that the appointment had gone well. She thanked Laura. 'I'm glad you're not Dr Williams.'

'Why, what was wrong with poor old Dr Williams?' Laura had replaced him in the practice; he'd been a Ravensdale GP for almost as long as Gerald.

Aimee shrugged. 'Exactly – old!'

Laura smiled. 'Make another appointment on your way out then.'

Aimee went to the reception desk to talk to Sheila as her father came out of his room into the crowded waiting area. 'What am I, a pen-pusher or a doctor?' He waved a sheet of paper, ignoring the curious glances. Aimee stood to one side. 'How did this land on my desk?'

Sheila studied the form. 'I'm sorry, that should have gone to Philip.' It had to be filled in to explain what had taken him out of the system for several hours while he delivered Alison Lawson's baby girl.

'Yes, but the point is, it's still more paperwork. Bureaucracy gone mad. Not only does it cost us to attend a home delivery, accounting for hours lost et cetera, but here we are filling in more forms in triplicate.'

Aimee noticed nods of agreement amongst older patients. She'd heard it so often across the dinner table, morning, noon and night, that she'd begun to think her father's moaning wasted more time than anything else. By contrast, someone like Laura got on and did it with minimum fuss.

'Leave it with me.' Sheila slipped the form under a notepad.

'You know you're due at the geriatric unit at Low Royds in less than five minutes?'

But it would take him longer than that to get rid of his irritation. Aimee swung out of the door, letting it bang shut, hearing him still sounding off in front of the patients.

# CHAPTER FOUR

'Gerald doesn't realise you have to bend with the prevailing wind,' Philip explained to Laura.

She was due to see Dot at Town Head on a social visit, and was looking forward to a big tea of home-baked scones and cake. 'Doesn't it ever make you a teenie bit weary?' The day had gone from bad to worse. Gerald had come back from Low Royds fuming about the level of funding for geriatric care.

'Not really. I know it's because he feels he's letting his patients down. It drives him crazy.'

'But you look as if you're feeling the strain.' She thought he must be going down with something. His eyes were shadowed and red-rimmed, and he seemed to be moving at half speed.

Philip stood by his car in the dark car park. 'Nothing to do with Gerald, though.'

'What, then?' Philip had had some kind of shock, perhaps. 'How are things? Are the kids OK?'

'They're fine.' He struggled in his pocket to find his car keys. 'It's Juliet. She says she wants to leave me.'

Laura took his hand. 'Oh, Philip!'

'She told me last Friday out of the blue. Well, not really, but I wasn't ready for it.'

'She hasn't gone yet?' Laura had seen her car at Bridge House that morning.

'No. She's been to see Luke Altham.'

'I didn't think he did divorces. He concentrates on criminal cases.'

'Yes you're right, he does. Maybe he's doing her a favour.' He spoke in a daze, as if letting out the secret to Laura had made everything suddenly real. 'She says she can't get over the affair, won't even talk about it. Sorry, Laura, it's all pretty sordid.' He didn't want to involve her; Mary had been her close friend.

'Not when it's happening to someone I know and like,' she assured him. She almost said 'love'. Philip and Juliet had been wonderful to her since she arrived. She hated to see either of them in pain.

He looked up. 'What did you do when it happened to you?'

'With Tom?' Her divorce had been a major reason for her move up to Ravensdale. 'I felt rejected, went to pieces, tried to pretend I hadn't.' Laura still held Philip's hand. 'I was the one who was doing the moving out but I was devastated all the same. It took me years to pluck up the courage to leave.'

'Like Juliet. Well, months anyway.' He thought back over the autumn, the winter.

'Where will she go?'

'I don't know. It should be me, shouldn't it? She should keep the house.' The decision struck him as painful and just. He wanted to go straight home and tell his wife.

'If there's anything I can do ... ' She released him and watched him climb stiffly into the car.

'Thanks, I'll let you know. There is one thing.' His voice choked. 'Look after Juliet for me, will you? Make sure she copes.'

He slammed the door and drove off, headlights raking down the empty lane.

Low rays from the sun made the powdery snow glisten

underfoot as Laura and Matthew tramped up Ravenscar the following Saturday. Apart from the sun's pink halo, the sky was silvery white, the pine trees around the tarn silhouetted tall and straight.

Looking back down the valley they saw isolated barns standing in white fields, dark trees dotted alongside frozen streams, patches of deep blue shadow, and snowdrifts sloping against walls like mountain glaciers.

Matthew had been expecting to have Sophie and Tim at Hawkshead for the second weekend running, but Abigail had cancelled at the last minute. Instead, he and Laura had made the most of the unexpected time together by climbing up Black Gill past Joan's Foss. Now they stood close to the frozen tarn, braving the full force of an easterly wind.

'Has Philip left the house?' Matthew held her gloved hand as they strode through flickering light and shadow between the scaly trunks.

'Not yet. I can't tell whether or not that's a good thing. On the one hand, as long as they're still together there's a chance they can sort things out. On the other hand, this half way situation must be tearing them both apart. They look dreadful.'

'Do you think it's ever final?' Matthew asked.

Laura stopped and looked at the branches overhead. 'It is for me.' She never wanted to see Tom Elliot again. It was too dangerous even to let him into her thoughts, with his bitterness, his self-righteous anger. However, she realised it wasn't like this for other separated couples. 'How about you?'

He walked ahead a few paces. 'I don't think it stops. There isn't a cut-off point.'

'Maybe not when there are children.' She'd steeled herself for his reply. Didn't she register his tone of voice whenever he spoke to his ex-wife on the phone? Deep and guarded, but with echoes of an old intimacy: 'Hello, Abbie, it's Matt. How are you?'

He turned. 'That doesn't mean I love you less.'

'I know.' She walked to join him, turning up her collar. Laura could not explain that it was much more complicated than a stand-off between herself and Abigail. Abigail was outside the door in a storm of grief and loneliness. Would he shut her out for good? Or, if he let his ex-wife in for the sake of the children, where would that leave him and Laura?

'Come on.' She saw the Hall through the trees, and diverted herself with Gabriella Blackwood's invitation to call in. 'Let's go and see if we can persuade them to give us a cup of tea before we go back down.'

'No one's home.' Matthew stood back from the door and looked up at the blank windows while Laura knocked again. A minibus stood parked in the yard beside two other vehicles still silted up with snow. Paths had been cleared between outhouses, but the overall impression was still one of inaccessibility and silence.

'Let's try round the far side.'

So they walked round the Hall, peering through low, narrow windows into empty rooms. Evidently there was no school party in residence, perhaps because it was the weekend. Laura spied the kitchen in spotless order, and a games room with table-tennis, darts and snooker.

'They've made big changes.' Matthew remembered the Hall from his childhood as a rambling, decaying building with legends attached. There was one about a servant who had ousted the master by drawing him into gambling debts and driving him to suicide. 'Kids round here said he blew his brains out by the tarn. The property fell into the servant's hands; an ex-farmboy from Hawkshead. He thought he was going to be kingpin from then on. But the place was jinxed after that. Anyway, we all said it was cursed.'

Laura enjoyed the details of the story. She glanced across the stretch of sloping, open land to the shore of the tarn, picturing the gory scene; blood in the snow, a mangled corpse. 'Did anyone live in it when you were young?'

'On and off. Someone tried to run it as an old folks' home once, but it was too cut off to be a success. A recluse had it at another time. He lived by himself and kept the blackout blinds from the last war permanently drawn. There was a stuffed owl perched up there.' He pointed to an upstairs window which overlooked the water.

'Did you dare each other to play tricks on him?'

'Probably.' He linked an arm round her waist. 'I was only here in the holidays, remember.' Experiences from his child-hood tended to drift on to unused shelves at the back of his memory.

Caught in the wind on this exposed side of the house, they were deciding to cut back across Ravenscar to the shelter of Black Gill when a door banged and footsteps crunched across the yard.

They went round the end of the house, in time to see Jim Blackwood at the wheel of the minibus, red tail-lights winking as he disappeared through the gates. Gabriella was standing at the open door, trying to catch his attention. When she saw Laura and Matthew she hesitated.

Laura went forward. 'Hi. Is this a bad time to drop by?'

'No, it's fine.' Gabriella managed to conceal whatever it was that seemed to have been wrong. 'Jim has to drive into Merton, but come in anyway. You must be freezing.'

So they made the introductions: Matthew to Gabriella, who insisted on them calling her Ellie, then Matthew to Paul Miller, who came into the square reception hall at the sound of voices. He was dressed in sweatshirt and jeans, looking as if

Sunday was definitely a day off, unshaven, dishevelled, but getting away with it. He was impressive anyway, with a litheness in spite of his muscular build and a good, clean bone structure; all the advantages that lent him an unselfconscious confidence.

When he placed Matthew as belonging to Hawkshead Hall, Paul was immediately interested. Matthew explained he was the latest in a long line of family members to manage the estate; as a New Zealander Paul was eager to soak up the sense of history. It wasn't long before Matthew was inviting him to Hawkshead, and Paul was reciprocating by offering to show Matthew the routes he'd set up for the orienteering and rock-climbing groups who came to Ravenscar.

'Leave them to it,' Ellie said. 'Come and have coffee.'

So the women watched the men wrap themselves up and set off on a trek towards the tarn and the snowy scree slope of Upper Ravenscar while they stayed warm behind a door marked Private, which led to a suite of rooms where Jim, Ellie and Paul had their quarters.

'It's a bit cramped.' Ellie apologised for the tiny lounge lined with paperbacks and furnished with assorted old armchairs and a desk in one corner. 'Silly really, when you consider the size of the place.'

'It must be difficult to run smoothly.' Laura accepted her cup and sat next to the window. She suspected from Ellie's remarks that living at Ravenscar wasn't all she'd anticipated of a grand house standing in acres of grounds in the heart of the Yorkshire Dales.

'Not really.' She shrugged and smiled. 'Jim has everything worked out like clockwork. You have to in our line of business.'

'Still, there's no way to avoid unexpected hitches.'

'You mean, like kids getting lost and spraining their ankles?' Ellie grimaced.

'I meant basic stuff like snow holding up food deliveries. I expect you've had plenty of that lately. Or staff leaving suddenly. It's like running a big hotel.' Laura didn't seem to be able to steer clear of sensitive issues; presumably the Blackwoods had had to cope with Paul's wife leaving them in the lurch.

'Yes.' Ellie sighed. 'Marianne. Jim certainly hadn't planned for that.' She sat a while, then decided to open up. As she spoke, her small, pointed, pretty face grew flushed and she moved her hands in animated gestures. It was a subject that upset her.

'We thought we had it all sorted out before we came. None of us walked into it blind, it was clear what our roles were. Jim's the organiser. Paul's good with the kids. I've got the medical knowledge – I trained as a nurse,' she explained. 'Athletes have pretty short careers; you have to have a day job to fall back on. And Marianne knew about catering. She used to work in a hotel in Leeds. That's where she met Paul, when he came over to play rugby. We thought we had it all sewn up.'

'Why did Marianne pack it in? Didn't she like it?'

Ellie looked away. 'She did and she didn't. At first she was the one who fell in love with Ravenscar. She went on about the fact that you couldn't hear the traffic, and you can walk for miles without seeing anyone.'

'Yes, I remember that.' Laura had felt the same awe when she first came. 'You wake up, and all you can hear is the birds singing. So what went wrong?'

'She changed her mind. It turned out she missed the traffic.' Ellie was flippant, then sorry. 'If you really want to know, things went wrong between her and Paul.'

In the silence Laura pictured this; a break-up that caused ripples beyond the personal hurt, one that must have happened in public, in front of a houseful of teenagers, before the eyes of a second couple who were relying on the Millers staying together. 'Ouch,' she said quietly.

Ellie nodded. 'We didn't know if Paul would get over it. And then he thought there might be problems over his citizenship. They hadn't been married that long.'

'He seems OK now.' Paul Miller looked and sounded like a man who had coped with his problems.

Ellie said nothing for a while, watching the distant figures of Matthew and Paul scramble up a slope towards a dark copse. Then she turned to Laura. 'It's strange; this is a hard place to settle in.'

'Ravenscar?'

'Yes, and Hawkshead itself. People seem, well, suspicious!' She seemed surprised by her choice of word.

Laura laughed. 'I know what you mean.' Had she not been brought up in Yorkshire before she went away to train and then practise in London, she would have seen some truth in the old stereotype that harsh country ways breed a peculiar mix of thrift, taciturnity and quarrelsomeness amongst members of the old farming communities.

'I can't pin it down, but I suppose I find them a bit blunt as well.' Ellie shared her worries, perhaps for the first time.

'You get used to that. It's a kind of challenge, to see how you react. That's how they behave to us off-comers. It's nothing personal.' But as a young woman GP still relatively new to the dale she knew what it was like to scale a wall of suspicion. It must be similar for Ellie and her team.

'Anyway, I try to stick up for myself. This is something I chose to do, and I want to make a go of it. I'm not going to drop it just because the locals don't welcome me with open arms.' Ellie described how she would approach farmers for limited access to sheep grazing areas, only to be met with point-blank refusal; how they turned with a 'What now?' whenever they saw her coming.

43

'Don't worry, I still have patients who refuse to accept female doctors. I was considered an oddity. A year and a bit later, they're just getting used to me.' She warmed to Ellie's predicament. 'Like you, I think there's an element of choosing your bed. I did know what I was letting myself in for, after all.'

Ellie nodded. 'Why did you opt to come here?' Laura's answer seemed important.

'Yes, why?' The big question. Why Ravensdale rather than Camden?

Looking out at the tarn, seeing how the wind had slanted the trees, noticing the wide open horizon, she found the answer. 'For the peace and quiet. Why did you?'


The phone rang as Matthew and Laura arrived back at Abbey Grange after their visit to Ravenscar.

'If it's a patient for me, tell them Gerald's the one on duty!' She let Matthew answer it as she unlaced her boots and took off her jacket, glad that the whole house was warmed by the ancient Aga which she'd inherited from Lilian.

'It's OK, it's for me.' He took the phone into the study and closed the door.

From the way he did it, Laura knew that it was Abigail. Irritated by the flare-up of emotions that such a small thing could cause in her, she went into the kitchen to begin an evening meal. There was satisfaction in taking out the board, chopping and dicing vegetables, moving methodically from task to task. It was a long phone call.

When he came to join her, Matthew's face had lost all the freshness and exhilaration of the afternoon's walk. He looked tense and told her that Sophie was in bed with a bad headache. 'I said I'd go across and see her.'

'Now?' Laura stopped setting the table with knives and forks.

'I said I would.' He sounded apologetic and looked guiltily at the simmering pans. 'Abigail says she keeps asking for me.'

She felt snarled up inside. 'Has she called a doctor?'

'Not yet. It came on suddenly after tea. Abigail put her straight to bed.'

There was a pattern to Sophie's illnesses, obvious to everyone except her parents. They were minor, the symptoms were usually invisible and they cropped up with amazing regularity on a Sunday evening, keeping her off school for a day or two.

'Do you have time to grab something to eat before you go?'

'Sorry, Laura. It sounded pretty bad.' He would have to set off straight away on the hour and a half's journey to York.

So the meal was put off and Laura spent the evening quietly reading and catching up on paperwork. Ellie Blackwood rang to say how much she'd appreciated the afternoon's chat and to arrange a return visit to Abbey Grange the following Saturday. Laura made the usual call to her parents in Wingate and planned to meet them on her next day off. At eleven o'clock, when she was turning off lights and locking doors, she heard a car crunching up the gravel drive, still icy and patchily covered with snow. It was Matthew.

He came in and flung his car keys on the hall table.

'How is she?'

'Sleeping. She was asleep when I got there. Three hours there and back for nothing.'

'Was Tim in bed too?' Laura saw how weary he was. He rubbed his eyelids with his thumb and forefinger and nodded his head.

'I asked Abigail why she didn't ring me on the car phone to put me off when she realised there was no point in me going after all.'

'What did she say?'

'She'd lost the number. I expect she'll find it again as soon as she needs something.'

'Come and have a drink.' She led him into the sitting room. 'And next time, get her to let you speak to Sophie on the phone before you go rushing across.'

Matthew sank into a chair. 'You think I'm too soft?'

'No, I understand what it must be like. But I think we need a strategy to deal with it.' She bent to kiss his forehead. 'And before you tell me yet again that it's not a contest, I have to tell you, my darling, that that's exactly what it feels like.' She gave a wry smile but, deep down, she too was wearied by it.

'I feel battle-scarred, Laura.'

'Did Abigail try to waylay you again? Did she hope you'd get snowed in?'

'Something like that.'

'What exactly? An indecent proposal?'

He sighed. 'A bit more subtle than that. She wants a cooling-off period on the divorce. She's suggesting that we all go somewhere to talk through the problems the kids are having.'

Laura listened. 'Family therapy?'

'She reckons she knows someone good.'

'Will you go?' She'd retreated to a far corner of the room, cradling her glass and swirling the whisky around its sides.

Matthew fell completely silent.

Seeing his dilemma, she felt sorry for him and terribly angry with Abigail. 'I think you should go. Let Sophie and Tim see that you care. And maybe the therapist will be able to smooth out some of Abigail's problems.'

'And get me off the hook?' He stood but didn't try to come near her.

These days their remarks took unintentional side turnings, got lost down cul-de-sacs of fear and resentment. What she'd loved at first was the clear, unambiguous nature of their relationship. 'Let's not argue,' she pleaded.

He took her glass, put it down and held her for a moment. 'When I was driving back, all I could think of was wanting to see you. I knew how late it was, but I couldn't go straight home. You don't mind?'

Laura smoothed his dark hair from his forehead. 'I'm glad you did.'

'You know that the kids are the only hold Abigail has, don't you?'

She nodded. Matthew's voice soothed her. It was deep and soft. With his arms around her, she thought that nothing could shake her.

'I only want to be with you.'

'I know.'

'Nothing else matters. As long as we're together we can sort things out.' He tilted her face between his cupped hands. 'I don't want Abigail to come between us.'

In bed everything was simple again, caught up in each other, sure of their love. Laura folded herself to him, for the warmth and strength of his body. He revelled in the closeness, letting it seep through his skin, before he began to kiss her and stroke her, tracing his hands up and down her back, knowing that she would arch towards him and hold him close.

Letting go, being in the moment, their tenderness soon gave way to desire. His mouth kissed her face, her breasts; his roughness against her creamy smoothness, one of her hands tangled in his hair, one pressing hard against his back. It was clear and uncomplicated; a passion rising through lips and fingertips, the sweep of soft hair against a shoulder, the curve of hips, limbs entwined.

# CHAPTER FIVE

Everywhere the snow melted, except on the highest hills, and by early February the grey-brown haul towards spring had begun.

It was with mixed feelings that Philip noted the emerging snowdrops in the garden at Bridge House amongst tree roots on a bank that sloped to the river's edge. The tiny, bell-shaped flowers always seemed too optimistic, anticipating the approach of warmer weather long before it was due.

'Philip, the phone for you,' Juliet called from the back door. 'It's Maisie Aire.'

With a last glance at the cold, clear rush of water over mossy stones, he turned and went in, fighting his way past packing-cases to the phone in the hall.

Maisie had rung to say she was worried about her granddaughter, Sophie. 'We've had the children staying here over the weekend. They were due to go home to their mother last evening, but Sophie seemed too ill to travel. Matthew took Tim back to York as planned, but I've hung on to Sophie. I thought you'd better come and take a look.'

Philip agreed to go over to Hawkshead Hall straight away, left a message with Sheila, and drove out of town over the bridge towards the Aires' imposing house in the valley. The child's illness was probably nothing serious, but he was aware

48

of two more recent confirmed cases of meningitis in York, and of the heightened concern.

Through the stone gateway, past the empty lodge and along the drive, his main preoccupation was still the situation at home; the nightmare division of possessions between himself and Juliet as he prepared to move out.

Maisie came down the steps of the main house to meet him, smart as ever in a dark red tailored jacket and black skirt, her grey hair worn up in a stylish fashion, her graceful, birdlike movements conveying an air of anxiety. 'The poor child has a headache and a stiff neck. I've kept her in bed.'

He followed her up the steps into the panelled hallway. 'Has she been vomiting?'

'No, but she says she feels sick.' Maisie took him straight upstairs, pausing at the end of a long gallery with bedrooms leading off. 'I'm a little out of practice with childhood ailments, I guess.' She looked apologetic. 'I hope I'm not overreacting.'

Maisie had made plenty of adjustments in the couple of years since her husband, Geoffrey, had died. From being the wealthy and indulged wife of the biggest landowner in the dale, with a cosseted New England girlhood behind her, she had had to face up to unexpected financial difficulties to do with the estate, as well as coping with her grief. One son, Christopher, had led her down the risky path of putting their land on Ravenscar up for sale to a multinational quarry company. The local furore had cast her in the role of chief villain, and when the scheme had failed, Christopher saw fit to keep a low profile by moving abroad, leaving Maisie to try to regain her standing and to recoup some money from the sale of other property.

Fortunately, she still had Matthew to help her and this time the outcome had been happier for all concerned. Laura, who had been househunting at the time, had bought Abbey Grange from Maisie.

'I'm glad you brought me in,' Philip told her now. 'Let's see if we can put your mind at rest.'

She led him into Sophie's room; a large one altogether too formal and precise for a child of seven, with its ornate ceiling, mahogany furniture and heavy red curtains.

'Hello, Sophie. Remember me?' He smiled at the small figure in the bed. He'd known her since babyhood and had been called in by Abigail on numerous occasions until she and Matthew split up.

She sat silent, propped up by pillows, a round-faced girl with long dark brown hair and her father's grey eyes, wearing a serious expression.

'I hear you have a bad headache?'

Her eyes glistened. She nodded and stared back at him. 'And a sore throat,' she whispered, on the verge of tears.

'Don't worry, we'll take a quick look.' He shone a light into her mouth and ears, spotted slight inflammation. The pupils showed nothing untoward, however, and the temperature was normal. 'Good girl. Your grandma will keep you tucked up in bed nice and warm. I'll give you some banana medicine to make you better. Have you had it before?'

'Yes.' The tears began to fall.

'Don't cry. You'll soon be up and running about again.' He tucked the bedclothes tight around her, wondering whether it was as simple as it seemed. He glanced up at Maisie.

'Daddy will be here soon,' she promised, taking over from Philip.

The name sent a spasm of sobs through the little girl's body.

'Don't cry, Sophie, you'll make yourself feel more sick.' Maisie tried to comfort her with a shabby teddy bear flopping off the side of the pillows.

Philip lingered by the bedside. 'You don't have any more pains?' He crouched and stroked her hot, wet cheek. 'Any tummy ache?'

50

Through her tears Sophie nodded.

'She gets so many,' Maisie said. 'It's difficult to know how much attention to pay.'

He stood up. 'Does she miss a lot of school?'

'Yes. Abigail's given up trying to get her in when she feels this way. Apparently, Sophie begs not to go. There are always tears.'

'Don't you like school, Sophie?' At seven, most children had got over their separation anxiety and dived into each day with enthusiasm. School phobia was often a symptom of greater distress. 'Don't you like your teacher?'

'Yes.'

'Do you have lots of friends?'

'Some.' The replies were guarded, weighing up the right from the wrong from her seven-year-old viewpoint. 'Where's Daddy?' she pleaded, obviously unwilling to answer any more questions.

When Philip and Maisie got out on to the gallery, he was frowning.

'I know.' She shook her head. 'Don't say it. I have one disturbed little grandchild in there.'

'Is it since the break-up?'

'Yes. It's all psychosomatic, isn't it?'

'Not quite. She does have a slight throat infection.'

Maisie sighed. 'She used to be such a happy child.'

'Perhaps she exaggerated her illness at the weekend so she could stay here longer? Is she unhappy in York?' He trod carefully, trying to assess the depth of the problem.

'With her mother? No. She loves her mummy. But she loves her daddy too. I think this may be her way of trying to get them back together.'

They heard a car arrive, so they went downstairs to meet Matthew in the hall. Philip filled in the latest news on Sophie.

'A behavioural problem?' Matthew seemed to sag as Philip

51

described the pattern. Once more he'd been asked to stay over in York. This time he'd been too tired to refuse. He'd spent much of the night as the recipient of Abigail's rambling anxieties.

'Yes. Minor ailments, school phobia. Some people would say she was trying it on to get her own way. But in her case, given the circumstances, I'd be inclined to pay it more serious attention.' Philip knew enough about the situation to realise that this was a difficult one for Matthew.

Aware of Maisie hovering, he advised professional help. 'It's not easy to commit yourself to family counselling, but outside opinion would probably help shed some light. Do you want me to refer you to a clinic?'

Matthew showed him out and stood for a moment on the top step, looking out across rhododendron bushes to landscaped gardens and a small lake. 'I'll have to talk to Abigail.'

Back pain, burns, food poisoning; the standard fare. Philip was pleased with himself for diagnosing Ménière's disease in an elderly woman at Low Royds, whose symptoms of dizziness and vertigo indicated an abnormality in the inner ear, easily treated with diuretics, oddly enough. He explained to the care assistant that it was to do with water metabolism. They'd been afraid that she was heading for a stroke, and were relieved.

If only it were all so simple. At lunchtime Philip forced himself to call in at home. He had to decide which stuff to take with him to his newly rented place in Askby. He'd found the house through Addy's estate agents, said yes to the first thing that came up; a semi-detached box in a new complex by the old mill workings, overlooking the race. He was due to move there the following weekend.

'Take what you need,' Juliet had insisted.

He didn't want to take anything. Dismantling Bridge House

would signify the real end. Left intact, there was the possibility that his move would be temporary.

But she was determined to divide things fairly. The furniture from his upstairs study was to go with him for a start, and a bed, a table, a sofa. Then there were smaller items, electrical and domestic. And his books. 'You can't live without them. There are boxes in the cellar. I'll get Dot to help me pack them.'

And today was packing day. Juliet had taken time off work especially. He arrived at Bridge House to find the two women methodically packing items he would need: kitchen equipment, lamps; and ones he knew he would never use: an old typewriter, a pressure-cooker.

'An iron!' Juliet suddenly decided this was a matter of life and death. 'You must have an iron.'

'I can buy one.' He sat at the kitchen table.

'No, I don't want you to. You take this one.' She brought it from the utility room, put it into a packing case.

Dot worked on, carrying empty boxes, tactfully disappearing upstairs to the study.

'Would you like a coffee?' Juliet aimed at normality. Each morning she dressed and put on her make-up, arranged the practicalities. It was Juliet who had phoned their three sons to break the news, she who remembered at the last minute to redirect his mail and all his professional phone calls.

'Yes.' He hated the new gaps on shelves, the air of disarray. Sometimes he thought it was a heavy price to pay for one short affair.

'Are you going to be all right?' She sat at the table with him.

'I don't know.'

'Maybe you could take some time off work?'

'I want a wife, not a mother.' Philip felt bitter.

'You didn't want one last spring.'

'I admitted it, didn't I?' He still didn't really accept that his affair with Mary had cancelled out all that Juliet and he had felt for one another.

'Only when you had to. If you could have got away with it, you would have.'

'For God's sake, where's your compassion?'

'And what about your loyalty? It's not a lot to ask. I thought I could trust you.' She sat trembling, refusing to look up at him.

'"As we forgive those who trespass against us!"' he quoted. Saint Juliet, the wronged wife.

'I have forgiven you, Philip.'

'What's all this, then?' He gestured towards the packing cases gathering in the hall.

She ignored the question. 'I said I'd be the one to move out. It didn't have to be you. That was your choice.'

'Some bloody choice.' He paced up and down behind her chair. 'Are you telling me you're not angry with me any more?'

'I'm not angry. I feel sorry –' She stopped.

'For me?'

'For us. For the boys. And yes, I feel sorry for you.'

He caught hold of her wrist, bent over her. 'What does it take to get us back together?'


'What did I tell you?' Gerald was on his way out when Philip arrived for afternoon surgery. 'I've just had another call out to Ravenscar. Every day, something different.'

'What now?' Philip asked Sheila, staring at Gerald's back. 'Was it Jim Blackwood?' His patient's last blood pressure reading had niggled at him ever since he'd noted it down.

'No, his wife. She made it sound urgent.'

Philip went through to his room.

'Bad luck on Gerald,' Laura called. She came out to speak to him. 'Have you seen the rain? He'll get soaked.'

She followed Philip into his room and shut the door behind her. 'Are you OK?'

Laura was the one person at work from whom he didn't have to hide anything. 'Lousy,' he confessed. 'I've just seen my home being taken apart. My wife won't listen to reason. And the worst thing is, I probably deserve everything I get.'

Laura sighed.

'It's so bloody mercenary, dishing out the belongings; one for you, one for me. Women seem to be better at that.' He sat heavily in the chair behind his desk.

'I wasn't. I left Tom without taking a single thing. I couldn't face packing up. My style was more cut and run.'

'But you wanted to leave,' he reminded her.

She paused, hand on the door. 'I wouldn't say *wanted* to. But I knew I had to if I was going to survive.'

'Is that how it is for Juliet? Would staying with me be so bad?'

'I guess it's as hard for her as it is for you.'

He nodded and sighed. 'I move out on Saturday.'

Philip and Laura had handled most of Gerald's patients between them, as well as their own, before he reappeared, wet through as Laura had predicted, his hair and jacket streaming.

'That does it!' He shed his wet things and banged about in Reception. For a moment Philip imagined some further trivial occurrence at Ravenscar. He went out to investigate.

'I knew this would happen sooner or later.'

'Did they call you up there on a wild goose chase again?' Philip expected to hear that another pupil had gone missing, or got stuck on a cliff face.

Gerald blew his nose and wiped his glasses. 'No, it was for real this time.'

'Is someone badly hurt?' Laura was the first to tune into the serious tone.

'Worse. Someone's dead. Jim Blackwood. It's pandemonium up there at the moment. Everyone's reeling with shock.'

'When? What happened?' Philip was stunned.

'Earlier this afternoon, not sure when. By the time I got there it was too late. We dragged him out of the water but there was nothing we could do.'

'You're saying he drowned?'

'Yes. Heart attack, fell in, drowned.' Gerald's businesslike tone was belied by a fumbling attempt to shift documents into order on Sheila's desk. 'There was water in the lungs. Not dead until after he hit the lake.'

'You found him in the tarn?' Laura pressed for details.

'Under it. The surface is still frozen. We had one hell of a job getting him out.'

Philip's mind flew back to Jim Blackwood's last appointment; the high b.p. reading, the man's refusal to make any allowances for his condition. Looking at it now, it seemed certain that he had been concealing chest pains and other signs of angina. 'Who raised the alarm?'

'Two kids in a rock-climbing group on their way back to the Hall. Apparently they'd been expecting Blackwood to come down Black Gill to supervise them. When he didn't show up they headed home past the tarn, saw an arm sticking out. The rest of the body was twisted under the ice and submerged.'

'Poor kids.' Laura imagined the shock. 'What about his wife?'

Gerald shrugged. 'It's her I feel sorry for. She seems to be taking it fairly well at the moment. She doesn't seem the crying sort.'

'Maybe she just hides it well.' Philip felt angry with himself.

Why hadn't he pushed Jim Blackwood harder on the hypertension issue? Proper treatment could have avoided this tragedy.

'What will happen to the school party at the Hall?' Laura decided to go up and see Ellie. A good friendship had developed quickly between them and she wanted to offer support.

'There's that young New Zealander to help keep things going.' Gerald gave up on the papers and handed them to Sheila. 'See if you can find the death certificate. I put it in there somewhere.'

'Are you issuing it straight off?' Instinctively, Philip felt he would rather take his time on this one. Although the patient's diabetic condition could lead to sudden death, on this occasion it didn't feel quite right.

'Why not?' Gerald was at his most dismissive, his voice curt, attention elsewhere as he rummaged now through a pile of case notes. 'It's simple enough, myocardial infarction due to angina in a severely diabetic patient. You saw him within the last fourteen days, I take it?' He pulled out Jim Blackwood's envelope of notes.

Philip nodded warily and glanced at Laura who also looked worried.

Sheila handed Gerald the appropriate form. 'Do you need a cremation certificate as well?'

He shook his head. 'The wife wants burial. She says he wouldn't have wanted cremation. He was dead set against it, apparently – no pun intended. She says she'll arrange it with the vicar.'

This made things worse as far as Philip was concerned. At least with cremation, Gerald's signature would have to be backed up by a second doctor and the certificate screened by the Registrar's office. 'Hang on. Let's think this one through.'

'What's there to think about?' Irritated, Gerald drew Philip to one side. 'Look, all I'm trying to do is help that poor woman who's been left to cope with what amounts to a bloody awful situation. You know what happens if I don't issue the certificate. It means police autopsies and all the rest. All for nothing. They open him up and find advanced heart disease. Why prolong the agony?'

'Maybe.'

'More than maybe, Philip. How many time have we seen it before? The chap's going along fine with his insulin injections, controlling his diet, coping with his symptoms. All the while the problem builds up; arteries clog, b.p. rises.' He tapped the case notes. 'You know that better than anyone.'

'Look, I admit he was hypertensive. I'm not denying that. But I've no evidence of actual angina.'

'It's a fair bet.' Gerald stuffed the notes back into the envelope. 'And I'm not prepared to mess about with this certificate.'

Philip pursed his lips. 'No witnesses I take it?'

Gerald glared. He wrote his name on the form with a flourish, took off his glasses and slipped them into his waistcoat pocket. 'I don't know why chaps like him have to go charging about climbing everything in sight. Don't they consider their wives?'

Philip felt that Gerald was taking a dig at him; another husband who had ridden roughshod over his wife's feelings. Though he hadn't discussed his separation from Juliet with Gerald, he knew whose side he would take.

'And what about the people who risked their necks trying to save him? A couple of eighteen-year-old kids and his poor wife? When I arrived they were still trying to drag him out. I tell you, it's no picnic dealing with a dead weight, trying to lift it clear of thin ice.'

Philip understood Gerald's anger. Jim Blackwood had paid the ultimate price for what some would regard as his foolhardiness, but the cost to his wife was great too. He pictured the scene; the struggle to recover the body in driving rain and sleet, the hopelessness of the effort. Reluctantly he sighed, nodded and gave in.

# CHAPTER SIX

That evening Aimee sat in the Falcon listening to the swell of gossip amongst her friends about the incident on Ravenscar. She didn't feel like joining in. They were raking up old stories about ghosts and how the place was known to be haunted, mostly for the benefit of a group of boys from the Hall who were sitting at a table by the fire, probably doing their best to forget the day's trauma.

'They're always finding dead bodies in the tarn.'

'Maybe there's a curse.'

'What do you think, Aimee?'

She played it cool. 'People get ill, drop dead. The end.'

'Do you remember the time someone committed suicide up there? A hosepipe from the exhaust into the car job.' The rumour-mongers were in full flow.

'It gives me the creeps, that place.'

The gang of boys came over with their glasses of lager and told stories of floorboards creaking, possessions disappearing in the dead of night.

'You should have been there when they dragged the body out,' one said. He was stocky, with short black hair, heavy eyebrows and eyes that were too close together. He welcomed the attention that his eye-witness account drew from Aimee's more gullible friends. She sat back, unimpressed.

'His eyes were wide open, but you could tell he was dead.'

'How?' There was a sudden drop in the noise level. Other regulars in the pub listened in; the old farmers at the bar, Brian Lawson.

'You just could. His lips had gone blue.'

'Gross!'

'He looked like he'd been under a fair while before we got to him. Sean ran for help and they rang the doctor. When he arrives, he gets to work, punching his chest and pressing up and down for a while. He keeps checking for a pulse. Nothing.'

'What then?'

In the warm, crowded room, the blow-by-blow account seemed distasteful to Aimee. She noticed one of the boys sitting more quietly than the rest; thoughtful, not so full of himself. He kept dropping his head and staring at his hands.

'The doc can't get his breathing going. We know the score. But he has to listen and check with a light which he shines in the eyes. Zilch. Dead as a doornail. The doc tells Mrs Blackwood that's it, there's nothing he can do.'

'That's Aimee's dad,' someone said in the unsteady silence. People turned.

'Don't look at me.' She shrugged. 'He never tells me anything.' In fact, she'd known something had upset her father; he was criticising everything, fiddling and fussing. She'd come out of the house to get away from the atmosphere.

'So how did he get in the water in the first place? Did he fall in?'

The witness faltered. 'Search me. No one saw it happen.'

'I bet he didn't. He wouldn't just fall in – not Jim Blackwood. Have you seen that scree slope? It's nothing. Even if he was taking a short cut, there's no way he'd lose his footing on that.'

'Unless someone pushed him.' Bushy-eyebrows took up the reins and charged on.

'Don't be daft.'

'That's stupid.'

'Why is it?'

'Who?'

'What for?'

'Bloody hell, Steve, the bloke's dead, isn't he?' One voice pulled them back from unseemly speculation. It was the quiet boy, who seemed more upset than the rest.

'That's the whole point, dummy!'

'Well then?'

'Well then, what's someone like Jim Blackwood doing, slipping on some piddling little slope and falling into a lake? He's climbed frigging Everest!'

The other boy shook his head. 'Leave it out.'

Aimee stood up, making it clear that she didn't agree with the gossip. She scraped her stool and went to the bar. Other regulars showed their unease too by backing off into their own corners and shaking their heads. Next to her, she overheard Dot Wilson's disapproving comment.

'Why can't they show a bit more respect?'

Aimee ordered a Slimline drink and stayed where she was, avoiding questions about her father's role in the incident. After a few minutes, the quiet boy also slid up to the bar to escape the barrage of rumour and counter-rumour.

'You're the doctor's daughter?' He paid for his drink but stayed put.

'Aimee Scott.'

'Sean Armstrong.'

'Were you there when it happened?'

He nodded. 'But I don't want to talk about it.'

She preferred this. Seeing someone die was a pretty private business. 'How long are you staying at Ravenscar?'

'Until Saturday.' He looked directly at her for the first time. 'Unless I decide to shoot off before then. I can't take much more of Steve Wallis and his big mouth.' His face was thin, his dark eyes heavily lashed, his voice slurred, out of shyness probably.

'Shoot off where?'

'Back to Leeds. It's nice and peaceful in the inner city. Everyone minds their own business.'

She grinned. 'And people don't drop dead on you?'

'Something like that. Honest, I thought I'd be going off my rocker with nothing to do out here. How wrong can you be?'

Soon they were deep into conversation. He asked her about being a doctor's daughter. She said she didn't recommend it. Sean was finishing A-levels, like her, but doubtful about going to college. He wasn't sure about grants and stuff. He said he'd never be able to afford a loan. They discussed exam grades, agreed they hated the system.

'You're different from how you look,' he ventured. Others were drifting out of the pub, calling for him to walk back to the Hall. He ignored them.

'How come?' She was interested. Sean didn't have the big-I-am style she loathed but he didn't lack confidence either. His ideas were pretty clear and honest and he got straight to the point.

'From a distance you looked like you might bite.'

'Maybe I do.' She felt a glimmer of resentment, the old leave-me-alone impulse.

He dipped his head, then looked up at her. 'So will you be here tomorrow?'

'Could be.'

'I'll see you here, then.' He went off quickly without waiting for an answer.

Do I look like I might bite, she asked herself, glancing in the mirror behind the bar. For the first time in ages she didn't altogether detest what she saw.

As soon as Aimee reached home, she wished she hadn't. She

saw Philip's car leaving, and found her mother trying to talk sense into her father. The issue was something about a death certificate; gloomy stuff. She tried to slip upstairs.

'For heaven's sake, Janet, the man was a prime candidate for an infarct. Can't anyone get it into their heads? He was hypertensive, his stress levels must have been sky-high trying to set up that centre.'

'But he was Philip's patient, and Philip isn't so sure.' For once her mother spoke her mind. There were red blotches on her neck and a tremble in her voice.

'Philip wasn't on the spot. He wasn't making the decisions.' Gerald waved his arms. 'Neither were you. What makes people think they know best all of a sudden?'

'We're not saying that, Gerald.'

'No? I'd like to know what you *are* saying, then.' He spotted Aimee on the stairs as he strode into the hall. 'Why not add your tuppence-worth? What's your brilliant theory; natural causes or suspicious circumstances?'

She carried on upstairs. His scorn bit deep. At the top she steadied herself and made her reply as pointed as she could. 'On a rough vote at the Falcon, I'd say it was two to one in favour of murder.'

There was a pause before her mother too came out of the lounge. 'What do you mean?'

'Pub gossip.' Gerald brushed it aside. 'Wouldn't they just love a scandal?'

'But Gerald, that's what Philip's bothered about. He'd rather the police were informed. You heard what he said.'

'I hear, I hear! Suddenly I'm wrong, and every other silly sod in the place is right!'

'No, we're saying better safe than sorry,' she pleaded.

Aimee watched the tussle with interest. This was her father's inevitable reaction to a challenge; injured pride, bombast, stubbornness. Surely her mother could see his opinion hardening like concrete.

'Better for whom?'

'For you. For the practice.' She sounded genuinely worried.

'It's not me I'm bothered about. That's what so galling.' He rounded one last time. 'You know me; minimum fuss wherever possible, for the sake of the family. Just because some idiots with wild imaginations want to kick up a fuss, it's no reason to withold that certificate. Trust me, Janet, I know what I'm doing.'

'What about Philip? It's unheard of for him to step in like this.'

'Philip has troubles of his own.' He opened the door to his study, paused and turned. 'Like the rest of us.'

'Gerald.' She took a step towards him; smaller, quieter, infinitely more patient than her husband.

Up went his head. 'Anyway there's nothing we can do about it. I've already issued the certificate and that's that. Gabriella Blackwood is planning the funeral for Tuesday.'

# CHAPTER SEVEN

The Sunday after Jim's death was the first day that Laura could go to see Ellie at Ravenscar, though they'd already talked on the phone. She wanted to give as much support as she could, imagining how isolated the widow must feel in the midst of her grief. Laura herself needed a bit more of the loneliness and space afforded by Ravenscar; at Abbey Grange and the health centre everything was tangled and cramped. Matthew's doubts over Sophie and Tim plagued him, while Gerald and Philip had embarked on a war of attrition, each determined to make their point about the hastily issued death certificate.

For a moment after she'd parked her car in the yard she stood looking up at the house. Solid as rock, thick-walled, Quaker-plain, it withstood this latest crisis unchanged. There were no drawn curtains, no hushed air. On the contrary, windows stood ajar to let in the first breath of spring. She could hear someone hammering in a downstairs room. Entering through the open door, she crossed the hall to knock at Ellie's flat.

Footsteps sounded along a corridor, then Paul Miller appeared, hammer in hand. 'Do you want Ellie?' His thick checked work-shirt, open at the neck, rolled back at the cuffs, and his open manner suggested another normal Sunday. 'She's out training on the moor.'

'I'll come back later.' Laura was taken aback.

Paul put the hammer on a mantelpiece and came to open the door for her.

'No, don't stop what you're doing. I don't want to interrupt.'

'I'm only fixing a window frame. Anyway, Ellie won't be long.' He led the way into the flat. 'She'll be pleased you dropped by.' Turning in the narrow passage, he shrugged. 'Not pleased exactly. You know.'

'How is she?'

'Pretty good. Ellie isn't the sort to sit and cry. She knows that's not what Jim would have wanted.' He went ahead again, into the kitchen. 'I don't think it's hit her yet. I keep expecting her to crack up for a while, get it out of her system. But no, she keeps trucking on.'

'What about you?' Ellie's lack of reaction wasn't altogether surprising. Laura saw this on occasion; the wife or husband whose nerve held up in an incredible way for several days following the partner's death. After the funeral was usually when the full impact hit.

'I never knew how crook he was,' Paul confessed. 'He didn't talk about it. I mean, not once.'

The picture Laura had built up of Jim Blackwood as a man who made no concession to his illness was heightened yet again. Most diabetics made no secret of their condition. In fact, many made sure to broadcast it by wearing an identity bracelet in case of difficulty. During a hypoglycaemia attack, when the body couldn't cope with levels of insulin in the blood, it was essential that those around knew what to do. 'I'm sorry,' she told Paul. 'You must be going through a bad time.'

'What do they say; this place is jinxed?' He grimaced, then smiled briefly. 'But there is just one thing.' He leaned against the kitchen table and folded his arms. 'What if there'd been

67

someone around when it happened? Would it have made any difference?

'I mean, I've read about it. Diabetics get dizzy and faint. You have to loosen their collars, clear the airway, get ready to give mouth-to-mouth. I can't help feeling that if Jim had had someone with him who knew what to do . . .' He tailed off, looking to Laura for reassurance.

'He'd still be alive?' She shook her head. 'As far as I know, what happened on Thursday wasn't what we call a vasovagal attack, one of these fainting fits. It was a heart attack. He must have felt it set in, lost his balance, slid down the slope into the water and drowned. It says on the death certificate that it was MI; a heart attack, followed by drowning.'

Paul took a deep breath.

'Completely unpredictable and unpreventable in the circumstances. No one could have done anything.'

He cleared his throat. 'At least he went the way he would have chosen.'

Beneath the surface, Paul was obviously traumatised. Laura wondered what the future would be for him now. Could the two of them, he and Ellie, keep the centre going? She asked about their plans, and found that they intended to carry on.

'If we can. We're fully booked until July, then we start running courses for managers.'

She wished him luck, heard a door swing open and closed and turned to see Ellie at the kitchen door.

She was dressed in a bright tracksuit and trainers, her hair in a ponytail, and was breathing hard after her cross-country run. There was a sense of strain in her exchange of pleasantries as Paul backed out of the room.

'Training doesn't get any easier,' Ellie admitted, leaning forward to catch her breath. 'I keep telling myself I'm thirty-five; time to slow down.'

Laura waited until she was ready to talk about Jim,

prepared to avoid the subject altogether if this was what Ellie wanted. They mentioned the thaw and the first signs of spring, working round to funeral arrangements for Tuesday.

'He wanted a spot in the churchyard at the Abbey,' Ellie said. 'We talked about it once. It seems strange now. There's a space by the wall near the river, surrounded by rough headstones made out of limestone. He said that was his ideal grave.'

Laura knew where she meant. 'It's covered in snowdrops at this time of year.'

'Typical Jim. No fancy stone, no religious verses. Just a chunk of limestone with his name on it.' She grew silent.

'Does he have other family?' Laura asked quietly.

Ellie shook her head. 'Both his parents are dead. He didn't keep in touch with cousins and so on.'

'Do you have anyone?'

'My father. He's in Spain. He might not make it to the funeral. He and Jim weren't on the best of terms.' She said this simply, without regret. 'Being married to Jim often meant giving up other ties. He wasn't a compromiser. I lost count of the number of people he managed to offend.'

Laura was chilled by this. In certain ways it reminded her of her ex-husband. Where a matter of principle had been involved, Tom hadn't minded whose feet he trod on. 'He must have been pretty single-minded.' She remembered various newsreels and newspaper reports where Jim Blackwood had featured on remote peaks, wearing dark glasses and rough beard, set against a fierce blue sky and white mountains.

'Utterly. Luckily, so am I. We each achieved everything we could in our own fields. Ravenscar was the latest great project; the last, as it turns out.'

'Paul says you plan to stay on?'

Ellie nodded.

'If you need any help . . .' Laura offered.

'Professional or otherwise?'

'Both.'

She spoke in such a way that Ellie's defences suddenly broke down. 'Don't,' she pleaded. 'I can't cope with people being kind.' She hid her face behind her hand.

Laura put an arm around her shoulder and waited until the sobbing stopped. Everyone was the crying sort when it came to it, she thought.

'I'm sorry.' She wiped her face. 'But you've no idea.'

'Tell me.'

'He broke my heart. He really did.' Ellie cried again and turned away. 'It sounds corny, but that's how it felt. I was torn apart.'

'What by?'

'Jim had another woman. Only, with him, it couldn't be just an ordinary secret affair. He didn't go off like most people. It happened under my nose.'

'Here at Ravenscar?' Laura couldn't tell how far back the hurt went.

'I oughtn't to be telling you. It's like trampling on his grave.' Ellie spoke in a slow whisper. 'No one else knows about it, except Paul. He was the one who found out. Marianne broke down and told him.'

A new picture built of what must have gone on for Ellie in the past year. 'Jim and Marianne?'

'As soon as we all started living under the same roof. It didn't mean that much to Jim, as it turned out. He could have put a stop to it whenever he wanted. But Marianne really loved him.'

'But didn't Jim realise what he stood to lose?'

Ellie's attempts to pull herself together succeeded at last. 'You mean me? He knew he wouldn't lose me.'

'Had he done it before?'

'A couple of times. He would have done it again, no doubt.

But Marianne made the mistake of thinking she was the only one. She wanted too much from him. He refused. She went and told Paul everything. Then she packed up and left. That's it in a nutshell.'

'I don't think I could have stayed either, if I'd been you.' Laura tried to measure her own reaction. Tom had used other women to get back at her since their separation, but not before.

'What makes you think I could stand it? We had rows. One or the other of us was always on the point of leaving. Me or Paul, I mean. There was never any doubt that Jim would stay put. You remember that day you first came here with Matthew?'

Laura recalled the uneasy first few minutes.

'There'd just been a terrible scene with everyone yelling. It was probably over nothing; who should drive the minibus down to Merton or something. We kept having these flare-ups. Paul wouldn't back down, any more than Jim.'

'Where did Marianne escape to?'

'She got her old job back in Leeds but we haven't seen her since she left.'

'Do you think she knows about Jim?'

Ellie shrugged. 'It was in the newspapers.' She squeezed Laura's hand and stood up. 'A mess, eh? And yes, I do wonder why I put up with it. Only, you would have to have known Jim. For him, it was so cut and dried. Other women were a passing interest but I was the real one. He always said that I was the only one who mattered.'

'But the damage! Did he know he was hurting you?'

'I guess he thought I could take it. After all, I chose to stay married to him. And now I'm the one who gets to bury him.'

She cried again, then rallied. They were talking calmly through practical affairs when Laura's mobile phone rang. Dot Wilson had been taken ill and had collapsed in church.

\*

71

Laura reached St Michael's to find the service broken up and the congregation gathered outside the church in small clusters. Dot was lying unconscious in the central aisle.

Marsden Barraclough, the vicar, had covered her with a coat but had not attempted to move her into a recovery position so that Laura's first job, as she listened to his rapid account of the collapse, was to tilt Dot's chin and put an ear to her mouth to listen for breathing. Hearing nothing, she put a hand on her chest to find there was no movement there.

'It happened without any warning. One moment she seemed normal, singing the hymn. Next thing we knew, there she was laid on the floor. She must have been trying to leave the pew but got no further than this.' He hovered, uncertain how he could help.

'She must have only just stopped breathing.' Laura could still feel a faint pulse in the carotid artery. The sight of Dot, ashen and motionless, was a terrible shock. She felt inside her mouth for a clear airway then immediately punched her chest at the lower end of the sternum, repeating this several times. 'Call an ambulance!' Her hair fell across her face and she grunted with the exertion.

Someone ran down the aisle with a message; Dot's grown-up, married children, Valerie and John, had been informed.

Now Laura pressed more evenly with both hands, released the pressure, did it again. She felt for a pulse. I have to get her to breathe, she told herself. 'Come on, Dot!'

'What is it, a heart attack?' The vicar bent over them.

'Yes, I'm doing all I can.' Not another one, she prayed, so soon after Jim Blackwood. Dot had no history of heart disease, had seemed as spry as ever last time Laura had seen her. Expertly she applied mouth-to-mouth, waiting for the lungs to shudder into life.

More footsteps, more news; the ambulance would arrive in five minutes. Not soon enough. Once more Laura had to resort to chest compression. They were reaching the limit for recovery. She began to fear they would lose her.

Then they heard a dry, crackling intake of air, and saw the thin chest heave. In, out; the breathing resumed. Re-oxygenated, the skin lost its deathly pallor, the pulse grew firmer.

Marsden Barraclough offered a prayer, his voice lost in the high rafters. Laura rearranged her patient face-down until the paramedics arrived and stayed kneeling in the aisle.

'What now?' The vicar clasped his hands and looked anxiously for further signs of life.

'They'll take her to Wingate. She'll probably be in intensive care until she recovers consciousness and they make a proper diagnosis.'

'But she's always been so active.'

Laura felt her own reaction set in. She desperately didn't want to lose Dot, her first friend in the dale and someone on whom she still relied.

Again the doors swung open, and this time two paramedics came running. Laura stood up, told them briefly what had happened and said she would travel in the ambulance with them to Wingate. The vicar would re-direct the relatives to the hospital. As the system took over, Laura controlled the trembling under her ribcage and steadied herself against the end of a pew.

'Good work,' the green-suited paramedic said as he picked up one end of the stretcher.

Laura nodded and looked up at the stained-glass, then followed them out of the church and into the ambulance.


'That's the disadvantage of working in a small community.' Philip welcomed Laura to his new house. She'd gone there from the hospital to tell him about Dot. 'Sometimes we get too involved.'

'According to the cardiologist, she'll make it OK. Valerie's there, waiting for her to come round.' She didn't take in her surroundings, simply sank into a chair and took a drink from him.

'It's at times like this that you wish you were tucked away in some quiet little research lab, surrounded by microscopes and test-tubes with no human beings to feel sorry for.'

'Or be angry with.' Careful not to betray Ellie's confidences, she explained her feelings about Jim Blackwood. 'Of course, I didn't know him, but I realise I could never have liked him, to the point where it might even have interfered with my treatment. How did he strike you?'

'Tough. Someone who got things done.' Philip gave a short laugh. 'You're right, he wasn't an endearing sort. Interesting, though. And you have to admire his achievements.'

'I don't know that I do. He seems to have been brilliant with mountains and lousy with people. I think I prefer it the other way round.' She relaxed and began to look round. Philip had left cases unpacked in the middle of the room. The house was a modern box, fully carpeted and fitted with units, but impersonal. It seemed he was intent on disregarding it.

'It takes a certain unyielding personality,' he admitted. 'If you see a mountain, climb it. If it's a person, dominate it.'

'Some people are like that.'

'Men especially?'

'Maybe.' She laughed back.

'It's OK, you don't need to spell it out.' He followed her gaze around the room. 'I haven't had time to sort anything out yet ... All right, it's a lie. I haven't the least inclination to do it. No, that's not right either; I haven't the heart.'

'It must be strange.'

'When I think of all I took for granted. Bridge House is part of me but I didn't know it until I had to leave it. I never realised I was so attached to the place.' He stopped himself

74

short. 'There is one feature of this house that saves me from going completely crazy, though. Come and look.'

She watched as he drew aside curtains from the French windows, opened them, and stepped out on to a narrow balcony. Cold evening air rushed in. Outside there was a deceptively warm pink tinge to the sky, but nearby trees were stark and blowing in the wind. She heard the thaw-swollen river running close by.

'The water.' He leaned on the iron railing and gazed down. 'If I close my eyes and listen, it doesn't seem too different from what I'm used to.'

Laura went to join him. Beyond the small, bare garden, the bank dropped sheer into a white, racing surge of waterfall and rocks, the current twisting through narrow channels, frothing over harder outcrops. She stared, fascinated by its unstoppable force.

'What's Matthew decided to do about those two kids of his?' Philip asked.

'The best he can, I guess.' He'd finally agreed with Abigail to begin sessions with the counsellor, starting the following week. 'He doesn't have a lot of faith in it, but he knows he has to do something.'

'I hardly need to tell you to keep an eye on Abigail.' Philip rested his elbows on the railing.

'Have you seen her lately?'

'Once, in the Falcon. She's still the same old Abigail. What I mean is, she doesn't let go.'

'I know but what can I do? Apart from keep on telling Matthew that we can work it out. Sophie is doing what all kids do when parents split up. The important thing is how we handle it.'

'Which doesn't necessarily mean giving in to every whim?'

'But Matthew's afraid to make a stand. He knows how easily Abigail could influence the kids against him.'

75

'And would she?' He looked straight at her.

Laura sighed. 'You tell me.'

He considered it. 'She doesn't have the self-restraint not to.'

Another deep breath. 'I wish,' Laura began, then stared down at the water.

'That you two had a clean slate?' he guessed.

'Yes, but I can't un-wish the children. One of the things I like about Matthew is how much he loves his kids.'

'It does make for complications though.' He mentioned his own three sons, variously shocked and outraged by their parents' separation. 'Even though they're grown-up, there's terrific pressure from them for us to stay together. That's one reason why Juliet took so long to decide.'

'But in the end, it's your own life.' Yet she remembered the times, pre-Matthew, when she'd argued vehemently the opposite; that parents should be reconciled for the sake of the children. 'Oh, Philip, I don't know what I'm talking about any more.'

'Me neither. I think I do – I just have it nicely sorted out in my own mind – then suddenly something knocks me flat.'

'That's what makes choices so hard.' She said goodnight to Philip then drove home with the image of black waters running at her feet.

# CHAPTER EIGHT

Within twenty-four hours Dot was out of intensive care. When Philip dropped by, she was sitting up in bed in a general ward looking embarrassed, even cross with herself for landing up in hospital.

'What's this little spot of bother you've got yourself into now?' Philip had checked her notes on the way in; there were no plans for immediate surgery, but a fair chance that she would need it eventually.

Her eyebrows flickered upwards. 'All those contraptions.' She protested that she'd come round to find herself connected to various tubes and drips.

'Those contraptions, as you call them, helped to save your life.' He smiled as he sat on the edge of the bed, not used to the sight of Dot out of her uniform of neat cardigan and sensible skirt.

'Nay, that was Laura who did that. Without her I'd have been a goner.' They'd told her about her collapse. All she recalled was a pain in her chest as she hurried to church, growing worse as the service proceeded, and a bungled attempt to get clear of her pew.

'You were lucky she was on hand,' he told her. 'Now, what are we going to do with you?'

'Get me out of here, please.' Loss of independence was hard for her.

'You hold your horses. No rushing about Hoovering for a while.'

'I don't want an operation,' she insisted. 'I want them just to give me something to get me back on my feet.'

Philip said she must discuss the options with Mr Walker, her specialist. 'It's angina, Dot, which means your heart isn't pumping enough oxygen because the arteries have narrowed. This chest pain – have you had it before?'

'Now and then. Not bad enough to bother me. You know me, Dr Maskell, I don't like to make a fuss.'

'Well, this was a warning shot. You'll have to take it seriously from now on. For a start, they'll prescribe a drug for you to take before any exercise.'

'And what about my little jobs?'

Besides cleaning at Bridge House, Dot helped whenever people needed her. But her idea of 'little' was pulling heavy furniture away from walls to dust behind. He warned her that there would be no more of that. 'Light work maybe, but nothing strenuous.'

She assimilated the facts, keeping a steady eye on Philip's face. All her life she'd kept herself busy. Town Head was immaculate; a reflection of her upright self.

'I don't mean you'll be laid up in bed,' Philip continued. 'But you'll have to recognise your limits, take care of yourself.'

'You put it off, you know; admitting that you've grown old with the rest of them.' She was over seventy, a survivor of vast changes, upheaval that younger generations could scarcely imagine.

'Take your time, Dot. Build up your strength and wait and see what you're able to do.'

Pressing her lips together, she nodded. 'Aye, I'll be right.'

He stood up, ready to leave. 'And you'll let us look after you?'

'If you promise to get me out of here as quick as you can.'

The old spirit flared. 'I can't be doing with all these little nurses flitting around, and people bringing me menus to tick, and doctors round the bed. They look like children some of them, bless their hearts.'

Philip promised to do his best and called in on his way out to see David Walker, Dot's cardiologist. They discussed how best to stabilise her condition and agreed to put her on the bypass list which meant a probable wait of six months. Meanwhile, she should be carefully managed. The professional, detached prognosis was at variance with Dot's own hopes of getting back to an independent lifestyle.

In the car park Philip came face to face with Juliet. She was carrying red tulips, dressed in her navy blue coat and a bright silk scarf, looking composed. She stopped to speak instead of rushing by, as he feared.

'How's Dot?'

'An impatient patient.'

'Trust her.' Juliet smiled. 'Valerie came to see me last night after she'd collected toiletries and things from Town Head. She found it hard to take it all in, poor thing. She says she can't thank Laura enough.'

'I'll tell her.' The focus on Dot was a relief.

'We're worried that she won't know how to take things easy. And Valerie says that if Dot can't carry on with her jobs there's a money problem too. She needs her wages from cleaning to keep Town Head going. There are lots of overheads in a big place like that.' Juliet pointed out problems that Philip hadn't thought through. 'Of course, she can keep on coming to our house, doing what she can. I wouldn't expect her to take on the heavy work any more.'

'She won't like charity.' Philip was knocked off-balance by the picture of 'our house'.

'That's not what I'm offering.' Juliet frowned. Perhaps she'd recognised that the unobtrusive pronoun carried connotations. The colour rose to her cheeks and she lifted the bunch of tulips to indicate that she should be getting along.

Philip didn't want her to vanish from the windy car park. They stood sandwiched between rows of cars, edging to one side as an ambulance crawled past. 'Meet me for lunch?'

She paused, then said, 'As long as it's just lunch.'

They arranged to meet at the best teashop in Wingate; neutral territory. Philip told himself not to pin too much on it as he hurried along to his next meeting.

This then was part of the amicable set-up Juliet had imagined. Lunch amongst the potted palms of the stately spa town, their conduct monitored by waitresses in black with white lace collars, and kept within the rules of the game by silver salt-cellars and trolleys laden with cakes.

The next day Philip stood in the churchyard, seeking shelter from the wind and rain beside the Abbey's ruined walls. Funeral services here were conducted with an especially sombre sense of man's impermanence. Round Norman arches in the stonework gave way to soaring Gothic, before these too crumbled. Walls six feet thick, witness to the stonemason's skill, withstood only five hundred years of winter rain, then conceded defeat. The eighteenth-century gravestones eroded and became illegible.

Hawkshead Abbey had become a tourist attraction of late, and was laid out with gravelled walkways and smart notices which explained the layout of kitchens and cloisters, nave and chancel. Surrounded by shadowy yews, overlooking a peaceful bend in the river, in the summer it was an attractive place to walk, to study mortality, and marvel. On a bitterly cold February morning, however, it was desolate.

Philip watched the mourners emerge from the church adjoining the ruins. St Michael's had been snatched from decay with the rest of the Abbey and restored during the second half of the last century as a parish church for Hawkshead and Askby. Today it still served its mixed community of landowners, farmers, commuters and young families; a stronger influence than might be supposed by outsiders who saw only history in the crumbling stones and lichen-covered graves.

He wasn't sorry to have missed the service for Jim Blackwood, though a sense of duty brought him to the church for the interment. In Gerald's absence, it was enough for him to put in a late appearance and offer condolences if needed. He watched as first the pallbearers bore the coffin into the rain, followed by Gabriella, who walked alone, then Paul Miller and a small group of strangers. No one from the village had come, except Laura and Matthew.

As the train of mourners trickled by, Philip joined them. Raindrops splashed cold and wet on his face. He turned up his collar and became part of the huddle around the open grave. Marsden Barraclough's hopeful words battled against gloomy skies and spirits. There were no tears, only a feeling of emptiness as dust returned to dust.

Then Paul Miller stepped forward to help Gabriella from the graveside. She looked bewildered and had to be guided to a waiting car. Philip stared at their receding backs; tall man, small woman in black, his arm around her, both heads bowed.

He glanced in surprise at Laura standing close by. For a moment he thought he had mistaken shared grief in Gabriella and Paul for something other. It was natural, surely, for her to cling for comfort and Paul's intimate response was what any friend would have given.

But the picture stayed with him long after he'd passed between the flat tombstones with their Victorian wrought-ironwork and had seen the funeral cortège drive away, mourners screened behind rain-spattered windows. It made such an impression that he decided to mention it to Laura when they got back to the health centre later that morning.

He cleared his throat. 'I'm hoping that the answer's no, but did you notice anything about Gabriella Blackwood and Paul Miller at the funeral?'

'The answer's no.' Laura was confident. 'Think about it, Philip, who else could she turn to?' Her father hadn't shown up from Spain; hers was a family short on relatives.

'Are you sure?' Normally he wouldn't push it further.

'Yes. Why?' She screwed the top on to her pen and rested both hands on the desk as she looked up.

'It would be another twist, wouldn't it? Something going on between them.'

'If it were true, I suppose it would.'

'Call it my fertile imagination, but if Gabriella and Paul were an item, it might cast a new light on things.'

Laura stood and went to lean against the wall and looked out of the window at the misty hillside. 'Say what you mean, Philip.'

'It occurs to me that they might have got what they wanted with Jim's death. I know it's a harsh thing to say, but with him out of the way and just the two of them together . . . Am I being ridiculous?'

'You are if you think Paul killed Jim Blackwood.' Laura's reply was measured as ever.

Philip looked over his shoulder, closed the door and spoke quickly, quietly. 'Laura, if Gerald missed something up there by the tarn, signs of violence on the body, for instance, he's in it up to his eyes!'

'But he says not.' Hands on hips, she faced him. 'He was categorical; death by natural causes.'

'Yes, and I wasn't happy at the time, remember.' Philip's thoughts swung back to the newer doubt. 'What if Paul did have a strong motive?'

'I don't believe it.' Laura was firm. 'I talked to him on Sunday. He asked whether anyone could have done anything to help Jim if they'd been on the scene. He was having a genuinely bad time coming to terms with it. Either he's a damn good actor and I'm a lousy judge, or . . .'

'I'm a suspicious fool.' Philip shrugged. I hope you're right.'

# CHAPTER NINE

'Why do you run yourself down?' Sean Armstrong asked. He and Aimee had followed a green track from Ravenscar over to Ginnersby, one of the old lead-mining villages high in the dale. He'd come back to finish a special project for his A-level geography course and arranged to meet her again. It was almost a week since his party had packed up and left.

To either side of the track, heather carpeted the hillside, brownish-black in the gloomy afternoon, until a weak sun came through and lit up ridges and further tracks and silhouetted disused mine buildings and what was left of a tall smelting-chimney.

'I suppose it's to save other people the bother.' She sniffed and turned, so that the wind blew her hair clear of her face.

Sean picked his way across the foundations of vanished buildings and pointed out entrances to tunnels now roughly boarded up. 'Some of these go for hundreds of metres. Come on, we can get into this one. Let's take a look.'

Aimee hesitated. 'God, it stinks.'

'Wimp.' He felt his way along the shaft, stumbling against loose bricks, and heard his own hollow footsteps echo. 'It meets up with another one. They probably go on for miles, like a maze. Imagine tunnelling your way down here for lead, on your hands and knees.'

She still refused to follow him. The mine held no attraction, only horror when she thought of men slipping to their deaths, or slowly dying of lead poisoning. What was left of them now except empty tunnels, piles of rubble where their houses once stood, and vast tips and grooves in the hillside where they'd dammed streams to search for ore?

Sean felt his way back towards the entrance. He emerged, rubbing his hands on his jeans. 'You can't see much anyway.'

'I wouldn't want to. It's primitive to force men to do that for a living. It gives me the creeps.'

'Good job you weren't living here a hundred years ago, then.'

She walked on, following the fast-running stream that cut through the heathery slope. 'Sometimes I wish I wasn't living here now.'

'Swap,' he offered. 'My life for yours.' He loved the feeling in the dale that the world wasn't an overcrowded planet after all.

'You wouldn't want it.' She was sick of trying to keep out of her father's way. If it wasn't her work, it was her appearance, her accent, her friends. All the good resolutions he'd made when she was in hospital, about trying to communicate and understand, seemed to have disappeared.

Sean stared at her. 'What *is* wrong with you?'

'Nothing you'd know anything about.' She regretted agreeing to come. It would have been better to have knocked him back, stopped him from phoning. She saw now that he wasn't her type. But she'd been fooled by the lean and hungry look; the feeling that his thoughts ran deep and might just coincide with her own.

He ran ahead and cut up the hillside towards a stone ledge, where he stood looking down at her. Then he swooped, ran into her, held her. There was a moment when she could have decided not to kiss him, until their eyes met and she was lost. His look was intense, challenging her to back out before it was too late. Their lips touched and the kiss went on and on. If

85

they stopped, would there be anything to say, any way forward?

At last he let her go. He rolled his eyes upwards, spread his arms wide and let himself topple back, flat on the ground.

Aimee laughed. 'I'm not picking you up!' Instead she scrambled up the hill.

He lay there looking up at the sky.

She turned. 'You'll catch your death.'

He too started to laugh. Then he rolled over and sprang to his feet. This time he ran up the hill towards her and kissed her again.


'Aimee!' She was in her room when her father's voice called her abruptly to the phone.

'. . . Yeah, I know, every night this week,' Sean began sheepishly. 'I'm ringing you from work.'

Work was as a part-time barman at a hotel in Leeds city centre. He fitted it around his studies, a couple of nights a week.

'Can you come into town and meet me?'

'When?' She sat on the bed with the telephone, surrounded by loose pages and ring-folders.

'Now.'

'Sean, I can't.' She would need a lift, and her mother was out at her painting class. She wouldn't dream of asking her father.

'It's important.'

'I could come tomorrow.' Friday. She would go on the bus, straight from school.

'Yeah.' He seemed to be in two minds. 'Yeah, come then. But I'd better tell you now in any case.'

'Tell me what?' This was different from Sean's usual style of phone call, which rambled and never got anywhere, except to tell her he was thinking of her, couldn't get her out of his mind, missed her, wanted to see her.

'Well, you've heard of a woman called Marianne Miller? I just found out that she works in this hotel.'

'Since when?' Aimee had never met Paul Miller's wife, but she knew that she'd only lasted a few weeks at Ravenscar.

'Not that long. She works in Reception. She must have heard that I was in Hawkshead when Jim Blackwood died. She came into the bar to talk to me. She seems pretty cut up. She wanted to know what happened.'

'Why couldn't she ask them herself? At the funeral?'

'She stayed away, something about Paul not wanting her around. There was a big bust-up.' Pips went in the payphone, while Sean shoved in more coins.

'Did you say you actually found the body?'

'Yes. She wanted to know all about it; what time, how quick it was likely to have been, all of it. I told her he had a heart attack and drowned.'

Aimee knew from the sound of his voice that Sean would have preferred not to have had the whole scene churned up.

'When I said "heart attack", she came in quick with, "who says?", which I thought was a pretty strange reaction. I asked her, didn't she read it in the papers? At that point she got really upset. So I told her I know you. I said if she likes, she can ask you or your dad about it.'

'Thanks, Sean.'

'Yeah, I know. But you should have been here. I've never seen anyone start shaking like that. She wants to know why the police aren't doing anything.'

Aimee sat cross-legged. Now she knew exactly why Sean had rung. 'What makes her say that?'

'According to her, it's off the wall. Heart attack is complete crap. She says Jim never had any heart problems. He was the fittest bloke she knew.'

87

'Yeah, with serious diabetes.'

'But get this. She says she left Ravenscar because she couldn't stand the rows. They were always at each other's throats.'

'Who were?'

'Jim and Paul Miller. When I say rows, I mean fights. Physical stuff.' His voice was cut off by more pips, the sound of more money in the slot. 'Listen, I'll have to be quick. It turns out they hated each other's guts. So when she heard about Jim, she put two and two together.'

'And did what?'

'Thought about it for a week, then went to the police. End of last week. They sent someone to interview her today. She reckons they'll soon be heading your way with some kind of request to dig up the corpse.'

In the background a door banged, a man's voice shouted. 'Aimee, I gotta go. Come over tomorrow. We'll talk about it.'

Slowly, she agreed. This was information she didn't know how to handle. Her first thought when she put down the phone was to ring Laura at Abbey Grange. She tried, but got an answer-machine message. Then she rang Philip; no reply. She would have to tell her father herself.

He was busy in his study as usual, stooped over his desk, a lock of grey hair falling over his forehead. He was wearing his off-duty outfit of grey ribbed sweater and open-necked shirt, frowning as he worked. He glanced up as she went in and held up a warning hand while he finished what he was doing.

When he was ready to listen, Aimee launched straight in. 'Sean's heard from Marianne Miller that the police might want to dig up Jim Blackwood's body.' If he hadn't treated her as a nuisance, she might have been more tactful. As it was, she saw his eyes flicker. He took off his glasses and swung them.

'Marianne who?'

'Paul Miller's wife. She works in the same hotel as Sean.'

'Oh, not this again.' He sighed wearily. 'First off I had it from Janet, then from Philip, now from you.'

'It's not my fault!'

'Isn't it? I don't hear you trying to put a stop to the gossip.' He sorted papers, knocking some off the edge of the desk.

As he bent to pick them up, an unguarded, vulnerable movement which showed the back of his neck, Aimee's irritation melted. 'Look, Dad, this could be serious. It's not just gossip any more.' She told him exactly what Sean had told her.

He listened carefully. 'The only thing this proves is the truth of the old adage that Hell hath no fury like a woman scorned.'

'But what if she can prove that Paul hated Jim enough to want to kill him? Won't they start poking around, finding out if he had an alibi?'

'You watch too much American TV,' Gerald began.

'Dad!' Aimee faced him across the desk. 'I'm trying to help.'

'You're interfering. You don't know enough about it.'

'That's right, blame me; I'm stupid. Mum's stupid. We're all stupid! You're the only one who knows anything round here. Why should *you* listen? We're only trying to muck things up for you.' It came out in a rush, eighteen years of pent-up frustration. 'No one's supposed to make a peep when you're around. We're all supposed to salute and follow orders. Ask Philip or Laura.' She stared him out, grew hot all over, felt her palms beginning to sweat.

'I don't hear them complaining.'

'That's because they don't know how to handle you any more. They're afraid you'll go off the deep end.'

'I don't know what you mean. I run the practice in a democratic way. We have our daily meetings. Everyone gets a say.'

'Who are you trying to kid?' She knew she'd pushed him to a point where he would lose his temper.

'Right, Aimee, that's enough. I won't have you waltzing in here shouting the odds.'

'So, send me to my room.' She stood fast in the doorway, then heard her mother come into the house behind her.

'Who's shouting what?' Janet Scott stepped in, wearing her common-sense manner as she made Aimee step to one side.

'Dad is. Ask him.'

'I am not shouting!'

'You are, Gerald. Calm down.' She came into the study unbuttoning her sheepskin jacket. 'What's the matter now?'

'Me. I'm the matter.' Aimee guessed it would be two against one. 'So what's new? I try to help, and all he does is dump his own bloody incompetence on me!'

'Don't you dare!' He strode up to her.

She didn't back off. Instead she stared right into his face. 'I'm the punch-bag round here. Go on, why don't you?'

Aimee was frightened but triumphant. She'd succeeded in goading her father further than ever before. His face was red, he drew sharp breaths and clenched his teeth, obviously wanting to knock her flat. They could do what they wanted now, him and her mother. In her own mind, she'd proved her point.

'Stop this.' Janet put a hand on Gerald's arm. 'What's going on? What incompetence? Will someone please tell me.'

'It's nothing.' He backed off, shaking his head. 'She and that boyfriend have cooked up a story between them.'

'Aimee?' Janet demanded a proper explanation. 'What is this about? Is it the Jim Blackwood business?'

'Bull's-eye.' Gerald went and sat at his desk, his face bitter now. 'Apparently the man was murdered, and I missed the vital clues.'

'I never said that.' As the mood in the room changed and

her father's voice dropped to a slow drawl, she felt more conciliatory.

'As good as. That's what everyone else will say; poor old Gerald Scott, he must be really past it these days. Doesn't even recognise a murder victim when he sees one.'

'I never said he'd definitely been killed. All I said was that someone's gone to the police.' Aimee appealed to her mother.

Janet drew a breath. 'But you didn't notice anything suspicious?' she asked Gerald.

'No black eyes, no bashed skull, if that's what you mean. I'm only obliged to check quickly, which I did.'

'In retrospect, wouldn't it have been better to . . . ?'

He closed his eyes.

'All right. We can all have twenty-twenty vision after the event,' she agreed. 'But what can you do now?'

'Wait and see.' The wave of emotion had cast him high and dry, stranded on a bleak shore. 'If the police find grounds for suspicion they'll go to the coroner for an exhumation order. If they find what they're looking for and a relative makes a complaint against me, the case will go to the GMSC, and I would be likely to lose.'

'Because you were negligent?'

He nodded and looked blankly at her.

Janet fetched him a drink, then talked it through and through; exactly what Aimee had found out from Sean, what was the timescale, how long it would be before they knew whether the police had decided to take action. 'Sit tight,' she advised. 'And Aimee, find out all you possibly can from Sean. Meanwhile, we ought to discuss it with Philip and Laura.'

Aimee wanted to slip away now. She knew her father would be shattered if it worked out against him. 'I'm sorry, Dad.' She bit her lip and fought back tears.

He looked up. 'Never be a doctor, Aimee.'

# CHAPTER TEN

For the first time Laura disliked the dark evenings at Abbey Grange. Winter was almost over, but still she found herself driving home after nightfall along the road by the river, hemmed in by stone walls to each side of the narrow lane.

Her house stood quiet and empty, surrounded by more walls and trees, overwhelmed by the bulk of Ravenscar which rose in front of it, more sensed than seen, with its soaring skyline, its folds of valleys and fast-running streams. She felt its lonely presence as she walked from car to house. For once, on the Thursday night when she knew Matthew was in York, she feared the secrets of the hill.

There were tactics she could use to divert herself. First, she closed the curtains to shut out the infinite dark. Then she lit lamps around the house, switched on radio noise and checked for telephone messages.

'Hi, Laura. It's Matthew.' Not Matt. For her, Matthew was always Matthew. 'I have to go to our first counselling session tonight. Did you remember? I just wanted to ring to say hello and that I love you.' His voice was hesitant, soft. 'See you later.'

The machine clicked. An automatic female voice told Laura that this was her only message. Since she'd missed speaking to him by only ten minutes, she considered ringing him back on the car phone but decided against it. Finding that she wasn't hungry, she toyed with a plate of cold food and longed for the spring, when she would be able to walk off her nervous energy up Black Gill, by Joan's Foss. As it was, the darkness trapped her within a circle of repetitive thoughts.

At eight o'clock, when Aimee tried to reach her with the news from Sean, Laura had escaped to the Falcon. Other people's conversation was in the end the only effective diversion from her own spinning doubts and fears.

Brian Lawson's warm greeting broke her mood. He reached straight away for her favourite drink, then launched into news of Alison and baby Emma. 'I promised myself not to talk shop when I saw you come in.' He grinned sheepishly. 'But I wanted to ask you about this crying business. I mean, is it normal for her to be waking two or three times a night screaming blue murder?'

'I take it you mean Emma, not Alison?'

'Oh yes, I see.' The smile broadened. 'Is she just hungry?'

Laura sat at the bar. She'd changed into a black mohair sweater and trousers and come out without make-up, her hair twisted up, but escaping from its clips. 'Does she stop crying as soon as she's fed?'

Brian admitted that she did. 'No need to worry, eh? I should know better. I've been through it once before. Mind you, that was a long time ago.'

'The only thing you have to worry about is your own loss of sleep. But that can't be helped. How's Alison coping?'

'Brilliant. Better than me. She's taken to it like a duck to water.'

Gradually Laura relaxed. She was glad after a while to see Alison herself come to serve behind the bar. She seemed at ease, and with a happy glow that meant the sleepless nights and constant babycare suited her as much as Brian had said.

'Where's Matthew tonight?' Alison chatted as she supplied an order to another customer.

'In York.'

'Seeing the kids?'

Laura let out a little information to repay the kindly meant interest. 'Yes, and Abigail. They've fixed up some family therapy sessions. They're a bit worried about Sophie.'

'Hard for you, though?' As usual, Alison was on target. She finished serving and came up close. 'I know what it's like. Brian has Nina from his first marriage, you know.'

Laura remembered the dynamics; outspoken, scornful teenager struggling to find a niche in the new family set-up after Brian had re-married. Nina visited the Falcon during her school holidays, had inherited her father's sporty physique, but not apparently his friendly, conciliatory nature. 'How does Nina like the baby?'

Alison cocked her head. 'She pretended not to show any interest at first. Said all babies looked the same to her. Then I asked did she want to hold her? That's when she fell for her hook, line and sinker. Now I can't keep her off the phone, asking how Emma is and when can she come and help look after her. Who'd have thought it?'

It sounded like a happy ending, or at least a fresh start. The pub grew busier and Alison was drawn away, drifting back occasionally to keep Laura company. Soon afterwards, she went upstairs to check on the baby.

'What are you drinking?' a voice asked at Laura's shoulder.

She turned to say hello to Luke Altham. 'Martini, please. Oh no, I'm driving. Just a tonic then.'

He settled beside her. 'No Matthew tonight?' He explained that he was in Hawkshead to visit a cousin, having come straight from his office in Merton. The cousin had gone on to play a squash match at the school gym. Luke, himself, was putting off going home to avoid a nightmare pile of undone housework.

'I veer between two extremes,' he confessed. 'On the one

hand, I firmly believe that a house has its own fine ecological balance. For instance, if I disturb the cobwebs, I do terrible things to explode the housefly population. And without several thick layers of dust, what would happen to the poor little dust mite?'

'On the other hand?'

'How long can I leave a half-full carton of milk standing on a windowsill without it turning into a health hazard?' He asked the question in all seriousness.

'You mean, how long can you hope to escape prosecution under the Public Health Act?' She threw him back a legal question.

'Lawyer in court for causing health risk? Can't you just see it in the *Merton Herald*? On the other hand again, supposing I had three hands, maybe I could weigh up the possibility of falling seriously ill from food poisoning and waking up to find an attractive young female doctor like you hovering at my bedside?'

Laura sighed and rolled her eyes.

'Sorry. A lousy line, eh?'

'Pretty much.' For a while they chatted to other regulars. Brian asked Laura how Dot was, and learned that she would soon be out of hospital, but by no means back to her old self. Luke talked to Kit and Harry Braithwaite about the death up at Ravenscar Hall.

'No inquest?' Kit sucked his teeth.

'Not if it was unnecessary,' Luke confirmed.

'Aye, that'd be throwing taxpayers' money down the drain.' Harry offered his thoughts between regular pulls at his pint of bitter.

'But who's to say it's unnecessary?' Kit knew Laura was listening in. 'A young chap in his forties drops dead in his tracks. I reckon they should at least open the poor fellow up and take a look at him.' He described Jim's death in gory detail, received second, third and fourth hand.

Luke refused to be drawn. 'Laura would tell us more.' He beckoned her across.

'She would if she were to be completely unprofessional and indiscreet, which she isn't,' she countered.

'But he was fit as a fiddle. I heard he ran up and down Ravenscar every morning before breakfast, come rain or shine.'

'That's his missus.' Harry was a stickler for facts.

'A chap like that has no reason to drop down dead.'

'What's reason got to do with it?' Kit's brother recognised the vagaries of fate. 'Fit young chaps keel over on football fields, anywhere you like. That's it, they've had their chips.'

'Aye, but there'd be an inquest.' Kit was dogged too. 'Ask Mr Altham here.'

'Not if the doctor decided to sign the death certificate then and there.' Luke frowned, realising they were on touchy territory, and glanced at Laura.

She signalled that it was her turn to buy him a drink.

He asked for a fruit juice. 'Why not have a proper drink yourself?' He gave her a long, hard look. 'Leave your car here. I can drive you back.'

Laura raised her eyebrows.

'No, that isn't just another lousy line. It looks to me as if you could do with a drink.' He ordered one before she had time to object. 'You don't take any notice of pub talk, do you?'

'No, but I suppose I'm worried that it could be more than gossip.' They took their drinks to a quiet corner. 'Maybe you could tell me; you're the lawyer.'

He grinned. 'I could if I were to be completely unprofessional –'

'No, no names. Purely hypothetical.' She grimaced at the use of the cliché, but went on. 'Say, for instance, there was a case of negligence. I know the ropes as far as the GMSC is concerned. The victim or the victim's relatives can follow a complaints procedure. GP gets hauled up to answer questions. It's tough. Very bad career-wise. Even worse for the ego. But what happens, say, if part of the negligence involves failure to spot a serious crime?'

Luke nodded. 'A capital offence? If it comes to light after the event, you mean? Well, the GP would have to give evidence at a public inquest, that's for sure.'

Laura tried to imagine Gerald brought to book by the coroner in Wingate. Why hadn't he spotted evidence of foul play? Where was his judgment when he examined the body? Or did he have reason to conceal the evidence? Knowing Gerald's reactions, his temperament and antipathy towards interference of any kind, she feared the worst. 'What else?'

'There's worse. He'd be called as a witness at any subsequent criminal trial.'

'That could drag on for ages.'

'At the very, very worst if the police considered that the negligence was deliberate, with some specific motive, the GP could find that he was the one in the dock.'

Luke's words sent the situation ballooning out of control; inquests, trials, a question of murder. She contemplated the repercussions for Gerald and for the practice.

'Of course, it hardly ever happens that they put the doc in the dock.' He studied her again. 'I'm not much help, am I?'

'Oh yes, you are.' She didn't want to seem ungrateful.

'Look, it isn't like you to sit and worry about hypotheses. I think of you as coming out fighting, seconds out; round three.' Luke had worked with the protest group against the quarry after Laura had enlisted his help.

They veered off into inconsequential topics. Luke's jokiness mellowed into a more attentive manner, while Laura dropped her defences. She found they had plenty in common beyond affairs to do with Ravensdale. It turned out that they'd studied at the same university, came from similar backgrounds.

'I was an idealistic youth,' Luke confessed. 'A law degree was my pass into the hallowed halls of influence. I wanted to make a difference.' He described his sense of vocation. 'That lasted a fair while, as a matter of fact, through the disillusionment of discovering that Law is largely a case of defending the indefensible and making money out of misery.'

'Just like Medicine. I try to cure the incurable.'

'But at least you don't make money out of them.' He said he salved his conscience by espousing worthy causes. 'Don't get me wrong. I believe in everything I do for my environmental groups. But I'm not naive any more. In fact, I've probably become more cynical than my most cynical opponent, whether it's a conglomerate stone company wanting to rip the heart out of the dale, or a spokesman for a multinational motor industry persuading a government minister to plough a route through.' He spoke with conviction now, frown lines appearing on his young-looking face. He had what Laura called Irish features; clear blue eyes, a straight mouth, everything well defined. They relaxed easily into humour, and switched just as readily into sympathy, concern, anger. Beneath the articulate, analytical guise which he'd worn throughout the quarry inquiry was a passionate core.

'It's strange. We both deal with people who are their own worst enemies.' She thought of bad diet, lack of exercise, drink, drugs, ignorance. The list of how people ruined their health went on. 'But I don't know if I could defend someone who I knew was guilty,' she added.

'That's just it; I don't *know* they're guilty. Not as a matter of empirical fact.'

'That's sophistry,' she objected. 'It's only because you don't ask the right question.'

'True. If a defendant pleads "not guilty", I have to use the facts as he presents them.'

'But what about your gut feeling?'

He shrugged. 'Do you stop treating a patient with lung cancer just because you have a gut feeling that he'll leave your surgery and the first thing he'll do is take out a cigarette?'

'But what if someone comes across as downright evil?'

'Most people aren't. Criminals are addicts of one sort or another. They lie to survive.'

'Why do they kill? Not only to survive?'

He thought a long time. 'I have to go to prisons to visit clients. Murderers. They're held for assessment in the hospital wing immediately after committing the crime. I walk in; rows of beds with bedside lockers. These men have usually killed their wives. On each locker there's a picture of the woman they've just killed. Every second is agony. Do you know how many murderers attempt suicide in the days after the crime?'

He gazed around the pub. 'There are no evil people. But the things people do may be evil. I think there's a difference.' When he looked back at Laura, it was with a clear idea of turning to more personal issues. 'I'll tell you one thing, though; these days I steer clear of divorce cases. Let others do the really dirty work.'

Laura smiled and nodded.

'And I've managed to avoid marriage myself. That's a promise that's not worth the paper it's written on.'

This time she couldn't agree.

'I only see the ones that break down. It gives a man a shaky idea of the whole edifice.' He drew another parallel. 'Like you, you know your way around the human body. You realise all too well what can go wrong.'

'True. I often think it's a wonder any of us get beyond twenty.'

Laura had managed to forget that her visit to the pub was a diversionary tactic. Against expectations, she'd actually enjoyed herself. But now it was time to go. She said she would walk home. It wasn't far, she wasn't afraid of the dark.

But Luke insisted on taking her. 'That was the deal. You could drink, I could take you home.'

They left together, Laura aware of his instinctively gallant manner; an old-fashioned word to fit the way he stood back from his stool to let her through, how he held the doors and made sure she was strapped into the passenger seat.

'Come in for coffee,' she invited. There was no sign of Matthew's car outside Abbey Grange.

'No, thanks. Time to tackle the cobwebs.' He stayed behind the wheel, waiting for her to get out.

'Poor spiders.' She smiled in at him.

'I know.' He peered out. She'd left lights on in the house, her head was framed by a yellow glow. 'Good luck, Laura.'

The remark threw her. 'Do I need it?'

'Do you?'

'Yes, I suppose I do.'

He nodded, eased the car out of the gate and was gone before she had entered the house.


Laura knew by the footsteps in the hall that Matthew was weary. He shuffled slightly and paused for a long time as he laid his keys on the table. When he came into the lounge, he'd put on a cheerful face that fooled neither of them.

'How did it go?'

He remembered to greet her with a kiss. 'How can you tell?'

'You can't with counselling. It's a long, slow proccess. How was Sophie?'

'The picture of health, actually.' He gave an ironic shrug. 'She was the one who did most of the talking.'

'And Tim?'

'He just stared round the room and answered yes and no when prompted. I think he wondered what the hell was going on.'

Laura reached the difficult question. 'Abigail?'

He turned down the corners of his mouth. 'Very earnest. Used twenty words where two would do, explaining what she thought was wrong with Sophie.'

'Did she blame you?'

'Not overtly.' He sat and stared at the fire, hands clasped. 'No, as a matter of fact, she seemed to think she should bear at least half the responsibility.'

'Well, she was the one who broke up the marriage.'

'She says she didn't realise the terrible effect it would have on the kids. Apparently Sophie talks endlessly about Hawkshead Hall, about living there, looking back to when we were a family.'

Laura's heart was squeezed tight. What more was there to say? She pictured the dark-haired child pining for the past. 'Did you get anything from the session?' Besides an unbearable burden of guilt.

He sank further forward to rest his elbows on his knees. 'It put me in the picture. I got a chance to listen to Sophie for the first time since we broke up. She usually clams up whenever I ask her anything. But this woman brought out a lot that I didn't know was there. That's good for a first session, isn't it?'

'Poor Matthew.' Laura knelt and put her arms around his neck.

With his head sunk against his chest, letting her arms stay there rather than responding, he told her his worst fears. 'What if we've ruined their lives between us? Done something that can't be repaired. I heard Sophie trying to describe what she liked about Hawkshead. At first it was her pony. Then it was her gran. Then her school. She made a story-book picture, left out all the rows. And I watched Tim. I can't read him any more. His face is blank.' Matthew's voice broke down.

'Give them time,' Laura whispered. She put her head against his.

'It scares me, Laura. That blank look. It's how I reacted when I was a kid at school and terrified of the older boys bullying me.'

'Trained yourself not to give away your feelings.' It happened to all children to a greater or lesser extent. It was how they survived. When people wondered why adults lacked the spontaneity of their youth, the answer was obvious to Laura. They couldn't afford the vulnerability that went with it.

When Matthew looked up, he was crying.

She kissed him. 'Don't give in. We can sort this out.'

He held her, kissed her back.

'I don't know if I can solve this, Laura. It hammers away at me, it's driving me mad.'

'I know.' She held him tight.

Gradually his head cleared. He held her, swaying to and fro, burying his face in her hair.

Then his kisses changed. They were more forceful. With his weight against her, he eased her backwards on to the rug, used his strength to press her down, his mouth on hers, his hands pinning her arms above her head.

She let him undress her, knew that this was what he liked. At the same time, she unbuttoned his shirt, felt the warm strength of his shoulders, smelled his skin. She was tender towards him, loved him completely. If part of this was the pain of his indecision and agony over Sophie and Tim, she must share it. 'I love you,' she whispered.

He didn't use these words in return but showed her that he did through every movement of his body as they clung to one another, her breast against his, hip to hip, his lips on her neck, her eyes, her mouth.

This was when he lost himself in her, when he would let go and frighten her with his intensity. But she knew he still recognised her, that she never became merely an object to satisfy him as he murmured her name, waited and caressed her until she travelled the journey with him to the passionate point in the distance that led to a moment no words could approach, beyond their everyday selves.

For a while afterwards they were content to lie in each other's arms. The fire glowed red, the world was warm and quiet.

He could hardly bear to let her go, he said. But he consented at last, and she was the one this time to fetch a bathrobe, a drink. They sat until after midnight, listening to music, limbs entwined. The fire burned down, logs collapsed in on themselves in a shower of sparks. They watched without talking. If only time would stop, if the rug by the fireside at Abbey Grange could be the still centre they craved.

Next day, Ellie Blackwood came to the health centre outside surgery hours.

'I think you should see her,' Sheila suggested, when Laura answered the internal phone.

'I'll come out.' She knew with a solid certainty that this would be about Jim's death.

'I need your advice.' Even now Ellie looked apologetic. 'I didn't know whether you'd be here. I just got in the car and drove down.'

Laura took hold of her arm and steered her to a seat in the waiting area. The building was empty except for Philip, who was working in his own room. 'Tell me what it's about.'

Ellie's face was pale with shock, she was trembling as she

103

took a letter from her pocket. 'It's from the coroner's office in Wingate.'

She read the information; not a request to Ellie, but a statement of fact. They were telling her that they'd granted permission for the exhumation of her husband's remains.

'I rang them straight back, said they couldn't do it.'

'What did they tell you?'

'They said the body is the property of the coroner.' She was bewildered.

'It's true,' Laura said gently. 'Hard as it seems.'

'You mean I can't stop them?'

'Not if the police have applied to the coroner and been given permission.'

'But it's incredible.' She looked to Sheila, to Philip, who had come out of his consulting room at the sound of her voice. 'Just the thought of it.'

Laura could scarcely imagine the trauma. That comforting phrase, 'Rest in peace', was demolished by the very idea of disinterment. 'Would you like Sheila to ring the coroner's office? We could try to find out more.'

She shook her head. 'Poor Jim. I want them to leave him alone. That's his special place, it's where he wanted to be.' The snowdrops by the wall, the rough gravestone.

Laura held her hand. Philip stood grim-faced.

'And I need him there.' She said she went twice a day to the churchyard to talk to him. 'If they take him away, I won't know where he is any more.'

'Only for a while,' Laura promised. 'The coroner will arrange another burial.'

Ellie shuddered, then sagged. 'I don't even know why they're doing it.'

Looking up at Philip, Laura realised that they were thinking the same thing. If Gerald had acted out of concern for Ellie in signing the death certificate straight away, his intention had badly misfired.

'Let us ring.' Philip was more determined in planning their course of action.

So Sheila got through for them and he went to speak, while Laura sat with Ellie listening to her blankly repeating the question, 'Why?'

'The exhumation's been requested by a detective inspector at Merton station,' Philip told them. 'They won't give precise reasons, but they say they gave permission as part of a possible murder investigation. The body will be exhumed, taken to the mortuary at Wingate General, and a Home Office pathologist will be brought in to conduct a post mortem.' He kept his voice steady and spoke quietly, letting the information sink in.

Ellie groaned.

Laura put an arm around her shoulder. Ellie's slight body shook. She covered her face with her hands.

They promised support and offered counselling. Philip rang Paul Miller to come down from Ravenscar to fetch the distraught Ellie. Only when she'd gone home could they focus on their own concerns for Gerald.

'I'll tell him,' Philip volunteered. 'Where is he now?'

'On call in Ginnersby, then on to Wingate for a fund-holder's meeting,' Sheila said. 'You will break it to him gently?'

'Is there a gentle way to break it?' Philip glanced into Gerald's empty room, at the untidy array of papers which he constantly shuffled around his desk, at the computer, largely unused, and at the framed family photograph of Janet, Nick and Aimee.

'It can't come as a total surprise,' Laura said, then recalled Gerald's trick of brushing aside bothersome details.

'I wouldn't be too sure.' Sheila knew him of old.

'What will he do?'

'Bluster. Take it out on someone.' Philip thought for a while. 'No, I think this could finish him off, if it turns out he's made a mistake.'

Sheila sighed and turned away. She disappeared into the cloakroom.

'Let's hope he hasn't.' Philip too was going, leaving Laura to sit for a few seconds in the middle of the light, clinically clean and cheeerful waiting area. 'Made a mistake, that is.'

She could see Ravenscar rising grey, banded with limestone ledges, old snow lying against the walls that mounted its higher slopes. She followed the line of its horizon, pictured the Hall and the tarn in its unlovely winter mood; water the colour of lead, frozen margins, black trees and dull grey scree. The still lake lying in its limestone basin, spilling down through great underground caverns, gushing into Joan's Foss and down Black Gill to the River Raven was the silent witness to Jim Blackwood's death. She sighed and got up. Ravenscar dominated them all, held the secret that was slowly unravelling before their eyes.

# CHAPTER ELEVEN

'One bus and two trains,' Aimee complained. Leeds station was crowded with early Friday evening commuters. Sean stood waiting at the ticket barrier.

'No need to tell me.' He'd done the journey several times in reverse in the past couple of weeks.

She kissed him lightly, he held her hand. 'How long have you been waiting?'

'Half an hour.' They crossed the wide forecourt, past bookshop and café, out into the drizzle and the blare of weekend traffic.

It felt strange holding his hand, shoulder to shoulder with the jaded crowd, most blankly making their way home from work to God knew what; a night in front of the telly, a row or two, an escape to the pub. Everyone looked worn out, worn into a groove, except her and Sean. They were stepping out along busy streets together for the first time, part of the world of bright signs, big shops, clubs.

He walked as if he wasn't really holding her hand, loosely, with a slight stoop and collar turned up against the drizzle. His battered leather jacket made him seem tougher than he was.

'Where are we going?'

'Where do you want to go?'

She shrugged.

There was a coffee place in the basement of the converted

Corn Exchange; a huge circular building with galleries and a domed roof, ribbed like the inside of the hull of an old sailing ship. They went there to talk. 'This Marianne Miller thing,' Sean began. 'I don't want you to get the wrong idea.'

'Like what?' Aimee flew on to the defensive, then checked herself. I'm like *him*, she thought. Like my father!

'That the woman's out to make trouble. She's not like that.'

She shook her head. 'If going to the police isn't making trouble, I don't know what is.' She'd refused milk in her coffee, and sat stirring the sugarless black liquid.

'Yes, but she doesn't mean it that way. That's not how she strikes me, anyway. You could talk to her, make up your own mind.'

'Where?'

'At the hotel.'

'Do you have to work tonight?'

'No, but she does. Look, why not? I'm giving it to you second-hand, saying the police might be up to something that affects your old man. But I don't like being stuck in the middle.'

'What's she like?' Aimee said slowly.

'OK, honest. I don't think she's bullshitting.'

'And she thinks her ex-husband killed Jim Blackwood?' She couldn't believe she'd come out and said it, sitting at the wobbly table under the genuine ancient bi-plane suspended from the roof. Why wasn't everyone staring at them? She sat in the middle of a kaleidoscopic world of disjointed pieces; cutlery, faces, palm fronds, iron stairs.

Suddenly Aimee made up her mind. 'I'd better talk to her, hadn't I?'

He nodded. 'Come on, then.'

It was back on to the dark streets, oily wet in the glare of lamps, through the city centre to a big hotel on the fringe of the university area. The Ridgeway; slabs of glass and white stone, layer upon layer, ten storeys high.

Sean led her through a side entrance into a wide, blue-carpeted area. A few people waited by lifts, or sat to one side of the reception desk in low, soft chairs.

'Where's Marianne?' he asked the man at the desk who'd nodded an acknowledgment.

'In the office.' He stared at Aimee's tight black jeans and short jacket and put her down correctly as one of Sean's student-type girlfriends. He gestured that they should go straight through.

The office behind the glitzy front desk was more of a cupboard than a room, lacking the glamour of front-of-house. Lined with shelves that were stacked with files and leaflets, it contained a small desk with a computer, and an empty chair.

Aimee frowned at Sean.

'Sorry, I forgot. She's on her break.' The desk clerk put his head around the door. 'You'll catch her in the canteen.'

The false start gave Aimee room for more doubts. As they went down the back stairs, with landings leading off to service areas and lifts, she wondered what she could possibly gain from meeting Marianne Miller.

'Too late to back out now,' Sean said, reading her thoughts. He showed her into a larger but still basic room furnished with tables and a self-service food section. A woman looked up at them from the far corner.

Marianne Miller's appearance didn't match Aimee's precon-ceived idea. From what little she knew, Paul's ex-wife would be polished, sophisticated, citified. She would be bitter about her broken marriage, and it would show in a hard-edged expression, a cynical air. In reality, the woman sitting at the table had natural light brown hair which she wore well-cut to shoulder length, a wide face and high forehead, and none of the off-putting superiority which Aimee had expected.

'Hi.' She was surprised to see Sean. 'I thought it was supposed to be your night off?' She smiled briefly at Aimee as they both sat down opposite.

'It is. This is Aimee Scott. I mentioned her to you.'

As the name slotted into place, Marianne made a gesture of apology.

'Do the police really want to dig Jim Blackwood up?' It came out more bluntly than Aimee had intended, but she was hopeless at prettying things up.

Marianne winced. 'They've applied to the coroner. That's all I know.'

'Don't they have to ask his wife first?'

'Apparently not.' She pulled out a pack of cigarettes and, when they refused, asked them if they minded before she herself lit up.

'I don't expect you want to talk about it?'

'Sometimes I do, sometimes I don't.' Marianne clicked her fingernails as she held the cigarette well to one side. 'It's always going on inside my head, though. That's why I wanted to hear it from Sean when I knew he'd been on the scene. Then I found out he knew you. Small world.'

Aimee nodded. 'Did he tell you how they found him in the tarn?'

'Yes, but the bit I want to know is what happened before that. They say heart attack.'

'Myocardial infarction.' Aimee mouthed the correct phrase. 'He was a sick man. It was on the cards for this to happen.'

'Not when I knew him, it wasn't.'

'Maybe he didn't like to talk about it.' Aimee thought it was likely that an action man like Jim Blackwood would try to hide any illness.

'No.' Marianne's mouth set in a determined line. 'Ask the others.'

'Gabriella and Paul?' Aimee frowned.

110

'Look, I'm not enjoying this.' She leaned forward. 'But I know for sure that Jim didn't have a history of heart problems.'

'How can you be sure?'

'He had to have a medical for insurance purposes when we first took on Ravenscar Hall. They checked and double checked his heart because of his diabetes. No angina. It's on the record.'

'When?'

'Less than a year ago. We needed a loan to set up the outdoor pursuits centre. There were all sorts of legal and medical hoops. We all had to have a full check-up.'

'Angina could have developed since then,' Aimee protested. But she wondered why Jim's wife hadn't mentioned the earlier medical report to anyone.

'In under a year? Anyway, Jim would have told me.' Marianne met her gaze. She couldn't have been more certain.

Sean broke the silence. 'So, is this what you told the police?'

'Yes. I also told them things were going badly at Ravenscar.'

'Financially?' This was the first time anyone in Hawkshead had heard this. People in the village were surprised by how busy the place was.

'No, relationship-wise.' Marianne looked down at the table, apparently reluctant to say more.

Sean realised he would have to steer them on to a different subject. 'Which police station did you go to?'

'The local branch in Merton. They decide on whether or not they want to investigate.'

'Investigate who, for God's sake?' Didn't Marianne realise who was in the firing-line? 'You know my father signed the death certificate?'

She picked up the challenge. 'That's not my problem. What

the police have to do is find out Jim's movements before he died, who was the last to see him and so on.'

'*If!*' Sean reminded them.

'Yes, *if* they find anything when they cut him open!' Aimee said. You couldn't beat about the bush. This is what they were talking about; a post mortem on a body that had been dead and buried for nearly three weeks.

'Well,' Aimee protested. Sean had invited her back to his house, but on the way he told her that she'd been too tough on Marianne. 'It's my father I'm worried about.' She stopped in the middle of the pavement. 'I don't believe I just said that!'

He laughed. 'I understand. You have to stick up for him.'

They walked on. 'I suppose that must be it. I must be having daughterly feelings. Normally I just mind my own business and he ignores me too. The story of our lives.'

'Even when you were younger?'

'You've heard of the Invisible Man? Well, you're looking at the Invisible Girl. It was all Nick, Nick, Nick with my father. Or else someone was dropping dead somewhere in the dale, and he had to rush off to revive them.' They sat on the top deck of a bus on a ring-road, in the rain.

'What about your mother?'

Aimee stared out of the window and thought about this. 'It's all right for her. She loves him.'

'You want to talk about something else?' He slung an arm around her shoulder.

'Yes.' Anything rather than imagine what it would be like if Marianne Miller turned out to be right and her father was wrong. His reputation, his job, his sliding self-respect were all on the line. 'Except for one last thing.' She wanted to set things straight in this potted history of the Girl Who Could Never Please. 'It was different last year, when I had my

112

accident. He dropped everything, stayed by my bed. I have to say that for him.'

They talked on as the bus swayed and swung round roundabouts, passed through one small shopping centre then another. Sean described his own family as ordinary. 'One brother, one sister. Me in the middle. I'm the one who passes exams. Mark left home, lives in a squat, turns up when he runs out of money. Lisa's the blue-eyed girl.'

'Not like you then?' Sean's eyes were rich brown.

'Not literally. Metaphorically.' If they hadn't been sitting on a creaking bus at traffic lights, with two women on the seat behind, he would have kissed her.

Aimee blushed and glanced out of the window. 'How far do we go?'

'As far as you like.' The bus lurched forward. Was she annoyed by his stupid joke? 'Come on, this is our stop.'

They scrambled downstairs just in time. Sean's house was near the bus stop on the main road. As they went up the path, she realised there were no lights on.

'No one's in.' He took out his key and opened the door.

'*Quelle surprise!*'

'OK, I admit it. My folks are away for the weekend. I planned it all in advance. I got you here to watch a video under false pretences.' He took off his jacket and slung it over the bannister.

'You're mad.'

'So are you.'

'Not as mad as you are if you really think this is going to work.' She was businesslike as they went into the kitchen to make coffee. It was a corny line, easy enough to handle if she felt like it. 'Anyway, if I'm so mad, why take two trains and a bus to come all the way to Hawkshead to see me?'

'To finish my project, of course.' He forgot the spoons, the mugs, the kettle, and turned to kiss her.

113

'Am I a project?' she asked softly.

'More of a challenge. You give off these signals. I'm trying to make sense of them.' He made sure not to rush things, was ready for her to change her mind and pull away from him.

'Don't do that,' she warned. 'I don't understand them myself.'

'Let me ask you a question.' He led her by the hand into a room with a sofa and a TV. A ginger cat was curled up asleep on one of the cushions. Sean let it be and sat cross-legged on the floor instead.

'Serious or funny?' She sat opposite him.

'You decide. This is it.' He seemed to rehearse it before he spoke. 'How many times should people go out before they sleep together?'

She laughed. 'Is there a rule?'

'I want to know how you see it.'

Aimee flicked her hair behind her shoulders, leaned forward and rested her hands on his knees. She kissed him gently on the mouth. 'The answer is, let's see,' She counted the occasions when they'd met. 'Four or five times. Depending on chemistry and stuff like that.'

'How's your chemistry?'

'Pretty good.' She'd never expected this bubbling desire to laugh as she kissed him again.

'Seriously?'

'I am, Sean.'

'Stop smiling.'

'I can't.'

He looked genuinely surprised by the turn of events.

'I could still leave if you want me to.' She shuffled closer until their knees met. 'Or I could ring home and say I'm staying over?'

114

# CHAPTER TWELVE

By the middle of that Friday evening, Philip had made and reversed the same decision a dozen times over. The house at Askby was a lonely place at the end of a difficult week. He convinced himself that he needed company and drove into Hawkshead to the Falcon. But the conversation there didn't interest him; football, tabloid scandal, and of course the big news, the exhumation.

Dick Metcalfe was unwise enough to tackle him about it. 'What's this I hear? They want to dig up a dead body?'

'News travels fast.' Philip tried to move from the old man's domain; a corner of the bar permanently reserved for the flat-cap brigade.

'It doesn't sound right to me.' Dick fixed Alison Lawson with his Ancient Mariner stare. 'If you ask me, they should leave a chap decently buried once he's been given a Christian burial. Mind you, they'll have a hard job. Ground's frozen solid. It'll take some doing to dig six foot under.' He meditated a while. 'Could be all to the good, though.'

'How come?' Alison winced in disgust.

'The body should still be in one piece. Like being in a fridge, see.'

This time Philip made a more definite move. He would call in on Juliet at Bridge House, after all. It had been on his mind for a while; a casual, unannounced visit.

As he walked out into the drizzle on to the square and cut across it to take the riverside road on foot, he rehearsed his reasons yet again. Against: revisiting his old home would churn him up, Juliet might not be in, might have company. It wasn't part of the game plan, which so far had involved occasional meetings on neutral ground. For the idea: it would show they could still see each other without bitterness, it would give them a chance to talk. He walked on, knowing that Juliet might well slam the door in his face.

He couldn't tell whether he was wise or foolish, brave or crazy, as he hesitated by the gate, looking up at the mullioned windows, reading the blurred date carved in stone over the doorway: 1624.

She came to the door and didn't slam it. It did, as he predicted, churn him up.

'Philip.' She sounded surprised to see him.

'Can I come in?'

Nodding uncertainly, she held the door open. 'I was on the phone to Jim.' She had her reading glasses on, was dressed in what he recognised as her weekend outfit of trousers, long sweater, flat shoes. 'But we'd finished before you knocked. He sends his love.'

'How is he?' Philip stepped inside. Nothing had changed. The arched fireplaces, the heavy beams and uneven floors resonated with centuries of family living.

'Fine. Impecunious as usual.'

'Shall I send him a cheque?'

'No, let him struggle to make ends meet,' she said, leading him into the lounge.

'Well, let me know if it gets serious.' Of their three boys, Jim tended towards the profligate. He trusted Juliet's judgment over whether or not to bail him out. 'Have you heard from Simon or Ian lately?'

'Simon's very good. He rings me practically every night. Bean's got other things on his mind.'

'Girlfriend trouble?' Philip sympathised.

'Do they keep in touch with you?' Juliet hovered by the fireplace, keeping the conversation ticking over, but obviously wondering why he'd come.

'Pretty well.' Not as well as they did with her, he realised with a twinge of resentment.

She paused. 'Philip, don't keep me in suspense. What do you want?'

'I wanted to see you.' It was odd to feel his heart race, the tension stringing him out like this. He saw a look in her eyes that warned him off. 'And I wanted to talk to you about a couple of practical things.'

'Luke's dealing with that,' she said hastily. 'At least, not Luke personally. It's Martin Wood who's handling it.'

'I know. I had a letter last week.' A thick, creamy white envelope, a dignified letterhead. 'I didn't mean that kind of practical stuff.' He leaned against the window, comforted by the sound of the river flowing under the nearby bridge. 'I was thinking more about Dot. They're going to discharge her on Monday. She says she wants to go back to Town Head.'

'And you don't think she's fit?'

'She doesn't realise how serious her condition is. She thinks she can go on as before.' He'd tried to persuade Dot to go and stay with her daughter, but this had been turned down flat. 'She says she doesn't want to be a burden. There's a steep hill to walk up to get to Town Head for someone with a serious heart complaint. I'm not satisfied that she'll cope.'

'But it's her choice.' They both knew Dot was an astute and determined woman. Independence was not something she would willingly relinquish. 'I think she does know how ill she is,' Juliet said quietly. 'She told me as much when I last visited her.'

'What did she say?'

'That she'd be glad to get back home. She wants to put a few things in order.'

Philip smiled. 'As if she didn't have everything meticulously arranged already.'

'She hates being looked after. What's her phrase? "I like to do things my own way".'

'I'll bet she gives the nurses a hard time.'

'No, poor thing. She manages to bite her tongue. She's ever so sweet to them.'

They agreed that Dot should have the support in place to allow her to go home.

'We'll look after her,' Juliet promised.

'There's something else I wanted to ask you.' The strain in the situation was receding. He chose to sit on the arm of a chair near the window. 'About Gerald.'

'I saw him and Janet earlier this week. They came here for dinner.'

'He didn't mention it.'

'I suppose he was being tactful. He seemed to be on good form, berating the system as usual.'

Philip outlined the situation over Jim Blackwood. 'We only found out today, but it's already common knowledge. I just came from the Falcon. Everyone's talking about it.'

'Hadn't you better tell Gerald?' Juliet was all for picking up the phone. 'You can't let him hear it second-hand.'

'It's OK, he's not at home. He's in Wingate with Janet, at the theatre. I plan to go and see him first thing in the morning.'

'He'll take it badly, won't he?'

Philip nodded. He pressed his fingers to the bridge of his nose. 'The thing is, he may already be losing his grip. He bangs on and on about funding and top-heavy management so much so that you learn to ignore it. But really I think it's a smokescreen to disguise some of his own inadequacies. His record-keeping's chaotic, for instance. Laura spends hours sorting it out on the quiet. And although he's still good in hands-on situations with patients, he doesn't keep up to date with new treatments. Now it looks like he missed something vital over Jim Blackwood.'

Juliet sighed. 'There must be hundreds of GPs like Gerald. They've practised all their lives, pillars of small communities. Suddenly all they've known gets swept away. They have to start crunching numbers instead of caring for patients.'

'As well as,' Philip reminded her.

'Yes, but one day you feel as if you know the job inside out. People look up to you. Next thing you know, it's all changed. You have to account for every movement. No one trusts your judgment any more. No wonder he's losing confidence.'

'You agree that he is?' He stood up and went over to her. 'It's not my imagination?'

'No, I think you're right.'

'What should I do?'

'You'll have to tell him what to expect over this exhumation. Don't let him brush it to one side. It is serious, isn't it?'

Philip nodded. 'He should have withheld the death certificate until the police had taken a look.'

Juliet took a deep breath. 'Then tell him straight. Say it affects the whole practice, so you'll deal with it together. How long will you have to wait for the pathologist's report?'

'We should have it within the week.'

'And that will prove things one way or another?'

He nodded again. 'Natural causes or foul play.'

He went to the Scotts' house early next morning. The short month of February had fled. March brought in a stiff breeze, with brisk, light clouds scudding across a blue sky.

Philip arrived on the doorstep at the tail end of an argument.

'Janet, did you hear this message from Aimee?' Gerald's voice carried through the stained-glass door panel.

'Yes. She's staying with a friend in Leeds.'

'Is it that boyfriend?'

'Sean,' Janet agreed.

Gerald expressed profound shock. 'And you agreed?'

'I didn't have any option. All I got was the message on the answer-machine when we came home last night.'

'Why didn't you tell me?'

'What would you have done? Made a fuss, driven over to Leeds to drag her back?'

There were noises, a door banging, then Gerald's voice again.

Feeling self-conscious, Philip rang the bell.

Janet answered. 'I hope you're wearing your flak jacket,' she warned.

'Do you want me to come back later?'

'No, come in. Gerald won't play the heavy-handed father now that you've arrived. Will you, dear?'

He came out muttering, looking his age, Philip thought. Minus his conservatively tailored work suit, in an old patterned cardigan and open-necked shirt, the slack skin under his chin, the scrawny neck were apparent. He'd caught Gerald before he'd combed his grey hair back into its faintly dandyish quiff, with sleep still written in the creases of his sharp-featured face.

'It's not work, is it?'

'Indirectly, yes.' The front door banged shut in the wind. Gerald glared at it. 'Sorry.' Philip stepped further into the tiled hallway.

'Coffee?' Janet suggested.

They went through to a long, sunny breakfast room. The

house reflected her liking for flowers and for early twentieth-century watercolours. She had good taste in both, composing colour schemes around an ornate lily-adorned lampshade or a special summer landscape which she'd picked up at an auction. There was an element of the Edwardian about Janet herself with her curved figure, lavish head of grey hair, her uprightness.

'Daughters!' Gerald shook himself. 'I could be going mad on the heath in a thunderstorm for all she cares.'

Philip couldn't help but smile at the melodramatic comparison with King Lear.

Janet put the cups and saucers primly before them. 'What he fails to accept is that an eighteen-year-old girl is a young adult.'

Gerald looked offended. 'I'm allowed to worry about her, aren't I?'

They granted him this. The sun shone warmly through the window, defying the season for once.

'Indirectly work, you say?' Gerald's attention was back on Philip.

'Well, directly then.' There was no avoiding it. 'We heard some news from Gabriella Blackwood yesterday afternoon, when you were out.'

Gerald narrowed his eyes. 'Let me guess.'

Philip glanced at Janet, whose gaze was fixed on Gerald. From the tension between them at his mention of the name, it was clear that the subject had come up before.

'They're going to exhume the corpse.' Gerald was matter of fact. 'I've been half expecting it.'

He stayed calm as Philip gave him the few details they had. 'The request came through from the Merton police, Mike Jackson. Coroner's office granted it and informed the widow yesterday. Exhumation on Monday or Tuesday.'

'Waste of time.' He shrugged, stood up to clear his cup. 'They won't find anything.'

Philip recalled Juliet's advice about not letting Gerald brush the news aside. If he didn't take it on board now, he wouldn't be able to approach the pathologist's findings with anything like a realistic view, and the shock of any significant failure on his part would be all the greater. 'But if they do?' Philip insisted.

'What can they possibly find? Thickened arteries, that's what. It's a pity they have to dig him up just for that.'

There was his usual certainty, his bombast, but beneath were signs of cracks in his self-control. Philip backed off for a while.

'I'm sure it's nothing to worry about.' Janet talked as if it was a formality to be gone through. 'It's unpleasant, of course. No one would like to have to cope with it.'

'What did I need in order to issue the certificate?' Gerald reeled off the criteria. 'One, the patient might be expected to die. Blackwood was hypertensive, a long-term diabetic. Two, he'd visited his GP in the previous fortnight. Three, the family was keen to avoid an autopsy. I met the conditions, did what I thought was best.'

Across the table, Janet nodded reassuringly.

'No one's saying you didn't do everything by the book,' Philip pointed out. 'But what it might boil down to is a question of judgment.'

Even now Gerald managed not to react. 'Ifs and buts. Mights and might nots. We can't say anything for sure until we've seen the pathologist's report.' He paused, then corrected himself. 'No, we can say one thing; there were no signs of struggle on that body. No wounds, no bruises.'

Janet shook her head, then left them to it. 'If you're talking shop, I'll leave you to the details. I have to go and collect Aimee from Merton bus station.'

As soon as she'd gone, Gerald's mood changed. 'No point worrying her,' he said abruptly. He could no longer sit still at the table, but go up and walked out into the bare garden, where daffodil shoots had begun to show at the base of trees, but the lawn still lay flattened and soggy after the snow. They stood side by side, hands in pockets, contemplating the heavy flight of rooks from one treetop to another.

'What if I did miss something? How will I be able to face that poor woman?'

'Ellie Blackwood?'

Gerald nodded. 'Not only could I do nothing to help when I got up to Ravenscar, but I mucked up the cause of death and she has to go through all this agony.' He turned away in self-disgust.

Philip pitied him sharply.

'I pride myself on getting it right when it matters,' Gerald went on. 'Forget all this twiddling, fiddling stuff we have to deal with. When it comes down to it I know what I'm about. I know medicine inside out, I know my patients.' Each point was re-inforced by a craned neck, a jutting chin. 'Or I thought I did.'

He inhaled and stood up straight. 'Tell me, Philip, you don't think I'm losing my grip?'

Philip had seen him at countless deathbeds, acting the emergency midwife, breaking bad news, chasing the best care for each and every patient on his list. He saw how he was held in affection and admiration and understood that it took decades to build up a rapport with the Dick Metcalfes and Dot Wilsons, the Brian and Alison Lawsons. Everything Philip knew about general practice he'd learned from Gerald.

When it came, battling through the surprising strength of his own feelings, Philip's reply was vehement. 'Not you, Gerald. You're one of the best GPs around.'

*

Juliet said she was glad. 'He needs you on his side.' She'd come over to Askby that evening especially to ask how it had gone.

Philip could tell she was startled by the removal boxes still half unpacked. It was the first time she'd called at the house. 'I haven't had time to sort things out,' he apologised.

'Don't worry, I'm not going to start doing it for you.'

'Who's that meant to be a sideways swipe at, me or you?'

'Both.' She said that one thing she'd learned was never to tidy up after anyone again.

'Where did you learn that?' He was pleased she could be light-hearted about it.

'Nowhere. I worked it out for myself. I'm enjoying not ironing your shirts. I once multiplied the number I ironed for you and the boys in one week by fifty-two, and then multiplied that by ten. It came out at nearly ten and a half thousand shirts in ten years. Can that be right?' She picked up books from one of the boxes, but only to flick through them and put them back. 'Four minutes per shirt made seven hundred hours' ironing, that's nearly thirty days. Oh God!'

He wasn't sure of the arithmetic, but he was interested in how she was handling their separation, glad in a way that she wasn't feeling sorry for herself.

'It's working out the way you wanted it?'

'I didn't want it. But that's the way it's working out.'

He let a silence develop. It was still hard to believe that they'd made the break, she was so recognisable in the way she stood, fingers spread and resting on a closed book, animated when she talked, with a half-smile.

'I'd better go.' She put the book down. 'I only came to ask you what Gerald's plans were.'

'Stay. Have a drink.' He showed her a shelf lined with bottles and glasses. 'See, I'm not totally disorganised.'

'No thanks, Philip.' The smile had faded. She looked round the anonymous space.

'I know,' he sighed, taking out two glasses and the whisky bottle anyway.

'You *think* you do.' Suddenly she was troubled, almost in tears. 'But you can't possibly know.'

'I'm only saying I realise how hard it is.' He loved this woman more than his life and he'd hurt her.

'Why? That's what I can't understand. Everyone must say that, mustn't they? Every wife in my position. Why did you have to smash everything for the sake of something so – shallow?'

He couldn't answer. He put down the glasses and closed his eyes.

'I don't blame her. Sometimes I don't even blame you.'

'I blame myself.' He'd been tempted. He'd seen Mary and wanted her, ignored the voices of his upbringing, said why can't I for once tilt off-balance, follow my longing?

Said to himself, no one will notice, no one will come to any harm. I can get away with this.

Worse, he'd convinced himself that something was missing in his marriage. He'd made the fatal mistake of not valuing what he had.

'I've told you before, what do I want with your guilt?' Tears streamed down. 'That's all I'm left with.'

'Then tell me, explain to me what it is you're going through.'

'Loss. I'm bleeding here.' She held her hands under her breast. 'Everything seeps away. Everything.' She was sobbing. 'It's an effort each day to cling to one thing that's solid, that means something.'

Philip couldn't bear it. He tried to hold her.

Juliet broke away. 'This isn't right. You're the last person I should tell. I'm supposed to be putting my life back together without you. That's what I'm meant to do.'

She stood stranded and crying in the middle of the room. There was no one whom he would ever know and love so well.

# CHAPTER THIRTEEN

Laura regarded Sunday as a day for herself after twenty-four hours on call. The demands on her time had included a visit to a patient in Waite suffering abdominal pain, where she'd suspected a stone in either the kidney or the ureter. This had involved a hospital admission. After that, she'd called at the Ginnersby cottage of an elderly patient whose husband had died two days before. Then on to one of her neighbours with emphysema, and back to the health centre to reassure an anxious mother about her son's asthma attack, worse than usual, but quickly responsive to treatment. A badly cut foot on a girl brought down from Ravenscar Hall by Paul Miller had rounded off a busy day.

In the evening she'd gone to Maisie's house for supper with Matthew, Sophie and Tim. Now, this morning, Matthew was keeping a promise made during counselling that he would take the children on a trip to a theme park near Wingate. There was an understanding that this was to be a treat undiluted by Laura's presence. Matthew would drive the children to York at the end of the day.

It was a rare opportunity to do as she pleased, and reminded her of one of the reasons why she'd picked out Ravensdale as the place to be after her stint in Camden. Where else could she look out of her bedroom window at valley and fields, a band of wooded hillside, a steep rise into heather-covered fells and limestone escarpment? The view was uninterrupted by houses or passing cars. The only thing to do, after she'd dressed and had breakfast, was to set out walking up into its inviting calm.

She took her favourite route up Black Gill, noticing the brave green shoots pushing through the battered autumn bracken and black earth. Joan's Foss was in full flood after the thaw. A torrent of white water splashed down rocky ledges into the pool below. On again, clear of the trees, to a barren stretch of moorland, where the wind pushed and pulled her along, across the dangerous limestone pavement above the dramatic cliff after which Ravenscar Hall was named.

Laura called in at the Hall without making a conscious decision. There it was, beyond the grey tarn, a silent house surrounded by a patch of green, backed by bare trees and scree. Only when she approached did the sight of vehicles, lights on inside the thick stone walls and the sound of voices break the impression of stern solitude.

A party of sixth-formers was departing at the end of their course. They carried rucksacks to the minibus and loaded a trailer with extra gear. Laura spotted the injured girl from the previous day hobbling on her bandaged foot. She'd gone through the painful process of having a toenail removed, and the damaged flesh bound tight. Later she would need a small skin graft.

She saw Paul when he came out to finish loading the bus. 'How are you?' she called.

'Good.' He swung the final rucksacks on to the roof-rack.

'Me too, see!' The girl held up her foot and hopped. Others helped her into the bus, then a teacher came out to take charge. Paul went with Laura inside the house.

'And how's Ellie?' Laura took off her gloves, examined her boots for mud and decided to take them off. The entrance hall was quiet. Outside, an engine started and the bus drove off.

'Not so good,' Paul admitted. 'She was doing OK until Friday when she got the letter from the coroner. Now she's in bits.'

'I'm not surprised.'

'When are they going to do it, do you know?'

'In the next couple of days. Ellie doesn't have to do anything herself, of course. She doesn't even have to know any details if she doesn't want to.' Laura followed him into the private section of the house. 'How about you, will you cope?'

He shrugged. 'I'll stick it out, I reckon.'

Laura knew to respect his privacy. 'If you need any help –'

'No, I'll be right, thanks.' On the point of going to fetch Ellie, he hesitated. 'She says the police will come poking around here.'

'They're the ones who requested the post mortem.'

'Will they want to speak to Ellie?'

Laura nodded. 'And to anyone else who was around when it happened.' It struck her for the first time that she didn't know what Paul himself had been doing at the time of Jim's death. 'Why?'

'I don't think she can take much more. This has got to be the worst thing that could have happened.'

'It's only the local police. I'm sure they won't be too heavy-handed.' She tried her best to be positive.

'What do they need to know?' He too was obviously nervous about what they would have to go through next.

'They'll probably want an account from Ellie of exactly what happened, and piece it together from various other people. I expect they'll want to interview my senior partner and the two boys who found Jim in the tarn.'

He frowned. 'I'll go and tell her you're here.'

Laura waited in the same small room as before, wondering whether it was her own heightened unease about the exhumation that had begun to chip away at her confidence in

Paul Miller. With all this going on for him – the split with his wife, the difficulties between him and Jim, and now the police – she would have expected him to show some reaction on his own behalf. Instead, the only concern he showed was for Ellie.

She had no more time to think about this before he and Ellie came back. Ellie could scarcely meet Laura's eye, her face was drained and her eyes red with weeping. Her hair hung loose and uncombed.

Laura's first thoughts were medical. She recognised the withdrawn look of a post-traumatic shock victim, when the mind fails to register anything beyond an obsessive, inturned fear or grief. There was no doubt that Ellie had spent the last two nights without sleep, and probably without food. Then Laura realised that right now she could probably be more use as a friend than as a doctor. 'I came to see how you were. Paul says you're not too good.'

'I'll be OK.' Her voice was a quiet monotone. 'They'll take Jim away, then they'll bring him back, won't they?'

Laura reassured her.

'I don't want to see the empty grave.'

'You won't have to.'

'Will you tell me when they've put him back, Laura?' She was fixed on the horror of the removal of the corpse. 'So I can go and see him again.' Ellie sighed and sat down. Her eyes filled with fresh tears. 'You probably think that's stupid.'

'No.'

'I was a nurse, you know. I've seen dozens of people die. I've watched the families trying to cope. But I never really knew what it was like before now.'

'Not many relatives have to go through this, thank heavens.'

'You know, I think he can still hear me. I say to him, "That's enough. This has gone on too long now, you can

130

come back." Part of me knows he won't, but I say it all the same. Then there are his clothes.'

'You don't have to tackle everything all at once. The clothes can wait. Or you can get someone else to do it if seeing them upsets you.'

'You know the things that remind me most of him? His shoes. Why should that be? And the thing is, when we pulled him out of the water he didn't look like the man I knew. There wasn't a single thing that was him, so soon after. Just empty. It was his face, but not his face. Do you know what I mean?

'I was here in the house. One of the boys from the climbing group came running. Sean Armstrong. I realised it was something terrible. He said I had to phone for a doctor, there'd been an accident. I didn't even have to ask, I knew it was Jim.'

'How?'

'The way Sean looked. He was scared to tell me, that's how I knew. But I didn't know how bad. I made the phone call, then we ran back to the tarn. There was the other boy, Steve Wallis, just standing there waiting for us. I was screaming at him to help. Do something, do something! Jim was face down in the water, but there was still a chance. People stay alive if it's cold. Their metabolism slows right down. I thought if we dragged him out, I could save him.' She was reliving each second. 'But it took ages to reach him. He was half-jammed under the ice, and it kept cracking and breaking around us. By the time we got him out, Dr Scott had arrived. We pulled him clear of the water and turned him over and I looked at the face and I knew.' She shook her head. 'He wasn't there any more.' Her features dissolved in a pitiful flood of new grief.

'I know Gerald did all he could,' Laura whispered.

'He did try, but it was hopeless. We had to carry Jim home between us, make the arrangements.'

As Ellie's voice slowed down and drifted to a halt, Paul grew agitated. He took Laura to one side. They stood by the window, overlooking the path they must have trodden when they brought the body back.

'She was fine till they decided to dig him up. It's driving her nuts.' He said he still didn't see what the police had to do with it. 'Who the hell brought them in, anyway?'

Laura glanced at Ellie in a new light, blaming herself for not realising how vulnerable Jim's wife was beneath her surface calm. 'Look, we'll get a clearer picture over the next few days. Everything may still be OK, you know.'

'You mean, in the end they might not have to come poking around?'

'Not if the post mortem confirms what's on the death certificate.'

He weighed this up. 'So they've got no other evidence to work on?'

Laura wished he would let it drop. Ellie needed someone with her.

'Sorry, I'm out of order.' Paul stepped to one side. 'But this is getting to me too.'

Laura accepted the apology 'She needs to get some sleep.'

Paul put his hand on her arm. 'Don't say anything, but I reckon I know who's behind this. There's only one person who would be out to get us. She'll be enjoying this.'

From his bitter expression, the deadness of his tone, Laura knew what was coming.

'My ex-wife. It's Marianne's style. She knows exactly how to twist the knife.'


'I'm out of my depth, I need some advice,' Laura confessed to Luke. The first thing she did when she got back home was to ring him.

'Shall I come across?'

'I could arrange to see you in the office tomorrow.'

132

'I'm not busy right now. Stay where you are, I won't be long.'

She was grateful to have someone to talk to. Paul's vehemence about his ex-wife had shaken her, made her think that the tangle of relationships at Ravenscar Hall must have a bearing on the way in which Jim Blackwood had died.

'I feel as though Gerald and the rest of us in the practice have been caught up in the backlash,' she told Luke. They sat at her kitchen table, looking out at the ruins of the old Abbey.

'What do you suspect was going on?' He'd arrived within half an hour of her phone call, looking relaxed in casual shirt and trousers, his dark hair cut shorter than when she'd last seen him.

'Suspect may be too strong a word.'

He smiled. 'So tell me what you know.'

From the confusion of her thoughts she tried to draw a clear picture. 'Start with the four of them; Jim and Ellie Blackwood, Paul and Marianne Miller. They set up a business enterprise together, thoroughly gone into, and they have all the expertise they need. But within a couple of months one of them backs out.'

'Leaving the other three up the creek?' Luke listened carefully, worked out the implications. 'Marianne Miller will want her money out of the business. Whatever capital she has tied up in it, she'll want back.'

Laura hadn't focused on this. 'As part of a divorce settlement?'

'Yes. And the other three will be in debt up to their ears; bank loan repayments, expensive overheads. No way will they be able to pay her off. Suddenly the whole venture looks shaky. Let alone the personal recriminations.'

'On top of that, Marianne Miller was having an affair with Jim Blackwood.' Laura broke Ellie's confidence to give Luke the full picture. 'His wife and her husband both know the score.'

'Is that why she left?'

'I guess so. According to Ellie, Marianne wanted too much from Jim. He backed off. She packed her bag and headed for the city.'

'What about Ellie and Paul?'

'As far as I know, Ellie had learned to accept Jim's behaviour. But Paul and Jim did have rows. They were both stubborn, so neither would quit the Hall, even though they must have hated each other's guts.'

'And that's what's bothering you?'

'Since the whole thing has blown up again over the exhumation and a possible police investigation, I can't help wondering about Paul in particular. He seems especially edgy about the police. And it occurred to me that none of us knows where he was when Jim died.'

'Well, you can leave that to Inspector Jackson. He'll no doubt follow pretty much the same line.' Luke knew the police officer involved. 'He's pretty thorough, but he won't jump to any conclusions.'

'Is that what I'm doing?'

He said she was. He also reminded her that it wasn't her problem. The legal process would take its course.

'I know, but you see what it means for the practice? It's looking more and more likely that Gerald was at fault.'

'You can't do anything about that either.'

'But that *is* my problem. Mine and Philip's. We'll have to carry Gerald through a public inquest, a possible GMSC complaints case, maybe even a murder trial. Imagine what that will do to him.'

Luke stood up and went to glance out of the window. Sunlight slanted across the stone-flagged floor. 'As I see it, it's still only your problem insofar as it affects the practice. You, personally, don't have to rescue him from whatever crisis he's going through. That's up to Gerald.'

But she knew that neither she nor Philip would be able to separate the personal from the professional responsibility. 'I feel for him, Luke. It's his life, it's everything to him.'

'Sorry, I'm sounding unsympathetic.' He came back and sat down again. 'I don't like to see you taking on too much.'

'I'm OK, I really am.' She poured herself some coffee, feeling clumsy now that the attention had swung her way.

'I've never heard you say otherwise.' He'd been on the scene when her ex-husband, Tom Elliot, had shown up in Ravensdale during the quarry inquiry. He'd admired how she'd handled that difficult situation. 'You're not the complaining sort.'

Laura wasn't sure how to respond. She was used to Luke providing sound advice; she respected him as a lawyer, and liked him as a friend. Up till now they'd kept their distance.

'I think I've worked it out. It's part of your "keep them at bay" mentality. Complaining how tough things are invites sympathy. It usually involves giving something away.'

Now she was irritated. She turned her back on him.

'What if we don't want to be kept at bay?' he insisted, following her to the window.

'Luke, if I need that kind of help, I'll ask, OK?' She glanced round to warn him off. Behind the careful working out of her personality defects, she was surprised to see genuine concern on his face.

'No you won't,' he persisted softly. 'That's why I'm offering it without being asked.'

'But there's nothing anyone can do.'

'What's Matthew playing at?' He reached out, turned her to face him.

She closed her eyes, shook her head. 'He's trying not to hurt the children.'

135

'Is he stringing you along?' Luke asked grimly. 'That's what it looks like from here.'

'That's not fair, Luke. What could anyone else know about it?'

'I know that it's making you unhappy. And that you don't deserve it.'

She shook herself free, resisted the urge to describe the turmoil she was in. What Luke was offering was just one more complication.

'Laura, let me near.' He held off, spoke with quiet intensity.

She turned her back on him with a final shrug. 'I can't, Luke. I'm in the middle of something with Matthew that I have to work out for myself.'

When he went and she could finally pull herself together, she saw his offer like a rescue ship on the horizon, its thin trail of smoke already receding as it charted its course elsewhere.

# CHAPTER FOURTEEN

Aimee was counting the calories, charting her weight on a meticulously kept graph which she kept hidden in a bedroom drawer. The line held steady, she was neither gaining nor losing. She looked at herself in the mirror and what she saw was satisfactory; straight lines and angles, no curves.

The doorbell rang. Thinking there was no one else in the house, she went downstairs to answer it. Whoever it was was standing in the rain which blew down the dale from the west and drove against the dark windows. It was Wednesday evening in the week when the local talk had centred on the exhumation of Jim Blackwood's body. Aimee herself had been drawn to the churchyard to stare at the deep, dark square of sodden ground. Its gaping emptiness shouted for attention amidst the daffodil shoots that had replaced the snowdrops at the foot of the wall.

'I'd like to speak to Dr Scott.'

A man stood in the shelter of the porch, holding up an identity card. Even without it, Aimee would have recognised the policeman in the way he stood; calmly observing, purposeful.

'Detective Inspector Jackson,' he told her.

'My father's not in.' She held on to the door, resenting his authority.

'Yes, he is.' Gerald emerged quietly from his study, still

dressed in his work suit, his tie loosened, his glasses in one hand.

'Sorry to bother you out of hours.' Jackson was polite as a matter of course. Once he saw Gerald, he ignored Aimee. She disliked him even more for his impersonal approach. He was tall and thin, with fair, receding hair and a darker moustache. As he stepped into the hall, he took a good look round at the furniture and fittings. 'We got back the pathologist's report on Jim Blackwood. I thought we should have a chat.'

Gerald nodded. 'Come in. Can we get you a drink? Or are you driving? Coffee or tea, then?' He led the way into the study.

Jackson said tea would be fine. Aimee took this as her cue and went off into the kitchen – tea-bag in the mug, set out a tray with sugar and spoon, take it quickly into the study in time to hear the detective discussing the autopsy report.

'. . . Some evidence of advanced heart disease.' Jackson said this as if he was repeating it for Gerald's benefit. 'According to the Home Office report, that much is conclusive. The pathologist is a woman called Sandra Gray. She found only mild thickening of some of the arteries and no damage to the heart muscle itself.'

Determined to stay, Aimee put the tray on the table beside the inspector.

Her father breathed out heavily and briefly let his head sink to his chest. Then he looked up. 'Not enough to kill him, then? So, what did I miss that I should have seen?'

'We're not suggesting it was something you missed. Of course, the pathologist has gone through it with a fine-tooth comb. She found things you couldn't possibly have spotted at the time such as minor contusions and abrasions on the underside of the body.'

'Occurring before death?'

Jackson nodded. 'Consistent with Blackwood having slipped

138

down the scree slope into the water. But no bruising to the face and arms. In other words, no violent struggle.'

'No foul play?' Gerald sat behind his desk looking pale and tired.

'I didn't say that.' The policeman dispensed information with the precision of a chemist. 'I said no violent struggle. There are plenty of other ways to commit a murder.'

Gerald flinched.

'But a few things still bother me in the report.' Jackson held them dangling on a string. 'Not things you could have been expected to spot.'

'Connected to the diabetes?' Gerald was ahead of him. 'Apart from the skin infection on the hands and feet?'

'You noticed that?'

'He was a long-term diabetic; you'd expect it. At his stage, he would also be experiencing some disturbance of vision, numbness and so on.'

The inspector nodded. 'Blackwood didn't wear glasses, though?'

'Not so far as I know. You'd have to check with my partner, Philip Maskell. Blackwood was on his list.'

'What other symptoms might he have been experiencing?'

'Ones that he would have been aware of? Well, unless he controlled his insulin intake carefully, he would tire easily and soon become breathless if he exerted himself. Too much insulin and he would suffer a hypoglycaemic attack; faintness, sweating, unsteadiness, ultimately falling into a coma. It's a notoriously difficult condition to manage. We're constantly managing and adjusting treatments in patients like this.'

Aimee appreciated how difficult it was for her father to maintain his self-control in front of the detective. The weeks of wondering and waiting were over, and the pathologist had proved that, on this one vital occasion, Gerald's judgment may have been lacking. It was the worst possible outcome.

'Excess insulin?' The detective picked him up on one point. 'I thought the problem for diabetics was supposed to be the opposite; that they can't produce enough.'

'That's right. Basically, the patient's body can't use sugar and starches because the pancreas doesn't produce insulin. The treatment is to replace or supplement this artificially through a controlled diet and insulin injections.'

'What's the point of the controlled diet?'

'The patient must reduce his sugar intake, partly to lose weight and ease any possible strain on the heart. Partly to lessen the need for insulin.'

'So, if for any reason he has too much of the stuff, how soon would he know about it?'

'Almost immediately.'

'And what should he do then?'

'Take sugar.'

It was so cut and dried, Aimee could almost forget that it was Jim Blackwood they were discussing.

'Are you saying that's what the autopsy has turned up; excess insulin?' her father asked.

The detective let him anticipate the answer during a long, non-committal pause. 'Too late to have detected that, I'm afraid,' he said at last. 'No, but what Dr Gray did find was a dramatically low level of blood sugar.' He watched Gerald's reaction. 'What do you think could be the reasons behind that, apart from excess insulin?'

Gerald considered. 'It can occur when a diabetic fails to eat frequently enough. If the level drops, he quickly gets confused. If it's bad, he falls into a hypoglycaemic coma. It all happens without much warning. That's why we have to monitor diabetics' treatment so closely.'

'And can anything else cause low blood sugar?'

'Well, we have drugs to induce it on occasions.'

'More injections?'

'Not necessarily. There's a whole range of drugs which can produce the desired effect. It depends on what suits the particular patient.' He frowned, as if his willingness to help was growing strained.

Jackson judged correctly that he'd extracted as much cooperation from Gerald as he would get that night. 'Well, I'm not giving away a state secret when I say that this is the picture we're getting from the pathologist: low blood sugar, leading to faintness. A fall on the loose stones on the slope by the tarn. He was unconscious when he hit the water. No struggle. Under he goes without regaining consciousness. Death by drowning.'

'There was water in the lungs. I got that bit right, at least.' Aimee trembled to hear it clinically discussed.

'But what really interests me is this stuff about using drugs to induce a low blood sugar problem.'

Gerald grimaced. 'You don't think that it was accidental, do you?'

'You can assume that from now on we'll be treating the death as suspicious. There may well be an inquest.' Jackson stood up to leave and Gerald showed him to the door.

'There's a smell about this one,' the detective insisted. 'Circumstantial stuff, I'll give you that. But, from what you say, I get a nasty feeling that someone somewhere made a plan for Jim Blackwood to die up there by the tarn. All nicely worked out and they nearly got away with it. Nearly, but not quite.' He nodded reassuringly to his fellow professional, turned up his collar and went out into the rain.

Aimee realised that under pressure people's bad habits grew worse. In the days after the detective's visit, her father couldn't read a newspaper without sounding off about this and that. He hummed and snorted, folded it in disgust and delivered an opinion in full bombastic flood. Easy targets came into his line of fire; squatters, scroungers, football hooligans, students.

'Nick's a student,' she pointed out. She hadn't noticed her brother rushing home to lend a hand during this family crisis. Their father had been to the coroner's court to give evidence at the inquest. He'd been criticised for failing to inform the Merton police about Jim Blackwood's death, a procedure which the coroner described as standard in this day and age for any GP called to the scene of an unexpected death.

'Nick's studying medicine, doing something useful with his life,' Gerald insisted. 'Not like most of them. Most can't even get themselves a decent job at the end of it.' He was eating breakfast, preparing to face the music at the surgery the day after the coroner's findings had been made public. Now there was to be a criminal investigation, based on doubts surrounding the cause of death. The coroner had signed papers for the body to be reinterred, but the case was still very much alive.

'And whose fault is that?' Aimee was exasperated. She ignored her mother's warning glance. 'They don't *want* to be unemployed, you know!'

'How do you know? Have you conducted a scientific survey?' He was savage with his toast knife in the butter dish.

'No. Have you?'

'Oh, please!' Janet sighed and stood up.

Aimee dug in. 'Anyway, if according to you it's all a waste of time, I might as well just chuck it all in and not even bother taking my A-levels!' She reached the door before her mother.

'You know he didn't mean to suggest that,' Janet implored. Her loyalties were constantly split. The more she conciliated, the worse the two of them grew. She watched Aimee storm upstairs, heard her bang doors, saw her reappear in her jacket. 'Where are you going?' Aimee was supposed to be at home on study leave, preparing for her prelims.

'Out.'

'I can see that. Where to?'

'Leeds.'

'When will you be back?'

'Later. I'll ring you.' She slammed the front door behind her.

Sean and Aimee met up in the Corn Exchange, their usual rendezvous. It was early morning in midweek, so the place was deserted. A hung-over air dominated the basement bars and the cafés. The shop-owners looked as if they were reluctant to open for the sparse business on offer.

'Let's re-wind and begin that again, shall we?' Sean could see she was in a bad mood. She'd scarcely offered her cheek to be kissed, let alone said hello. And she was looking peaky. Today her thinness was all spikes and angles, her dark hair a curtain across her face.

'What do you mean?' She slumped at a table. A coffee machine gurgled and hissed, the sandwich and cake racks stood empty.

'I mean, "Hi, Sean, how are you? Thanks for rushing into town to meet me when I ring you early one morning out of the blue!"'

'Sorry.' She pulled herself round for his sake. 'Hi, Sean, how are you?'

He smiled and kissed her across the table. 'What's up?'

'Everything. No, I mustn't exaggerate. My father, that's what's wrong.' She described how he was more opinionated, chauvinistic, and short-tempered than usual. 'He's so caught up with this problem at work that it's as if nothing else exists. And if the police do manage to arrest someone, it's going to get even worse. He'll have to go to court and give evidence again.'

'The police came to see me yesterday,' Sean said. 'I was at work. They came to the hotel to interview me.'

Aimee was jolted out of her own preoccupations. 'You're joking?'

'They'd been to talk to Marianne, then they dropped in on me.'

'Who did? Inspector Jackson? Tall, fair, with a moustache.'

Sean frowned. 'No, this one was was short and dark. I can't remember his name. He was from Wingate CID.'

'What did he want?' Aimee recalled the first time she'd ever seen Sean, sitting quietly in the bar at the Falcon, trying to keep out of the gossip about the body in the lake. 'They don't want you as a witness as well?'

He nodded. 'Me and Steve Wallis. If they send the case to the Crown Prosecution Service. I can't see them having enough evidence as things stand, though.'

'What exactly did they ask you?' She hated the way they were all snarled up in this. It was all anyone talked about these days; who the killer might be.

'Just what you'd expect. Times, places, sequence of events. I wouldn't say he was particularly friendly, though. He pointed out that some of the details didn't tie in with Steve's account.'

'He made you out to be a liar?' Aimee swore and went on. 'Next thing they'll be saying you did it.'

He grinned. 'Don't worry, I'm not a suspect.'

'So who is?'

'They didn't let on.' Sean fiddled with the spoon in his coffee cup.

'But you have an idea, don't you?'

'I heard it through Marianne. She came into the bar after they'd gone, saying they'd put her through it too. Where was she the morning Jim died? What was she doing? Who with? It looks like they're checking everyone who ever went within a hundred miles of Ravenscar Hall. Marianne says she can't take much more. She wishes she'd never opened the whole thing up in the first place.'

'So why did she?' Another couple came to sit at a nearby table. They were forced to discuss things in a whisper.

'I guess she couldn't keep quiet any longer. It was eating her up.'

'What did she have to tell them that was so bloody crucial?' If Sean did know more than he was saying, she wished he would tell her. 'Besides the stuff about Jim not having a history of heart problems after all?'

'I think it was something to do with Jim and her.' It was common knowledge in Hawkshead by now why Marianne had left Ravenscar in such a hurry. It was an old, old story with a new twist, in that the lovers and spouses all lived under the same roof.

'What, for heaven's sake?'

'As far as I can make out, the affair carried on after she left and came back to Leeds.' Sean mumbled as the other couple looked round and began to eavesdrop. 'Marianne says they were still seeing each other right up until he died. That's how come she knew he didn't have bad angina or anything.'

Aimee didn't see how they could have been so blatant. 'Did the other two know?'

'Marianne doesn't think that Ellie did.'

'What about Paul?'

He nodded. 'She says he definitely did know. There was a massive row the week before Jim died between him and Paul. And then on the morning itself Jim rang her up and told her it had all blown up again. Paul had gone off his head. He said she'd better keep a low profile for a bit. Paul was gunning for them both.'

'Is that what he actually said?'

'That's what stuck in her mind.'

'And she told the police?'

Sean nodded.

'Well, it's just a matter of time, then.'

They stared at their empty cups and let the hiss and bubble of the coffee machine take over from their whispered words. Aimee frowned. She could see that Paul Miller might have been pushed beyond his limits. It was all right *wanting* to kill the man who was screwing your wife, but how would he plan it? And if the two men did hate each other's guts, how had Paul Miller ever got close enough to Jim to give him the overdose of a lethal drug?

# CHAPTER FIFTEEN

Business as usual, Gerald insisted. 'Sheila, could you phone these cholesterol results through to Val Barraclough, please? And Joy, chase those referrals for the two Low Royds patients, will you?' He presided over the Thursday morning eight hundred with his normal swift decisiveness. 'What does the latest ECG print-out show on Dot Wilson?' he asked Laura.

She checked the results. 'Suspected dissecting aneurysm of the aorta,' she confirmed. 'Not good.' Her ex-landlady's condition had deteriorated since her discharge from hospital. It seemed that now some of the layers in the wall of the artery had been separated by leaking blood.

'I'll go and see her,' Philip said straight away. 'Leave it with me.'

They moved on to deal with paperwork; how they might push harder to meet targets set by the Department of Health over immunisation and cervical cytology, then an invitation for one of the partners to join a training system on the holistic approach to general practice.

Gerald snorted as Laura volunteered.

'Someone has to go.' Philip defended Laura's decision. And not everyone has your natural affinity with patients, Gerald.'

'Especially the dead ones?' Gerald glanced up over the rim of his glasses.

'Gerald . . .' Laura began. But she tailed off when she saw

him shove the offending invitation to the bottom of the pile. Suddenly the small consulting room seemed claustrophobic.

'Let's be clear, shall we?' He sounded off-hand and refused to meet their gaze. 'I'm not looking for sympathy over this Blackwood affair. I don't want you treading carefully around what you imagine to be my hurt feelings. And I certainly don't want either of you to go around defending what was obviously a very bad decision on my part.'

Laura glanced at Philip.

'What *you* want might not actually present the full picture.' Philip was braver than she was at handling their senior partner. 'Laura and I have some say in this as well, you know. Whatever the coroner put on the record, and whatever debate we had at the time about issuing the death certificate, I'd still like to make it clear that you have my full backing.'

'And mine,' Laura added quietly. The walls seemed to close in further. The artificial light and the lowered blind highlighted the focus of their concern. She watched Gerald's eyelids flicker, then open to look directly at them.

'This indwelling catheter they've fitted to Neil Summerfield,' he said abruptly; 'I want Joy to go over to Waite to check it first thing this morning. His wife rang to say he was having problems.'

So Laura went into her morning surgery not knowing how the practice would cope with its newfound notoriety. The coroner's report on Jim Blackwood would appear in the Wingate paper next day and then it would be the talk of the whole dale.

In simple newspaper terms, the police would be looking for a killer and Gerald Scott would stand as the bumbling local GP who had failed to spot a murder.

In public, Laura would have to be discreet but privately, her confidence in Gerald was shaken. She recalled his pig-headed determination to sign the certificate and felt convinced that

148

this time he'd fallen victim to his own blinkered viewpoint about the manner of Jim Blackwood's death.

Amongst her patients that morning she wasn't surprised to find Ellie herself. She'd been driven down from Ravenscar by Paul Miller, who sat outside in the car. It was obvious that Ellie had been incapable of driving herself.

'Come in and sit down.' Laura guided her to a seat. Ellie behaved almost like a child; passive, unsure, even dazed. Her pale grey eyes were red-rimmed and swollen, her skin roughened and patchy. 'How would you like to tackle this? I'm your friend as well as your doctor, remember.' Nevertheless, Ellie hadn't chosen to come and see her at Abbey Grange, but here in the surgery.

'Can you help me to sleep?'

She nodded. 'Of course. How about eating; have you any appetite?'

Ellie shook her head. 'And I can't concentrate. Luckily the Hall's empty this week. We're supposed to be getting ready for the Easter influx but I'm leaving it all to Paul, I'm afraid.'

'I'm sure he can cope.'

'It's been a horrible few days,' Ellie confessed. 'I think even Paul is feeling the strain.'

'But not as much as you must be.' She knew that Ellie had attended the inquest. 'At least now it's over and done with.'

'And Jim's at peace. I went earlier in the week to plant daffodil bulbs on the grave. They'll come up next year and you won't even be able to tell it was ever disturbed.'

'I'm glad.' Laura let her take her time. 'And I'm relieved you've come for help. I was afraid you might not.'

'Why wouldn't I?' She sat with her hands in her lap, slightly disorientated, slow to respond.

'Because of the death certificate muddle.' It was Laura's natural way to want things out in the open.

'Oh, that wasn't your fault. I know Dr Scott was only trying to help.'

It seemed for the moment at least that Gerald wouldn't have to face the tortuous GMSC complaints procedure. Laura eased herself back in her chair.

'I only wish the police had been happy to leave it at that.' Ellie sighed. 'Now it's all so complicated.'

'Have they been to see you yet?'

'No.'

'I expect they're letting you get over the shock of the pathologist's report before they come bothering you.'

Ellie thought about this. 'I expect they already know about Jim and Marianne. Paul's convinced it was Marianne who went to them in the first place.'

'Has he spoken to her recently?'

'We haven't a clue where she is. But Paul says it's the kind of trick she would pull. Anyway, it's paid off. She's gone and upset everything, hasn't she?'

'It seems like it,' Laura admitted. 'But if the police do follow this up, the worst they can do is ask a few distressing questions, isn't it?' She wanted to reassure Ellie that there was no reason to lose any more sleep. If anyone should worry, it was Paul Miller, she thought. 'Meanwhile, I'll give you a prescription for a mild tranquilliser. And I'd like to keep a close eye on you during the next couple of weeks. Can I come up to the Hall and visit?'

'If you like.' Ellie retreated into vagueness.

Laura signed the prescription. 'Take one of these three times a day before food.' She pushed it across the desk. 'That means regular meals too!'

Ellie stood up, ready to go. But then she suddenly changed her mind. 'There's one other thing.'

Laura sensed a deep reluctance to go on. 'Don't worry, anything you say here is strictly confidential. It's one of the few places where you can be sure that what you say won't be passed on.' She approached Ellie and spoke quietly, kindly.

'It probably isn't that vital.' Ellie's pale face flushed deep red. 'But there's something I wanted to show you.' She put her hand into her pocket and drew out a small white cardboard packet, obviously issued by a chemist and containing some kind of medication.

Laura took it and read the label. 'Glyclozide?'

'Jim's tablets,' Ellie confirmed.

'But I didn't realise ...' She'd personally checked Jim's medical record as soon as they got the pathologist's report. She was sure that Philip had only ever prescribed insulin on a regular basis. Glyclozide was a blood-sugar reducing drug prescribed to diabetics who could produce a small amount of their own insulin.

'Jim didn't get these from Dr Maskell,' Ellie explained quickly. 'He'd had them for ages, since his last expedition to Nepal.'

'Did he ever mention them to Philip?'

'I don't think so. You know what he was like. He decided to get hold of them for emergencies, on top of his regular insulin injections. He knew enough about the illness to realise that he was at a stage where the Glyclozide tablets might be a useful option. And of course if you're half way up the Himalayas in a snowstorm, with temperatures of minus twenty, it's much handier to take blood-sugar reducing tablets.'

Laura looked inside the packet. The prescription was for forty tablets, but the box contained only a dozen or so. 'And do you know where he got them from?'

By this time Ellie had turned pale again. Her hands shook as she pressed Laura to keep the tablets. 'I've no idea. I'd forgotten about them until Paul found them in Jim's filing cabinet when he was sorting through papers yesterday.'

'I think you should take them straight to the police,' Laura advised. 'They could be important evidence. Glyclozide could induce coma if wrongly used.'

'I can't do that.' Ellie backed away. 'Think how it would look if I did show them the half-empty packet and I told them how they'd turned up?'

Laura had a prickling sensation at the back of her neck. What was Ellie drawing her into?

'Paul was the one who found them. I know he was as shocked as I was about them, but the police wouldn't necessarily believe that. And it won't be long before they find out about the rows between Paul and Jim, if they don't know already.' She waited for Laura to draw her own conclusions. 'I want you to keep them for me.'

'This puts me in an impossible position, you realise?' She must try to make Ellie see sense. 'I'd be withholding evidence.'

Ellie snatched the packet back. 'OK, I'm sorry, it was too much to ask.'

'I want to help, believe me. But I can't see what good it would do. You must have realised what I would say, surely?'

'I thought you might keep them for me, give me time to think.' Ellie's mouth had set in a firm line. She took a deep breath. 'This is all completely confidential, remember?'

Slowly Laura nodded. She had the chilling sense of having been manipulated from start to finish of this conversation until she looked again at the strained, disappointed figure before her. 'I'm sorry,' she found herself saying. 'It must feel as if I've let you down.'

Ellie put on a brave face. 'No. You gave me the best advice you could. And I will think about it, honestly. Only, don't say anything, will you?'

Laura had no choice. Patient confidentiality came above everything else. Before she knew it, Ellie had nodded briefly and slipped from the room.

*

But the vow to keep the secret didn't slip so easily from Laura's mind. It edged between her and the rest of her patients on the morning list, interfering with her concentration.

In theory she had two courses of action. The first was to hold straightforwardly to the confidentiality rule, as promised. It was what she was professionally trained to do. And besides, Ellie was relying on Laura to keep her word.

But there was a second way which she couldn't ignore. This was to go straight to the police and tell them everything; a course of action which would relieve Laura of a heavy responsibility. If she told them about the Glyclozide, she would be rid of the dilemma. But ... but! Professionalism versus a desire to tell the truth; loyalty to Ellie versus an ingrained belief in justice. Doubt plagued her throughout the morning. It tired and frustrated her and made her look forward unusually to the end of the week when she would be able to relax with Matthew at a dinner for three to which Maisie had invited her.

'Tell Gerald he has my full sympathy,' Maisie Aire announced across the dinner table.

As predicted, the Friday paper had gone to town and led with crucial pieces of evidence from the pathologist's report which Gerald had overlooked. Axes were ground over the bar at the Falcon; Kit Braithwaite versus Dick Metcalfe, pro and contra Gerald. Alison Lawson reported back to Gerald, Philip passed it on to Laura.

'Dick loves to twist the knife,' he'd told her. 'Any chance he gets to take us stuck-up professionals down a peg or two he seizes with both hands. Now he reckons Gerald's past it. Or, in his inimitable words, "It were a bit nippy up on Ravenscar the day it happened. I reckon the doc just wanted it over and done with. He signed that piece of paper so he could get back to a nice warm fire."' Philip had imitated Dick's deep, gruff voice.

Laura had felt incensed, and now, after a day or so had

153

passed, she could see that real damage was being done. If Maisie felt it was her place to enter the fray on Gerald's side, it really did mean the rumours had taken hold. Well-brought-up Maisie usually thought herself a cut above the gossip.

'I know how it feels to fall victim to malicious talk around here.' Maisie poured the coffee, handed it to Laura and then Matthew with her eyebrows raised. She didn't let them forget that her own intentions over the sale of land on Ravenscar had been misinterpreted. 'One can decide on a course of action for perfectly good reasons and, before one knows it, one's name is blackened.' She'd always found Gerald a perfectly good GP during all the years she'd lived in Hawkshead. 'Not that I regret switching to you, Laura dear. Don't get me wrong.'

Laura smiled. They'd finished a leisurely, well cooked and beautifully presented meal, surrounded by Maisie's wonderful paintings, lamps and furniture; all chosen to emphasise the richness and antiquity of the architecture of the Jacobean Hall. Familiarity hadn't lessened Laura's love of the place. She'd been smitten at first sight by the oak and stone, the arched fireplaces and narrow, mullioned windows.

'Mother, did I ever tell you how much like Katharine Hepburn you've begun to sound?'

Very Yale, very gracious, with her gravelly voice and drawn-out vowels. Laura could tell she was flattered by the comparison.

'I only wish I *looked* half as good.' She patted her already perfectly swept-back and pleated grey hair.

'You know perfectly well that you do.'

'Yes, but at my age I'm permitted to fish for compliments.' As usual, Maisie was preparing to leave Laura and Matthew to drink their coffee alone. 'I think I'll go up, dears, if you don't mind.'

'But it's only half past eight.' This evening Laura found

herself wishing that Maisie would stay; perhaps because she wanted to avoid being thrown yet again into the never-ending search for a solution to Matthew's problems with Tim and Sophie. Tonight she didn't have the energy to be positive and strong.

'Yes. I want to check the children to make sure they're settled.' Abigail had dropped them off for an unexpected visit earlier that day.

'I can do that,' Matthew volunteered. He rose to his feet but Maisie insisted.

'No, I'll tell them a bedtime story. I'm growing sentimental in my old age.' She gave Laura a light kiss. 'And you two young things need to spend some time together.'

They took their coffee into Laura's favourite room; a lounge where the pale sofas and jade green of the patterned rug gave a lighter, more relaxed atmosphere. There was music playing, a soporific Eric Satie piano piece, and the cream curtains were tightly closed against yet another drizzly March night.

Laura curled up in the corner of one of the big sofas. Maybe, just maybe they could avoid the problems. The music was soothing, Matthew seemed happier than he'd been of late. He sat beside her and began to describe a game of football with Tim and Sophie.

'There was me in goal. Tim was chief penalty-taker.'

'What did Sophie do?'

'She was the referee. She kept blowing the whistle because she said I moved before I was supposed to. She was very tough.'

Laura rested her head on a soft cushion and turned to smile at him. 'She has a highly developed sense of fair play, that's all.' It was going to be all right. They weren't going to get strung out on a line of anxieties. Matthew had his arm along the back of the sofa. He was talkative, tender.

But the doorbell rang and he had to go to answer it. Laura

waited. She could hear voices; Matthew's and a woman's, then Maisie's light step coming quickly downstairs.

'Abigail, it's you!' Maisie's tone was jarringly bright. 'Whatever brings you back here?'

The lounge door was open so Laura heard Matthew's ex-wife come uninvited into the house. She swung her legs to the floor and sat stiffly, waiting for Abigail's reply.

'Sophie and Tim, of course!' Abigail laughed. 'Where are they? Didn't I give you a time?'

'We assumed when you dropped them off that you planned for them to stay over.' Maisie sounded perplexed. 'I guess I thought it was the usual weekend arrangement.'

'But they haven't brought their night things with them.' Abigail glanced into each room in turn. She saw Laura and waved. 'So where are they?'

'In bed.' Matthew spoke. 'They have spare things here. Sophie said you must have forgotten to pack them.'

'She's having you on. She knew perfectly well that they were only staying for the day. I've got something planned for the three of us in York tomorrow.' Abigail began to sound frustrated.

'You should have mentioned it to me,' he said stubbornly.

'Maybe you just didn't hear me, Matthew.' Abigail came frowning into the lounge where Laura sat. 'I'm sorry to break into your evening like this. It seems we all got our wires crossed.'

Laura stood up and slipped her shoes back on. She could see Matthew hovering in the hall while Maisie followed Abigail.

'Laura, have you met Abigail? Oh yes, of course I remember you have.' Behind the niceties she seemed to indicate that she didn't want a scene. 'Since the children are already fast asleep, why not leave them where they are?'

'But what about tomorrow? I can't cancel, not at the last minute.' Every casual movement seemed to reassert her

156

presence in the house where she and Matthew had lived as man and wife. She went and stood by the fire, flicked through the CD rack to see if there were any additions.

'Maybe Matthew could drive them over first thing in the morning?' Maisie looked to him. There was an awkward pause.

'Or maybe, if it comes to it, I could stop here? That would work, wouldn't it? Then I could take them off bright and early and that would save you a drive, Matthew.'

The Hall had many empty bedrooms. It made complete sense. But the idea was like a kick in the stomach. Laura waited for Matthew to make a stand. He didn't speak.

'Fine. I can put off what I was going on to later tonight, and I can cancel the babysitter in York.' Abigail went to make the phone calls, crossing paths with Matthew as she left.

Maisie looked apologetically at Laura, then shrugged. 'I guess we're all grown-ups.'

But Laura was sure that Abigail had set this up. While Maisie went off to sort out sleeping arrangements, she pulled Matthew into the corner of the room. 'What's going on?'

'Take no notice. That's just how Abigail is. She's clueless about arrangements.'

'You don't think she did this deliberately?' Laura was breathless. Her heart thumped. 'To spoil our evening?'

He shook his head. 'She probably didn't even know you were coming to dinner.'

Laura wasn't convinced. Abigail had sounded brittle. Her voice was full of challenge, daring them to turn her away. And wherever she'd been intending to go, it had involved dressing in a beautifully cut black jacket and trousers that made her short hair look blonder, her figure even more slender. She was well groomed and poised, with that ironic intonation in her voice, her air of still belonging to the Hall, despite the separation. Laura noticed in particular that Abigail was even able to railroad Maisie; no mean feat in her own experience of Matthew's self-possessed and socially adept mother.

'That's that.' Abigail came back with a cup of coffee and a satisfied sigh. Before long she was quizzing Laura about the Jim Blackwood fiasco. 'Poor Gerald,' she said without meaning it. 'It must be quite a blow to the old ego, making such a public balls-up of things.' She abandoned the coffee and moved on to a smooth malt whisky from the drinks shelf beside a bookcase.

Laura refused to be drawn. The struggle to stay calm was taking all her concentration. This was crazy; she was going to pieces over what was surely a series of innocent mistakes. We're all grown-ups; she recalled Maisie's phrase. For the first time since her divorce from Tom Elliot she began to doubt it. What she felt now was a straightforward, immature desire to run away.

'Why?' Matthew caught up with her on the steps leading down from the main door. Laura had endured Abigail's chatter and his silence for half an hour before she made her excuses and left.

'I just don't feel well, that's all.' She hurried down the steps. She'd wanted him to take charge in some way, not be pushed around. Yet she knew he'd taken the common-sense line. It was probably the best way to deal with Abigail; not to react and give her the satisfaction of knowing that she'd succeeded in upsetting things. Or was that Laura herself being infantile again? Oh God, she wanted to be at home at Abbey Grange, to take a shower, go to bed and forget the whole thing.

'Why are you angry with me?' He caught her by the arm before she could get into her car.

She saw in the dim light that he was genuinely confused.

'How often have I got to tell you that Abigail only calls the shots as far as the kids are concerned?'

'It seems to me she calls all the shots.' If Matthew couldn't see for himself why she was upset, what was the point of trying to tell him?

'What did you want me to do, throw her out?'

'Of course not.'

'Throw the kids out?'

She refused to answer this one. 'Let me spell it out. Abigail arrives unannounced. I go home. She stays. You stay. I don't like that, Matthew.'

'You're jealous?' Until that moment it had been beyond the scope of his comprehension.

'Yes, I'm jealous, if that's the way you want to describe it.' She pulled her arm free, flung open her car door and climbed in.

'Laura, wait!'

Shaking her head, she closed the door and slid away down the drive. In the silent privacy of her car, on the dark drive across the river and up the lane to Abbey Grange, scalding tears rolled down her cold cheeks.

# CHAPTER SIXTEEN

'Believe me, Abigail never does anything by chance.'

Matthew hadn't called Laura by lunchtime next day, but Luke Altham had. Needing to be out of the house, wanting to clear her head, she had arranged to meet him at the Falcon.

'How well did you know her?' She'd sketched in events of the night before, admitting that she'd been upset.

'We've met at formal social occasions; Maisie's dos at the Hall, rugby club dances, that sort of thing.' Luke finished his drink and offered her another.

'I feel dreadful even talking about her, really.'

'I guess most women would want to scratch her eyes out.'

She didn't want to be like that. 'What would most men do?'

'Tell her to piss off, probably.'

'And upset Maisie? If I'd made a fuss, Abigail would have dragged the kids out of bed and driven them home there and then.'

'Not your problem,' he insisted.

'But definitely Matthew's. She might even have used it against him to cut back on access by saying that visits to the Hall were disruptive.'

'So you play it her way and you and Matthew hit problems. Either way you can't win.'

'Who says we've hit problems?' She wanted to deny it but she'd spent the morning forcing herself not to be the first one to phone, and desperately hoping to see his car in the lane, to find that everything was all right between them after all. Instead, there had been a deafening silence.

Luke shrugged. 'Anyway, if it makes you feel any better, it's my guess that Abigail did set it up. So why not go ahead and blame her for any upset it causes?'

'You're right.' Laura got up, determined to throw off the cloak of anxiety.

'Where to?' He followed her to the door, nodding goodbye to Brian Lawson.

'Black Gill?' There would be few people around on this cold, windy day. They would be able to stride out and forget about Abigail Drummond.

Soon they left the village with its square of sombre stone houses and took the road up past Town Head. This way, they would approach the fast-running stream and series of small waterfalls which tumbled from the top of Ravenscar. They would take the easy route to the top, then pick their way down the steep gill side.

'This was my favourite place from the moment I came to the dale.' They'd made their trek up the limestone slope, and now they looked down into the valley at the river and the Abbey. She showed him Abbey Grange tucked into a bend on the river and he pointed out landmarks that she'd never noticed before.

'See that obelisk thing on the horizon?'

She pinned her hair back with one hand to stop the wind from whipping it against her face, then peered at a thin tower way over to the east. 'What is it?'

'A folly. One of those useless things they built in the eighteenth century when they had nothing better to do.' He seemed to be amused by the notion. 'In the middle of nowhere and of no earthly use to anyone. Brilliant, isn't it?'

He led her out of the wind through the trees growing at the

head of the gill. They splashed through shallow, clear puddles where a natural spring bubbled to the surface. This was the source of the stream that would gather force to rush down Black Gill into Joan's Foss, a beautiful clear pool at the foot of a horseshoe-shaped waterfall. 'I can see why you were anti-quarry. I'd forgotten how peaceful it was here.'

'You were anti too, remember.' They'd put up a hard fight, thanks to Luke's legal help.

'But with me it was more based on principle; fight the big conglomerate, stick up for the little people. With you, it's a passion.'

'Totally.' She soaked in the sounds of the water gushing over rocks, smelled the wet earth.

'That's good.' Luke had walked ahead until he came to the top of the waterfall. But now he stopped.

'What is?' She felt him studying her face.

'To see you passionate about something.'

He was intense, his eyes fixed on her face, waiting for her to respond.

'You've got it all wrong.'

'Have I?' He looked disappointed.

'About me.' Laura put out her hand. 'I care about things. I might seem cool and calm, but I'm not underneath.'

Before he could stop himself, he'd put his arms around her. She sank against him. His grasp felt like that of a life-saver. 'I think I'm going mad.'

'Over Matthew?'

'He loves me but he doesn't realise what he's doing to me. Maybe it's my fault; am I expecting too much?'

He soothed her, rested his face against her wavy hair, held her tight.

'And I want to help him but I'm part of the problem. If he wasn't involved with me, I know Abigail wouldn't be half so difficult and Sophie and Tim would probably be happier too.'

162

'Stop,' he pleaded.

For a second she had a glimpse of running out of a tunnel into a vast, brilliant landscape. But nothing was in its right place. Trees, sky, earth whirled. In any case, Luke was kissing her, and she kissed him back.

Abbey Grange; alone, safe. She wasn't on call so she took the phone off the hook and went out into the garden. Lilian's crocuses showed brave purple and gold, reminders of a lifetime's devotion to the small garden centre she'd run from here. All that was gone now, but Laura had inherited her old friend's appreciation of the traditional shrubs and perennials, and when she looked up at the soaring horizon, saw rooks torn by the wind across a grey billowing sky, she was glad she'd chosen a home so wild and out of the way.

She worked amongst the flower beds, carefully weeding around new shoots, investigating plants that she didn't recognise. She looked them up in an old book of Lilian's and identified hellebore and the fleshy, spiked growing tips of hosta, peony and sedum. Gradually the memory of being held by Luke, of returning his kisses as the waterfall crashed behind them, began to fade.

She was so absorbed in her garden that she scarcely heard the approach of a car down the lane. She only looked up when she heard the door slam and the crunch of footsteps up the drive.

'I tried to ring.' Matthew stopped, hands in pockets, watching her slowly straighten up.

'I took the phone off.' Laura slipped her hand out of her gardening glove and pushed her hair behind her ears.

'I came round earlier. You were out, but your car was here.'

'I went walking up on Ravenscar.' The stilted exchange and her economy with the truth made her fumble with the gloves.

163

She dropped one. Matthew moved quickly to pick it up. 'I needed some peace and quiet.'

'I thought you might. That's why I waited until lunchtime.'

Typical Matthew; taking her feelings into account and doing the wrong thing for the right reason. 'I wish you hadn't,' she said, troubled.

'I didn't sleep much last night, did you?'

'No.' Her smile was unconvincing when his lips brushed her cheek and he put an arm around her shoulder. 'Come on in. I was just going to take a break.'

They went into the comfortable, old-fashioned kitchen. Over tea and biscuits, it seemed that they might be back to normal.

'Mother was concerned about you.'

Laura shook her head. 'Tell her there's no need.'

'She sends her love. She realises it must have been tough and she's grateful for the way you handled it.' He paused. 'I let you down, didn't I?'

'It's not important.' She reminded herself of what Matthew had done for her in the past. He'd come on to her side in the quarry debate and stood up against his brother and mother.

For a while they talked about how Gerald was coping at work; about how Philip too was under pressure since his separation from Juliet. She didn't mention her own dilemma over Ellie Blackwell and the Glyclozide, though from day to day the doubts shifted and ground away at her.

'So, we're OK?' Matthew said tentatively, returning to the sore point. 'When you said you'd taken the phone off the hook, I feared the worst.' His voice wasn't much above a murmur and he sat still, fearful of her answer.

'I over-reacted. It just felt strange to be in the same room with Abigail, knowing that she used to live there. I don't like to be reminded that I'm following in her footsteps, that's all.'

'You're not. You're nothing like her, believe me.'

She stood up to clear the cups. 'Matthew, last night did

make me realise one thing.' She was busy at the sink, her back towards him. 'I think it might do us good to ease off for a while.'

'But you said we were OK!' He followed her across the room.

Even causing this much distress was almost beyond her. She so much wanted them to be OK. But last night . . . and now Luke. No, she must leave Luke out of it. What was one kiss? That had been gratitude, friendship, that was all.

'What do you want me to do?'

'It's not you, Matthew. It's the situation. I think we're getting trapped by it. If we saw a little bit less of each other until the divorce is worked out, it might take some of the pressure off.' He stared back, trying to judge exactly what she meant.

'I don't want to take the pressure off,' he protested. 'I want to be with you.'

'You are with me. But it doesn't mean we have to live in each other's pockets. I've got my house, you have yours. Let's make sure we never find ourselves in a situation where Abigail can interfere again. Because if she ever did a repeat of last night, I don't think I could cope.'

'I realise that. But maybe it's because we're neither one thing nor another. We're not living together nor apart. It gives Abigail the idea that she can still exercise some control.'

Laura lowered her gaze. 'So what are you saying, Matthew?'

'I want us to go more public. You know . . .'

'Live together?' Strange where an ex-wife's interference could push them. Until now, she and Matthew had valued their own space. He loved the Hall and being manager of the estate. She was happy gradually turning Abbey Grange into her home, running her own life.

'If you like.'

He'd done it again; flicked the decision over to her, failed to make a passionate case. Something stopped him; what was it? She gazed back, her eyes filling with tears.

'Do you want to?' he asked gently.

She let him stroke her hair. 'No.'

'What then? Can we go on as we are if we don't live together?'

'I don't know.' She felt weary.

'Don't say that, Laura. You're the one with the clear head. You always say we can work it out.'

'That's why I think we should ease off. It's as if we're trying too hard, isn't it?'

'But we can see each other?'

Don't ask me questions, she wanted to beg. Give me a firm statement, something to grasp on to. Instead she let the tears come in silence.

'I love you, Laura.'

She nodded. 'Let's just see what happens.'

Disbelief marked his features; there was helplessness in the way he backed towards the door.

He went, and the silence took over. She stood in the garden looking up at Ravenscar, but there was no consolation in the cold hillside; only a loneliness that for once drove her indoors out of its grey shadow.

# CHAPTER SEVENTEEN

It had been at the top of Philip's list to visit Dot Wilson at Town Head to discuss with her the results of her most recent ECG readings. The difficult news made him push it to the final task he undertook after his weekend on duty, however, and it was Sunday evening when he finally went on foot from the health centre into the village and up the steep hill to Dot's immaculately maintained, double-fronted Victorian house.

He knocked and waited, using the time to glance at the view across the stone roofs and winding streets to the narrow river plain and the Abbey in its sheltered position on the far bank. No wonder Dot didn't want to leave her home with its crow's nest vantage point.

'Dr Maskell.' She opened the door to him, firm and welcoming, dressed in her regulation tweed skirt and neat patterned jumper, head held high, shoulders back. 'Come in. Don't stand in the cold.'

He unbuttoned his coat and stepped inside Dot's ornament-filled hallway. She showed him into the sitting room while she went to make tea. When the tray arrived, it was set out with her best china and slabs of home-made fruitcake.

'I know why you've come,' she said easily, sitting opposite him at the far side of the hearth.

'For your cake,' he teased. 'It's the best in the village.'

'Yes, and for my W.I. news, and the latest recipe for

'rhubarb jam, I know.' She had a dry way with her, which was really a way of deflecting attention from herself.

'And to check how you are.'

She shrugged. 'Why don't you go right ahead and tell me?'

He explained clearly about the suspected aneurysm. 'We can't be sure from a single test result, but it looks most likely that we'll have to get David Walker to push you higher up his by-pass list and get you in for surgery as soon as possible.'

Dot sniffed.

'And meanwhile you must avoid exerting yourself. No heavy lifting, no running for the bus. Nothing that makes you out of breath, you understand?' He waited for her to react.

'I'll do my best.'

'You must, Dot. Take it easy for now, have your by-pass, take time to get back on your feet and you'll be surprised by how much better you feel afterwards.'

She gave him a sideways look. 'It's a good job I've known you a fair while, Dr Maskell, or I'd think you were flannelling me.'

'Well, I'm not. By-pass operations are generally highly successful.' He described how the surgeon would take a healthy artery from the leg and use it to replace the diseased aorta.

'It's amazing what they can do these days.'

'Especially when they have full patient cooperation,' he warned. 'There'll be no dashing about for at least three months after the operation.'

There was a pause, the first flicker of anxiety on Dot's thin, lined face.

'Might you consider going to stay with your daughter?' Philip prompted.

'Nay, Valerie has her own family to look after.'

'I'm sure she'd want you to. Why not discuss it with her at least?'

'Maybe. But if I can manage, I'll stay where I am, thank you very much.' Dot tapped her fingers on the arm of her chair. 'I'm growing old, Dr Maskell. I don't recommend it.'

He smiled. 'I'm no spring chicken myself.'

'How old? Under fifty? That's no age.' Another pause, a couple of shrewd looks. 'How's Mrs Maskell?'

'Have you seen her lately?'

'She popped in the other day with the Easter flower rota for church. I thought she was looking peaky myself.'

It was Philip's turn to falter.

'I hope I'm not speaking out of turn?'

'Not at all. I appreciate it.' He leaned forward to rest his elbows on his knees. 'I know she's not finding things easy.'

'She's been kind to me, though. She's holding my job open until such time as I feel up to it again. There's many that wouldn't. She says that now there's only her in the house, it's easy to keep clean.' Dot poured more tea, pressed another slice of cake on him. 'I hear Dr Scott's in a bit of a mess.'

'If you believe what you read in the newspaper,' Philip reminded her.

'I feel very sorry for him. There's nothing worse than groundless gossip. Mind you, there's plenty of people round here on his side.'

'I'm glad to hear it.'

'Bound to be. We've known Dr Scott a fair time. You don't turn around and believe the first bad thing you hear, not if he's someone who's delivered your babies and patched you up after an accident. He's always been liked, has Dr Scott.' It was typical of Dot to steer the talk away from herself and to show sympathy for others.

'I'll tell him what you say.'

She nodded. 'Between you and me, I did wonder whether he'd think about calling it a day over this business.'

'I wouldn't know about that. But I know that to Gerald,

resignation would look like defeat. He's a fighter through and through.'

'Poor man, it's a shame. You want to go out on a high note, feeling you've made a difference, not clinging on for dear life. And he's aged in this last year or two, since Dr Williams retired. Have you noticed?'

'So have we all.' Philip saw the chance to press home his own argument. 'Never mind Gerald, Dot. This is exactly what I'm saying about you having to take things easy. You can't go on like you used to.' He hoped he wasn't too hard on her. 'You mustn't let my advice go in one ear and out the other.'

'But it's different for me,' she said with dignified self-reproach. 'There's no pension waiting for me if I give up work, other than my widow's pension, and that's little enough. I have to keep going as long as I can.'

He thought this one through. 'How about taking in a couple of lodgers again, to supplement the pension?'

Dot sighed. 'Not all lodgers are like Laura,' she said softly. 'You can never be sure who you'll get.'

Philip got up to leave, feeling that they'd made some progress. He thanked her for the tea and cake.

'You look as if you need feeding up.' Dot eyed him critically as she held the door open.

He called her incorrigible and left in a better mood, promising to get in touch again as soon as the specialist gave him some firm news.


Easter blew in cold and rainy, disappointing all hopes of breaking with the winter routine of living behind closed doors and buttoning up against the weather. Philip had dealt with the usual mixture of bad news and good; a confirmed case of Parkinson's disease, still at its early stage of hand tremors, which grew worse while the patient was at rest but could actually disappear while he slept. The victim, Bill Shaw, had

170

been a potholer in his youth and was still only fifty-five. He took the news grittily and demanded the details. Philip had explained about the progressive degeneration of the nerve junctions caused by atheroma; a narrowing of the arteries. Bill had grasped on to the information like a man hauling himself along a narrow tunnel of dangerous rock. He'd sworn he would beat the disease if it were within human capability. Philip had offered no promises.

The good news of the week had included two healthy hospital births, a marked regaining of speech in a stroke patient at Low Royds and the discharge from hospital of an eight-year-old accident victim after months of physiotherapy to get her walking again. Sarah Bellamy was home for Easter, and her family was celebrating, Sheila told him as he left the health centre on Good Friday.

'Great!' He got ready to brave the rain.

'Oh, and there's a message here from Juliet.'

He stopped mid stride.

'She says Jim's due home. He left word on the answer-machine while she was at work. He's decided to come home for Easter. She wondered if you would like to call in. She said any time you felt like it.'

'Thanks, Sheila.' He brazened out her curious gaze. His brain scrambled as he swung out through the door. An invitation to Bridge House; the first since their separation.

He made himself wait until Saturday teatime, then he rang Juliet to check they were both in.

'Drop by,' she said. 'Jim's going out at seven, so you'd better make it soon.'

He knocked on his own front door, a stranger to the house. Juliet opened it shyly and let him in.

Jim was standing by the window in the dining room that overlooked the river. He was like a photograph of Philip taken

171

thirty years before; spare-framed like his father, stooping slightly because of his height. He was the youngest of their three sons, the last to leave home, the first to come back when things went wrong.

'What's up, have you broken up with your girlfriend, or are you skint?' Philip asked after an awkward greeting.

'Do me a favour.'

'Your mother told me you were. How much do you need?'

'I can get by, thanks. I have to go and see the bank manager next week, that's all. It's just that this weekend I'm out of cash.'

Philip nodded. 'How did you travel across?' Jim was at university in Manchester.

'I got a lift with a friend. Look, I didn't come purely because I was broke.'

'No?' Philip didn't know why he was getting at Jim. Before the break-up he could have got away with a straightforward bailing out without his son taking umbrage. 'Have some cash anyway.' He drew notes out of his pocket and put them on the table. 'How are things? Is the course OK?'

'Boring.'

'Exams coming up?' Another false move. Jim shuffled to the table and stuffed the money into his jeans.

'Yeah, thanks for reminding me.' He was in the second year of his art history course; penniless, world-weary.

'I could come in and we could start all over again, if you like?' Philip suggested. This was the first time he'd seen his son since Christmas, and the phone calls had been few and far between.

'What would you like to drink?' Juliet stepped in. 'Have you eaten yet? Jim's planning to meet some friends in Merton and they'll be eating out, but I could still knock a meal together if you want.'

She'd evidently forgotten her resolution not to mother

172

them. Philip declined. They were all feeling too ill at ease to relax over food.

'So what's new?' He persisted with Jim, wishing they could drop the social phrases and get down to something meaningful. 'Been to any concerts lately?'

He mentioned a couple of names that meant nothing to Philip. 'Look, I've got to go. Can I take the car, Mum?' He turned his back in casual rejection which he knew would hurt.

'Don't drink if you're driving,' Juliet called after him.

'He won't talk to me, but he'll take my money,' Philip complained after he'd gone. He'd taken Jim's place by the window. 'I take it he blames me?'

'You'd better ask him that. I don't know what he thinks. He doesn't talk to me either.'

How had they produced this surly, monosyllabic ingrate, he wondered. Was this what divorce inevitably did to children? But Jim had always been erratic and nervy. 'Who *does* he talk to? Does he have a new girlfriend now?'

'At least three. He believes in open relationships. Sweet, isn't it?' Sarcasm didn't suit Juliet. 'Actually I don't think he treats them very well either, so his bad behaviour isn't confined to you.'

'I won't take it personally, then.' He changed the subject. 'Dot was asking after you. I called to see her last Sunday.'

'I know. I visited her on Thursday. Has she got a date for her op?'

'Not yet. The sooner the better, though. And I wish we could find a way to sort out her money worries.' Unlike Maisie Aire when she felt the pinch, Dot didn't have spare property to dispose of.

'She's trying not to think too far ahead. One day at a time is what she says. She didn't look well when I saw her, Philip.'

'She isn't.'

'Poor Dot. It's hard for someone who's been independent all her life.'

'Hmm. Are you worried about Jim?' He guessed right, swung it back round.

Juliet nodded. 'I'm beginning to wonder about drugs.'

'No, I don't think so.' Philip made a swift judgment. 'He's not showing any of the signs.'

'But he does seem lethargic.'

'I'd say he was still fairly together. If he runs out of money, he comes home. He arranges to meet his mates, he's not secretive or withdrawn. No more than usual.' Jim had always been the self-contained one. 'Look, try not to worry. It's probably just me he's mad at. Perhaps I shouldn't have dropped by after all.'

'I thought it might help.'

Philip shrugged. 'He's protecting you, that's all.'

'Well, I wish the boys wouldn't take sides like that.'

He pondered for a while. 'The problem is, Jim's too much like me. He doesn't have your generosity.' Many women would set their sons against adulterous fathers, not encourage them to stay close. 'Is Jim the only reason you invited me?' he asked softly. She hovered at the other side of the room, keeping her distance.

'Yes.'

'You wanted him to see we could still be civilised?'

She nodded. 'They have to learn to make the best of it. I don't want them to be bitter.'

'I don't want you to be bitter either.'

She grew angry. 'Don't try to worm your way around me, Philip!'

'Just talk to me,' he pleaded.

'What about? There's nothing new to tell you. Nothing's changed.'

'How can you say that? I've changed for a start.' He didn't

move from his position by the window, and looked out over the water as he spoke. Neither of them could possibly have stayed the same through all this. He turned to face her. 'You've changed too.'

'In what way?' Juliet stood defensively by the door.

'You're angrier.'

'Oh, don't patronise me, Philip! It's good to express my anger and all the rest of it. Suddenly I'm some Amazonian heroine taking charge of my life? Spare me, please!'

'You're more definite about what you want, then.'

'But I always knew what I wanted. I had it. You took it away from me.'

He ended up at the Falcon where he found Laura and Matthew with some of Matthew's friends from Wingate. Across in another corner of the bar he spotted a surprising group; Aimee Scott and Sean Armstrong with Jim.

'I thought you were supposed to meet someone in Merton?' He offered them a drink which was readily accepted all round.

'They never showed up.' Jim scarcely raised his voice above a grunt.

Philip backed off from the wave of teenage hostility. He bought the drinks from a cheerful Alison Lawson.

'I take it you're not flavour of the month?' she guessed.

'Except when I'm paying for the drinks.' He took the beers to the youngsters and warned Jim to leave the car in the pub car park and walk home. It got the reception he expected; another, even shorter grunt. So he went to join Laura's group.

'I'm not even going to mention work!' he promised, putting his hands up in surrender.

Laura introduced him to two other couples at their table. 'It's a deal. No work. No murders. Gina already sees Hawkshead as a den of iniquity.'

'You must have been reading the papers,' he said.

'Yes. In the past I always wanted to move out here. I had this romantic picture of a little stone cottage with roses around the porch.' The woman laughed. 'A Dales backwater which would suit me fine.'

'Not any more?'

'We drove over from Wingate via Ravenscar. I changed my mind.'

'It's not at its best when it's raining.'

'Bleak,' Gina confessed. 'And spooky. I just imagined bodies in the lake.'

'Body,' Philip pointed out. 'Singular, not plural, we hope.'

Laura tutted. 'I thought we said no murder talk.'

'My lips are sealed.' He took a drink, pleased that he hadn't gone back to Askby to spend the evening alone. He let the talk flow, keeping one eye on Jim to see that he didn't drink away all the money he'd given him, but most of his attention on Gina, who seemed to have honed in on the lonely divorcee in him and had decided to cheer him up. She was a confident redhead, something in conference work; an organiser, evidently. If he tried hard, he found he could squash down the distress that had swamped him as he left Juliet. He could pass a pleasant evening; mundane, superficial, but easy. He was Philip Maskell, not a man drowning in a mid-life crisis.

Brian and Alison served on. Nina, Brian's eighteen-year-old daughter from his first marriage, came out from behind the bar to chat with Aimee. Philip noticed Jim turn on the charm. Three old-timers in the corner, Dick, Kit and Harry, propped up the bar as usual. Often Dot would have been here for a Saturday night out, but she was obviously not well enough tonight. There was the usual mixture of weekenders, walkers and villagers. Nothing untoward.

Until Paul Miller walked in. No one bothered to hide their curiosity. They stared as he stood in the doorway, looking round the bar.

'What's he want now?' Dick grumbled audibly.

Brian was determined to make it business as usual, however. 'What can I get you?' he called to Paul.

With all eyes still on him, Paul shook his head. He spotted Philip's group and came across. Close to, they could see he was under stress. His broad, square face was clenched tight, deep frown lines marked his forehead. 'I need to speak to you.' He singled Laura out by bending over her shoulder. 'It's Ellie.'

Laura eased sideways. 'It's not me who's on call. Try Gerald.'

He didn't listen. 'She wants to see you.'

By now, the noise level in the pub had dropped. Everyone tuned in to Paul pleading with Laura.

'She's sick. She won't see anyone except you.'

Laura glanced at Matthew, then Philip. 'And can't it wait?' Instinctively she wanted to help, but caution overlaid this response. Since Ellie's visit to her surgery there had been silence from Ravenscar Hall. Laura didn't even know whether or not the police had been to interview them or if Ellie had shown them the tablets.

'No, it can't.'

'Do you want me to go and see if there's anything I can do?' Philip volunteered.

Paul kept his gaze on Laura.

'No, thanks. But you'll have to give me a clue, Paul. I need to know what I should bring with me.'

'She's in bits,' he confided, his voice lowered to a whisper. 'I can't get much sense out of her, except that she needs to talk to you. I tried your house, then I came here.'

'OK.' Laura stood up with an apologetic tap on Matthew's shoulder. 'I'm on my way.'

Relief broke down his reserve. He seemed to forget the fascinated audience. 'Make it quick,' he pleaded. 'She's going nuts up there. She had a couple of policemen up to see her earlier today and she couldn't cope.'

Paul followed Laura to the door. 'I can't do a thing with her. She's throwing herself around the place.'

The cold night air hit Laura before Paul opened the car door and she could climb in.

He started the engine and took off across the square. 'You won't believe this, Laura, but she's convinced they're going to arrest her!'

# CHAPTER EIGHTEEN

'Why does Ellie think the police suspect her?' Laura held tight as Paul drove crazily up the winding road. His headlights picked up the rough stone walls to both sides, until they swung round a bend and climbed clear of the fields into open moorland. There were no stars, no moon; only blackness beyond the beams of light.

'Search me. She's got it into her head, that's all. Something's been happening to her these last few weeks. It's scary stuff.'

Laura could see the pinpricks of light belonging to Ravenscar Hall in the distance. Closer to was the dull gleam of the tarn. 'Were you here when the police came?'

'No, I was in Merton. They put her through it, though. When I got back I found her in her room talking all kinds of weird stuff about Jim, as if she didn't think he was dead.'

At last they pulled up in the yard and ran towards the house. 'Where is she now?'

'In bed. She took some of the pills you gave her.'

'Has she slept?'

'A bit. But she got worse again when she woke up. Now she says there's no point denying it. They're too clever for her, they twist everything she says.' He hurried inside, holding the door for Laura.

'Did the police get round to interviewing you too?'

He nodded. 'That's why I was in Merton. I had to go to the station there while the two from Wingate came to see Ellie and scare the hell out of her here.'

'And they're definitely making this a murder inquiry?' She wanted to get her facts straight.

'You bet,' he said grimly. 'They've brought in the big guns. Inspector Jackson has handed the case over to a Detective Superintendent Ford at Wingate CID.'

Laura glanced round the cramped sitting room. 'Shall I go up?'

'No, I'll fetch her. And thanks for coming. I'd have lost it completely if you'd turned me down back there.'

His confiding tone made her draw back. She shrugged off his gratitude.

He stood by the door. 'She's got to get it into her head that she didn't have anything to do with Jim dying. They could make her confess to anything, the state she's in now.'

'And you're sure she wasn't involved?' Laura wanted a categorical answer.

He came back towards her. 'What kind of question is that?'

'The kind I need an answer to. Can you be absolutely certain that Ellie didn't kill Jim?'

'Jesus!'

Laura wondered what on earth had directed the police interest away from Paul, the more obvious suspect, towards Ellie. 'Does she have an alibi?'

'She was here in the house, for Christ's sake. There were people around who can tell you that; kids setting off on different orienteering tasks, a couple of delivery van drivers, me. I was here too. I was talking to Ellie at about the time Jim must have died. I'm her alibi!'

And she's yours, Laura thought.

'You know we've been set up, don't you?' Paul's temper and

voice rose. 'And you know who by? My lousy ex-wife! It's got her stamp all over it, the conniving bitch.'

'But surely she'd want to lie low after Jim died? She was in the wrong for having the affair, if that's the way you want to look at it. Wouldn't she just want to get over his death and put her life back together?'

'You don't know her.' Paul lowered his voice. 'She doesn't think the same way most people think.'

For the first time, Laura caught a fresh view of Paul Miller. No longer the solid, easy-going man of action, he fumbled for words that would adequately describe his ex-wife. He stood with fists clenched, head bowed, frustrated by his own inarticulateness. She decided to switch back to the task in hand. 'What Ellie needs right now is help. I'll do what I can, but I also think she should find a good solicitor, just in case. Does she know anyone locally?'

'No, and she's not ready to see one; not the way she's acting right now.'

'If I can calm her down, I'll suggest someone I know.' She had Luke in mind. 'If she's right about the police and she is a suspect, she needs someone lined up to look after her. In fact, I think she should see him anyway.' She gave Paul Luke's name and number and promised to have a word with him herself. 'He does criminal cases, and Ellie wouldn't find him threatening. He's the best person I can think of.'

As Paul went to fetch Ellie, Laura had time to sift through the facts and slot them into place. She tried not to be swayed by this most recent development. There were various possibilities; firstly that Ellie's reactions to the police were neurotic. This would be understandable. Her normal responses were bound to be exaggerated under the circumstances. Even for a woman who wasn't the 'crying sort', acute grief was bound to take its toll.

On the other hand, there might be real grounds for Ellie's

fear of the police, in which case there must be substantial evidence which she was still hiding from Laura. In her own contact with her since Jim's death, Laura had found some disturbing puzzles, most notably in Ellie's disturbing revelation about the Glyclozide tablets.

Even at the time, Laura thought this made little sense. If Ellie had truly been begging her to hide them from the police in case they pointed suspicion at Paul, it had been a clumsy attempt to deal with the problem. Why not simply throw them away? In effect, it had highlighted their existence and, though Laura was sworn to secrecy, she now saw it was possible to read the situation yet another way; that Ellie had been trying to incriminate Paul deliberately and divert attention from herself.

She thought again about the missing Glyclozide. It was one of a family of diabetic drugs designed to reduce blood sugar, not known to the general public in the way that insulin treatment was widely recognised. In fact, it was probably only familiar outside the medical profession to patients themselves and to those closely connected to a long-term diabetic.

Laura came up against a jolting realisation. Ellie was certainly closely connected to Jim and she had trained as a nurse. She would know about this obscure drug, its uses and abuses.

An overdose; what would be the effect? It would cause irrational behaviour for a start, exacerbated by exposure to extreme cold. In such circumstances it could prove fatal. In the wrong hands the drug was a killer.

If Ellie were implicated ... would she have befriended a doctor who might put two and two together? Would she be this good an actress? Laura pictured her at the funeral, numb with grief; remembered her distress when Jim's body was taken from its quiet, snowdrop-covered grave. But did this fit the real circumstances of Jim's unfaithfulness? Why wasn't

Ellie more bitter? The truth slipped and slid away as she heard footsteps in the corridor announcing the return of Paul Miller.

'She's on her way,' he said quietly. 'I'll let you get on with it.'

'Wouldn't she prefer you to stay?' Laura wanted him in on this.

'You don't mind?'

'Let's see how it goes with you here. She obviously relies on you a great deal.' Laura took off her jacket and threw it over the back of a chair. The small room was warm and cluttered and the whole house silent, she realised. 'I thought you had a big group of students over Easter?' she said.

'We had to cancel.'

'Ellie couldn't face it?'

He stood to one side as she appeared in the door.

Anyone further from the slim, bright athlete whom Laura had first met couldn't be imagined. Gauntness had taken over, Ellie's face was pale and bewildered, every action slow and distracted. She turned to Paul.

'I did what you wanted.' He pointed to Laura.

Eyes fixed on him, she nodded.

'She knows you're sick.'

Post-traumatic stress. Laura made an instant diagnosis. Ellie let herself be led to a chair like a child and passively allowed her blood-pressure and temperature readings to be taken.

'You must keep her warm and give her plenty of fluids,' Laura told Paul. 'This is a form of shock. Do you think you'll know what to do?'

'What brought it on?'

'Who knows? Delayed reaction to the exhumation? She looks to me as if she's terrified.' She saw how reluctant Ellie was to be touched, how she shrank into the chair.

'Of the police?' He stood back to let Laura finish her examination. 'I'd like to know what they did to her!'

'Hello, Laura.' Ellie seemed to register her presence for the first time. Then she looked around the room for someone other than Paul and Laura. 'Did you come by yourself?'

'Paul said you wanted me. I've told him how to take care of you.'

Ellie pushed strands of lank hair from her face. She was wearing a loose black tracksuit which emphasised her paleness. 'I needed to see you. What was it? That's right, I gave the police the Glyclozide tablets like you said.'

Laura snapped her bag shut in silence.

'They took them away.' She looked at Paul, then back at Laura. 'I told them how I'd found them in Jim's bedside drawer.'

'*You* found them?' A new version. Laura frowned.

'Yes, when I was tidying up his things.'

'What are you on about?' Paul asked. 'Glyclo . . . what?'

Laura explained. 'It was something Jim kept for emergencies. Didn't you know?'

'No. I thought the insulin was all he had. Where did he get them from?'

Thoughtfully Laura put on her jacket. 'We don't know. Not from our surgery.'

'From me,' Ellie said slowly. 'I lied, Laura. It was me who got Jim the tablets when I was temping for my last agency. I took them from the hospital pharmacy, thinking he could use them on his next expedition. He's kept them in a drawer ever since.'

'Sunday must be my day for asking you for help.' Laura spoke to Luke on the phone. She hadn't seen him since Joan's Foss; hadn't risked making contact.

'Professional, I take it?'

184

'How can you tell?'

'From your brisk tone of voice.'

'I didn't mean to be off-hand.' Before she'd left Ravenscar Hall the night before, Ellie had pleaded for advice. Laura had promised to get in touch with Luke on her behalf. 'Are you busy?'

'No, I'm wallowing.'

'Not in self-pity, I hope.'

'In my bath. Avoiding work on the house as per usual.'

'Shall I ring back later?'

'No, I can wallow and listen at the same time.'

She gave a rapid account of Ellie's situation. 'She needs you, Luke.'

'It sounds like she needs somebody, that's for sure. Listen, make a record of this post-traumatic stress business in her file. It might be important if we have to put in a plea of diminished responsibility.'

'"We"?' She was pleased that he'd jumped in with both feet.

'The defence. If she does want me to act for her.'

'She does. She kept crying and asking for help.'

'What do you think, innocent or guilty?'

Laura paused. 'Innocent.'

'Is she seeing straight enough to ring me and get me to start work?'

'Probably not. But she's got Paul Miller to look after her. They'll be glad if you say yes through me. They're desperate.'

'Paul and Ellie, are they an item?'

'Does it make any difference?' Laura liked his directness.

'Yep.'

'Then you'd better make up your own mind.'

'So, what are you doing?'

'Now? Not much, why?' Matthew was in York for the day.

'Come over and discuss the case, Dr Grant.'

'Is that ethical, Mr Altham?'

185

'Off the record.'

'Even worse!'

'Come anyway. I'll cook lunch.'

'Isn't your kitchen a health hazard?' She hedged, torn between yes and no.

'I'll take you out instead. Come to my place. There's a bar I know just off the High Street.' Luke lived in town, five minutes from his office. 'Just say yes.'

A ring on the doorbell interrupted Laura's nervous preparations to visit Luke. She was brushing her hair, having changed out of jeans into smarter trousers and a short, soft cream sweater when Juliet Maskell arrived at Abbey Grange. Laura made her welcome, then rang Luke to say that she was delayed.

'I don't want to mess up your day,' Juliet said. 'I realise how precious your time off is.'

'You're not messing anything up.' She told herself not to be so jittery; she'd agreed to have lunch with Luke. No big deal. 'Something's wrong?' she said gently, leading Juliet into her sitting room.

'You can tell?' She was on edge, strained and washed out.

'Yes. How are you coping?' It was a delicate situation. From the beginning Laura had liked both Juliet and Philip, so she wasn't about to start taking sides. On the other hand, she wanted to offer Juliet some support.

Juliet sighed. 'What would you say; "As well as can be expected"?'

'It's awful, isn't it?' Splitting up was like standing at the edge of a cliff, feeling the ground crumble underfoot. Your life slid away from you.

'Laura, you know Mary Mercer well, don't you?' She sat forward on the edge of her seat. 'Would you mind if I asked you about her?'

186

'If I can tell you anything that would help.' Her guarded reply meant that she recognised the power of a misplaced word, a wrong judgment.

'I don't want you to dish the dirt.' Juliet raised both hands as if to steady Laura's apprehensions. 'I want your opinion. Do you think this affair was a shallow thing for Mary? One of a string, with no special significance?'

Laura guessed what lay behind the question. Mary's style was flirtatious and jokey. She lived life with a sense of drama, could ricochet from one relationship to the next. Since she'd gone to act in rep at Birmingham, they'd kept in close touch by phone. Mary was deep in yet another love triangle, but this time she was consumed by doubts and jealousy towards another actress who was making moves towards Mary's new man. Still, Laura couldn't answer 'yes' to Juliet's question. 'I know what you mean, but no; Mary was in love with Philip,' she said quietly. 'She even tried to behave well over him. You know she left Bridge House when she realised how she felt about him?'

'I guessed as much.'

'At the time?'

'No, since then. Everything fits into place once you discover the truth.' Again she sighed. 'I liked Mary, you know.'

Laura offered to put the two women in touch.

Quickly she shook her head. 'No, I couldn't do that.'

'Talk to Philip about her then?'

Juliet gave a worried smile. 'Whose side are you on? He's always telling me we should talk. But talking draws me back in and I get angry and hurt all over again. I've got so little resilience these days. Not talking to Philip is a method I've perfected to protect myself.'

Laura compared it with her own 'leave me alone' reaction to her divorce from Tom. She nodded. 'What else do you want to ask about Mary?'

'This next one's about Philip. Why do you think he did it? Apart from the fact that Mary's an incredibly attractive, sexy woman, of course.' She gave a flat smile.

'He'd been immune to attractive women until then, I take it?' A weak sun had begun to filter through the bank of clouds that had hung over Ravenscar for days. Laura glanced out at the still hibernating garden, picked out green buds on a hawthorn tree, the first catkins.

'Pretty much. He likes women's company, but he doesn't flirt. *Didn't*,' she corrected.

'Doesn't,' Laura insisted. She recalled watching Philp talk to Gina Wray in the Falcon. He'd been attentive but disinterested.

'So why Mary?'

'Mid-life crisis?' The answer came out too pat. Laura apologised. 'Juliet, listen, maybe you're not asking the right question. "Why" is the impossible one to answer, even if we're the ones involved. Why not accept that it happened and move on?'

'Because I need to know what I did to switch him off. It's not so much that he chose Mary, but that he rejected me. When it comes down to it, that's the devastating thing.'

Laura looked sadly at her friend. 'Philip would never say that he'd rejected you. I'm sure he didn't want you two to split up.'

Juliet flicked something from her lap; a gesture of dismissal.

'It looks as if you're punishing him.'

'Not intentionally. It's the way I've been brought up. Even if I don't like this puritanical streak in me, I can't help feeling that if Philip's miserable it's no more than he deserves.'

Laura thought for a while. 'But you're miserable too. And the boys, presumably.'

Juliet stood up.

'What can I do to make this come right again? I want to be

on good terms with Philip but I can't forgive him. I don't want to live in that great big empty house by myself yet I could never feel safe with him again. If he's done it once, he could do it twice, three, four, five times. They say people repeat a pattern; drinkers keep on drinking, don't they?' She stopped, suddenly exasperated. 'I know; to make one slip isn't a pattern, is it?'

'I never said a word.' Laura smiled.

'But I can see you thinking it.' The tension eased.

'When Tom and I split up, finally, I never had any of this debate with myself. It was like cutting the head off the beast. No ifs and buts and if onlys. Finished. Full stop. All I felt was relief.'

Juliet nodded. 'I envy you. Doubt is the worst state to be in.'

Laura took this to heart. Her own doubts about Matthew were always close to the surface. But she knew he was the person she must discuss them with. 'It knots you up,' she agreed.

'The trouble is, I'm too conventional.' Juliet joined her at the window. 'I've lived a sheltered life; born in Merton, married Philip and came to live in Hawkshead when I was in my early twenties, had three sons, looked after them. It was enough for me. Ordinary doctor's wife and mother.'

Laura smiled again. 'There's nothing ordinary about you.'

'Truth is a moveable feast,' Luke said. He and Laura hadn't yet gone for lunch. At one-thirty on Sunday afternoon they sat in the depot he called his kitchen, surrounded by packets of cereal, sliced bread, jars of marmalade, tins of soup.

'What about the truth, the whole truth and nothing but the truth?' Laura had confessed to him that Ellie's version of the events surrounding Jim's death was shot full of holes.

'You've been brought up on too much Perry Mason, that's your problem.'

189

'Before my time, actually.' She glanced round. There were walking boots on a work surface beside soap-powder and cartons of orange juice. She was bemused by the chaos.

'I'm still finding a place for things.'

'How long have you lived here?'

'Five years.' He grinned.

The house had been difficult to find. Laura had followed instructions and turned left off the High Street on to a narrow road called Tan Hill which climbed at a steep angle towards open countryside. Tan Hill was cobbled, the terraced houses a miracle of nineteenth-century design and engineering. Leading off, there were even narrower side streets called Folds, named after local landmarks. She passed Abbey Fold, then Scar Fold, before she came to Raven's Fold and Luke's house at the end of the cul-de-sac.

Number eighteen looked out on to fields. Inside, its style was solid stone, with ornate wood and plasterwork. Rooms were high and spacious, but obviously went unappreciated by their owner. Laura had glimpsed a kind of office to one side of the long, narrow hallway. It was stacked with papers, a computer, cardboard boxes. Another room might be a lounge. The curtains were still closed, a tall plant had withered in its pot. At the back of the house was the kitchen, where they now sat.

'I don't have a home-making instinct,' Luke explained. 'I think it's because I always feel kind of temporary, as if I might soon move on again.'

'Has anyone ever tried to domesticate you?'

'A couple of people.' He was deliberately vague. 'Would you like to see the one notable exception to the scenes of devastation around you?' He picked up his glass and their bottle of wine.

She followed him upstairs.

'The attic.' They'd climbed two flights to a large room with a sloping ceiling and a dormer window overlooking the fields.

'It's empty!' Laura laughed.

'Precisely. I just painted it white and left it. What do you think?'

She went to perch on the deep windowsill and looked out at the hills. 'It's perfect.'

'A few big cushions here and there, a music system in the corner. I come up here to get away from it all.'

'It works.'

'You have your garden. I have my attic.' He sat down beside her.

'You were asking me about Ellie,' she reminded him. 'I can't work out why she pulled suspicion her way by handing over the Glyclozide.'

'And I can't put my finger on what the police are up to. I rang the station but there's no one around today. Mike Jackson took two days off, I hear. I tried Wingate and they're not committing themselves either. All they'll say is that Paul Miller's ex-wife has come forward.'

'But she's not exactly an impartial witness, is she?'

'They've obviously got something else to go on. I'll find out when Mike gets back on Tuesday. And I'll get through to Martin Ford as soon as I can.'

'The superintendent at Wingate? What's he like?'

'Good at his job.' Luke drank the last of his wine then refilled both their glasses. 'I'm glad you came, Laura. Do you want to carry on talking shop, or can we change the subject?'

'What about lunch?' Laura sat with her back to the sun, felt it warm on her shoulders.

'Forget it?' His eyes were full of other, unspoken questions.

'OK,' she said slowly.

'Can we talk about you?'

'What are you expecting from me?' By coming here she knew she'd made a significant move. Being close to Luke, she felt the full force of the attraction she'd spent the week fending

191

off; the lightness in his grey eyes, the mouth that suggested humour. With Luke she felt she would be able to laugh.

'Not expecting. That's putting it too strongly.'

'What do you *hope* will happen, then?'

He shrugged. 'That we can stop playing games for a start. It doesn't feel right. I want to come clean and say that my interest goes way beyond the professional, and beyond the merely friendly. There, how's that?'

Laura stared at him. 'Mine too, if I'm really honest. But there's Matthew.'

Luke glanced down at his empty glass. 'I don't know how long I can keep on doing the decent thing as far as Matthew is concerned.'

'Me neither.'

'What would you say if I told you I think about you, Laura? At inconvenient times, like when I'm filling out Legal Aid forms or watching the nine o'clock news.'

'You hardly know anything about me.'

'What's there to know? That you're beautiful, that your face is imprinted in my brain? That I want to kiss you and make love to you?'

She felt the turn and tilt of her heart's rhythm, a melting disbelief. But at the moment when he leaned forward to kiss her, she pulled back. Though she ached to be held in this bright, light room without shadows, she knew she must refuse. It was Matthew's face that clouded her vision and brought tears to her eyes; Matthew's doubtful, vulnerable, loving face.

She guessed how Luke would love her, with a powerful mixture of desire and tenderness. He would take his time, speak his feelings. No silences, no fears.

He hung his head.

Cut deep by his own sudden defencelessness, she almost put out her hand to touch him. 'It's bad timing, Luke. And it's my fault, I shouldn't have come.' She spoke the words, the trite cover-ups. Inside, her world was disintegrating.

She tried to explain. 'What I want isn't straightforward any more. It was, when I first came to Hawkshead, after my marriage broke up. I knew I just needed to be left alone for a while, and that was fine. Then I got involved with Matthew, and now things are confused again.'

'These "things"; they're called emotions.' He listened, half turned away.

'Luke, I'm sorry.' Balance was what she'd striven for; peace and quiet. Now there were wild swings between desire and guilt, a jolting realisation that nothing stayed the same. 'Give me time. Let me talk to Matthew.'

He turned abruptly, opened the window, and stood looking silently up the dale.

# CHAPTER NINETEEN

'I'm here, aren't I?' Aimee wrapped a sheet around herself and stood up from the bed. Sean was putting her under pressure to say how she felt. Why couldn't he leave it and let things develop?

'What does that prove, apart from the fact that you hate your father and can't bear to be in the same house?' He lay on the bed watching her.

'I don't hate my father.'

'You act as if you do.' She'd come to spend Easter Monday with him after another row had flared up at home. His parents and sister were away, helping to bail his older brother, Mark, out of the latest heap of trouble he'd got himself into. Sean was supposed to be at home working for his exams.

'OK then, I do. He's a pain.'

Sean rolled off the bed and put on his jeans. 'Fine. Great. Fantastic.'

Barefoot, his thin, smooth torso hunched over as he searched for his shoes, he looked vulnerable. His bedroom reminded her of boyhood; sports shields on a shelf, old books and photographs. 'I thought I was the champion sulker in this relationship?' She went up to him and put her arms around his neck.

'I'm not sulking.' His scowl made him purse his lips, his dark lashes shadowed his eyes.

She kissed him. 'You are. All because I won't tell you I love you.'

He turned his face away, but he had his arms locked around her waist. 'Why not? I tell you, don't I?' Sean poured out his heart when they made love.

'It's only words. You know how I feel without me having to spell it out.' She tried to kiss him back into a better mood. His frown didn't worry her; she thought it was funny to see him trying to stay serious and resist her.

He turned her round and backed her against the bed, threatening to tug her wraparound sheet away. 'I'm trying to talk to you!'

She laughed, clinging on to the sheet and falling backwards. Then she rolled to one side and scrambled on to her knees. The sheet had come untucked, so she wrestled to gather it around her.

'I need to know why you're here stopping me from doing my work.' He crawled over the bed after her. 'Why you're distracting me and making me chuck my chances of a good grade. Why you come and tempt me with those big brown eyes and little-girl-lost look, Aimee Scott!' This time he backed her against the wall at the head of his bed. 'If it's not because you're as crazy about me as I am about you!' He put his palms on the wall above her shoulders and moved in to kiss her.

Aimee felt the sheet being tugged away and the touch of his skin against hers. She wrapped her arms around him, put her head back and held him tight. They slid down the wall and lay flat, tangled in sheets and pillows, sprawled across the narrow bed. The way he moved in on her, kissing her neck, her breasts, her mouth, roused her too. She ran her hands down his back, slipped her fingers through the belt-loops of his jeans and arched to meet him.

'Tell me what you like.'

'This.' She reached for his hand and put it over her breast. His long fingers caressed her, his eyes stared straight into hers.

Then he stooped to kiss her neck and breasts again, as she arched and sighed. Her hands fell back, her arms stretched wide.

'What else?' His lips were on her face, his whole body pressing against hers.

'Just love me,' she whispered. She turned her face into the pillow, felt him slide to one side, quickly undress and come back to her. Aimee rolled over and opened her eyes. Softly she stroked his thick, dark hair. 'I do love you,' she whispered.

'I know. I wanted to hear you say it.' He breathed against her cheek. It was the first time she'd admitted it and it felt amazing.

'I think you're wonderful. I never want to lose you.'

'You won't,' he promised. Their murmured words sealed the moment. Life would rush them on into jobs, other cities, perhaps other loves. But this was theirs; this precious second of knowing they were adored.

'I have to work tonight,' Sean whispered. 'Bank Holiday Monday. They're short-staffed at the hotel, so I said I'd go in.'

It was the hardest thing in the world to move out of the warm comfort of his arms. Aimee closed her eyes and pretended not to hear.

'Aimee!' He tickled her under her chin. 'We have to get up.'

She groaned.

'I'd have told them no if I'd known you'd be here. But now I can't let them down at the last minute.'

She curled towards him. 'What time?'

'Half-seven.'

'What time is it now?'

He propped himself on one elbow to look at his watch. 'Five-thirty.' Leaning across her, he took her mass of long, silky dark hair and spread it like a fan across the pillow. 'You can stay here if you like. My folks won't be back until tomorrow.'

'No.' She opened her eyes and smiled. 'I'd better go.' She would take the bus with Sean into town, then make her way home. Perhaps her mother would be able to give her a lift from Merton. 'Guess what, I'm starving.'

'You know where the kitchen is.' He kissed her once more, then got up. 'Would you recognise an egg if you saw one?' He told her there was bread in the bread-bin, bacon in the fridge, then vanished into the bathroom.

Robed in her sheet like a Roman senator, hair tousled, eyes smudged with mascara, Aimee cooked for two.

'Brilliant.' Sean peered into the smoke-filled kitchen. 'Smoky bacon crisps.'

She rapped the plates on to the table. 'Please yourself.' The fried eggs were split and the bacon frazzled. Still, she ate ravenously.

Sean said nothing. He gave her extra bread. 'Get a move on, or I'll be late,' he told her.

She headed for the bathroom, still chewing.

'And don't leave any of your long hair in the plug-hole, or my mum will kill me.'


In the end, it was a scramble for Sean to get to work on time. A fun-run had snarled up the city centre traffic so he and Aimee decided to jump off their bus and make for the hotel on foot. From there she would walk to the station and catch a train.

'Isn't a fun-run a contradiction in terms?' She complained at having to walk. Weary runners were completing a five-mile circuit through the streets, jangling tins for a hospital charity, many in fancy dress. Nurses in black stockings and suspenders were a favourite theme for male and female runners alike.

'Are you sure you'll be OK when you get home?' Aimee had

described her father's black mood; how he'd flipped when he heard that the police had targeted Ellie Blackwood for Jim's murder.

'He'll have calmed down by now.' Aimee had walked out early that morning in mid-rant. Her father was acting as if he were the one they were going to arrest. 'He'll probably ignore me as usual.'

They stood on the wide, white university steps opposite Sean's hotel. 'I'll give you a ring later on.'

She nodded. 'Do you think Ellie had something to do with it?'

The murder had become 'it' in everyone's minds. To Sean it was more graphic; a frozen hand stretched out of the ice, grasping at nothing. A submerged body, a white face and staring eyes. He couldn't forget the jolt of fear that ran through him when he first saw it, nor the dead man's face when they finally pulled him out. He shook his head.

Aimee took his hand. 'Sorry, I know you don't like to talk about it.'

But Sean needed to get it off his chest. He glanced at his watch. 'No one has a clue what it was like up there that day. It was freezing cold and pouring with rain. It came down so hard your face and hands felt numb with it. I could hardly see. We thought Jim must have called the climb off, the weather was so bad. Then, when it happened, and I had to run for Ellie, you should've seen her face, Aimee. It was like someone had shot her. She never expected bad news, I swear. How could she have reacted like that if she'd been involved?'

Aimee shook her head. 'So why do the police act as if she was?'

'I'll tell you something else weird,' Sean continued. 'Marianne Miller doesn't work here any more.'

Aimee shot him a surprised look. 'Did she leave?'

'Without working her notice. She just didn't show up on

Friday and left them in deep trouble. That's why they need extra staff to work over the holiday. I'm in Reception tonight.'

'Do you think it's got anything to do with this murder?'

Sean resented how much Jim Blackwood's death had come to dominate their lives. 'Dunno. The manager's pretty pissed off with her anyway. I told him she might be scared.'

'Because she came forward with the evidence?'

'Yeah. And as far as Marianne knows, the finger's pointing at Paul. Maybe she was worried that he would track her down in this new job so she's done a runner.'

Aimee sighed. 'I wonder what she told them that was so bloody vital.' She stepped down on to the pavement and turned up the collar of her jacket. Stragglers in the race shambled by. She put a hand in her pocket and drew out fifty pence to sling into their tin.

'We'll find out soon enough.' Sean squeezed her shoulder. 'At the trial. Marianne will be the main prosecution witness.'

By the time Aimee reached home it was dark. Her father was in his study talking to someone. The door was shut, but murmured conversation drifted into the hall. She flung her bag on the hall table and headed upstairs. Her mother was out so she'd had to wait ages for a bus from Merton. No bus, then when it did arrive, no change. The bus driver had made her feel a fool. Rain had accompanied the dregs of the bank holiday as a stream of cars crawled out of the dale. Happy holiday.

The study door opened. 'Aimee, do you have a minute, please?' her father called.

'I'm meant to be revising. What do you want?'

'Luke Altham's in here with me. He'd like a word.'

Not again, she thought. Her father had gone seriously paranoid if he thought he needed a solicitor. She sighed, went back downstairs and followed him into his study.

Luke sat to one side of the desk. Aimee didn't know him well, but she'd attended meetings where he'd spoken against the quarry and she had him down as totally calm and professional. With his pale grey eyes, straight eyebrows and smooth haircut she could see that older women would find him attractive. He wasn't the sort of lawyer that she would have expected her father to go for.

'Hi.' He'd hung his jacket over the back of his chair and had the sleeves of his pale blue shirt rolled back. 'You're looking well.'

She blushed and kept her distance, watching her father sit down at his desk.

'No long-term effects from the accident?' Luke asked pleasantly.

'I'm fine, thanks.'

'Luke's working for Ellie Blackwood.' Gerald swung his glasses and shuffled some papers. 'He's been taking details from me about her husband's death.'

She did a double-take. 'Oh, I thought . . .' She looked from him to Luke and back again.

Luke smiled. 'Your father doesn't need a solicitor, does he?'

'Sore point,' Gerald interrupted. 'But no one's suing me for negligence, so far as I know.' He touched wood, then went on. 'I've given Luke as much help as I can but it occurred to me that you might be able to add something through this boyfriend of yours.'

'Sean?'

'He was on the scene, I remember.' Gerald was belligerent, waiting for her to catch on.

Luke intervened between father and daughter. 'Look, it might be best if you just give me his phone number and I can ask him directly.' He cleared his throat and reached for his jacket.

'But Aimee's right here. Didn't your boyfriend say he knows where this Marianne Miller woman is working?'

Aimee swallowed hard. 'Not any more. I just saw Sean. Marianne Miller left her job.'

'When?' Luke grew more alert.

'Last Friday. He doesn't know where she is now.'

'Pity.' He stood up. 'It would have been useful to have a chat and find out exactly where she fits in.'

'I met her once,' Aimee said casually. 'She seemed OK, as a matter of fact.'

Gerald tutted loudly.

'She didn't start any of this,' Aimee said hotly. 'I got the impression she hated it as much as anybody else. But she couldn't let somebody get away with murder!'

Luke held up a steadying hand. 'Do you know what she actually told the police?'

'That the rows at the Hall went on right until the day Jim died. That her affair with Jim hadn't stopped, that Paul knew this, but Ellie didn't so far as she knew . . .' She listed the points on her fingers.

Luke nodded. 'That would go a long way to establishing a motive.'

'For Paul, not for Ellie,' Aimee pointed out. 'That's what doesn't add up. Why are the police going after her?'

'I don't know. There's something we've missed. I can't work out what it is. And I'm not getting much sense out of my client, I'm afraid. I went to see her before I came here and she claims not to remember half of what went on that day. There was one other thing, though. Ellie did say something quite odd. She said, "Ask Laura. Laura will tell you all about it."' He frowned and shook his head.

'Ask her then.' Aimee made the logical point.

'He can't,' Gerald said quietly.

'Why not?'

'Laura won't be able to divulge anything,' Gerald told Luke. 'It's against the rules. Patient confidentiality.'

'But if she *knows* why Ellie's a suspect . . .'

'Your father's right. And I wouldn't even ask her. Rule number one: what's said in a GP's consulting room never gets beyond those four walls. Poor Laura, it must put her in an awkward position.' Thoughtfully Luke made his way to the door.

'Shall I still tell Sean you'd like to speak to him?' Aimee asked.

'Yes please, the sooner the better.'

While her father showed the visitor to the door, Aimee made a quick getaway to her room. With luck, Gerald would be too wrapped up in his own problems to come and ask where she'd been all day.

But his footsteps soon sounded on the stairs and along the landing. He came in without knocking. 'You didn't tell us that you'd seen Marianne Miller!' His tone was accusatory, carrying a note of betrayal.

'You never asked.' She couldn't help herself. From being tiny, she'd always put her head into the noose of his bad temper.

Gerald closed the door firmly behind him. 'I'd like to know just what sort of people you're mixed up with these days.'

'Normal people for a change.' He knew what she thought of Hawkshead residents; a bunch of snobs and country bumpkins.

'Normal people go around murdering each other, do they?' he retorted. 'And sleeping around and leading double lives? Do you realise how embarrassing it was for me when you came out with the fact that you know this woman?'

His voice drilled through her. She hated the way he paced up and down her room. 'I didn't say I *knew* her. I said I met her once.'

'And conveniently forgot to mention it to your mother and me.'

Aimee turned away. 'I wish I'd never opened my mouth. I'm not allowed to express an opinion without you getting at me.'

'What are you mumbling about now? And another thing, this boyfriend . . .'

'Sean. Sean Armstrong. He's got a name!'

'. . . We don't know a single thing about him.' Gerald didn't even pause. 'He comes up here on some half-baked course, and the next thing we know you've practically moved in with him. What about his parents? Don't they see anything wrong with it?'

'No, they're not dinosaurs like you, Dad. They're normal. This is how everyone acts these days.' The more he exaggerated, the more she stoked herself up for a confrontation. She omitted to tell him that Sean's mum and dad didn't actually know she'd spent the night at their house.

'Not round here, they don't. And not as long as you're living under this roof. Don't you realise how much your mother worries about what you get up to?'

'Don't you know it's *you* who's driving her round the twist? Bossing us around, saying everyone's wrong and you're right. You're the great doctor, the pillar of this crummy community. Yeah, right. You don't even recognise a murder when it hits you in the face. You go ahead and sign the death certificate, nice and neat. You try to tell me what to do, and you can't even hack your job any more. That's you; clapped out, losing your grip. Get it? This is me telling you you're useless!'

All her life she'd been in awe of him. Until she was twelve years old, she'd thought his word was law. Now she saw him for what he was; a vain and insecure man too stupid to acknowledge his mistakes.

When the impact of her words sank in, Gerald's shoulders

slumped forward. He put a hand to his forehead, then dragged it down his face, pulling at the loose skin beneath his eyes, pressing his fingers into the hollows of his cheeks.

'Dad . . .'

He turned away, fumbled with the door handle.

Immediately she regretted it. There was a bitter taste in her mouth and tears in her eyes. Words, once spoken, were irrevocable.

He turned. 'Is that what they're saying?'

'No. It's me. Probably no one else says it. Forget it.' Quickly she rubbed the tears away and sniffed.

'That's what they're thinking, though.' At last he managed to open the door. The years weighed him down, his shoulders were hunched, his head bowed. 'And the worst thing about it is that every word you say is true.'

# CHAPTER TWENTY

The week after Easter was an uneasy one for the practice. Though no new major crises disturbed the routine of eight-hundred meetings, surgeries and home visits, there was an air of ill-temper around the health centre which Philip could readily attribute to Gerald. Sheila took the brunt of it as the one responsible for organising the use of the doctors' time in the diary. Gerald spent the week in fussy, nattering mode, blaming their receptionist for landing him with meetings he didn't want to attend or not shielding him from the pharmaceutical reps. He would run his head against problems instead of using tact and diplomacy, and finally today had failed to secure a much-needed psychogeriatric place in Wingate for a Low Royds patient. Philip and Laura had only been able to look on in dismay.

'What stage of senile dementia does a patient have to be in these days before we can get them any help?' he demanded, slamming down the phone on a helpless hospital administrator. It was Friday afternoon and the end of a long, dreary week.

Philip glanced through Gerald's door. He wanted to get away to call in on Dot Wilson with a date for her by-pass surgery, but his senior partner demanded his attention. 'Is it still the place for Sarah Jennings that you're after?' He knew the history all too well; Sarah was a ninety-three-year-old lifelong resident of Hawkshead, never married, with no surviving family. At the age of eighty-nine she'd reluctantly agreed to go to Low Royds to be looked after and her home in a small terraced house on the main square had been dismantled and sold to pay for her care. Now she was in an advanced stage of dementia.

'The poor woman can't even remember her own name. She's sweet-natured as ever, but she can't feed herself and she can't even stand up without help. One of these days there'll be another fall, hypostatic pneumonia, and that'll be it.' Gerald snapped his fingers.

'Why not try York?' Philip suggested.

'I've tried bloody York, and Leeds, and Bradford. It's the same story everywhere; according to them, not a single psychogeriatric bed in the entire county!'

'Then Low Royds will have to cope for a while longer. Would you like me to call in and tell them on my way up to Dot's?'

'No.' Gerald implied that he was perfectly capable of doing it himself. He turned his back on Philip to riffle through some file drawers.

Joy Hartley came across the waiting area in her navy coat and hat, heading for home. She raised her eyebrows at the sound of Gerald's peevish voice. Everyone was tired, wanting to be away from the wear and tear of work.

At least the news he took to Dot's was good, Philip thought. David Walker had scheduled her surgery for the end of April.

'I must be pretty bad, then,' she said quietly when Philip gave her the news. She sat in a chair by her living-room window, overlooking the steep cobbled street. 'If they've jumped me up the list as quick as this.'

He sat down beside her. 'And I thought you'd be pleased!'

'Chuffed to bits,' she said flatly. Then she pulled round. 'I'm sorry, Dr Maskell, don't mind me. I'm really very grateful for all you've done.'

'Well, we did know your case was urgent,' he told her carefully. 'The ECG readings were a fair warning of what was happening to the main arteries and Mr Walker's tests soon confirmed it. You'll just have to reconcile yourself to a week in hospital and a fairly lengthy period of convalescence.'

'At least they must think I'm worth the trouble.' Her tone remained dry but she was beginning to look on the bright side. 'I can't be a complete waste of their time, can I?'

Philip reassured her again about the success rate for the surgery. 'And afterwards it should give you a decent quality of life, Dot. That's the main thing to remember.'

'Aye well, I'm not enjoying having to sit around all day at present, I can tell you,' she confessed. 'It's not my way, you know, Dr Maskell. I like to be up and doing.'

He sympathised with her frustration. 'And we miss you.' Dot was part of village life; she kept them in order with her astute opinions and he feared she was part of a fast-dying breed.

'No one to boss you about, you mean?'

'We need you to take a lead sometimes. Take this Jim Blackwood business, for instance.' He directed the conversation away from medical matters. In no hurry himself, he knew he had a long weekend on call ahead of him and only an empty house in Askby to go home to.

'Nay, I know nowt about that except what Dick tells me and I don't set much store by that. He can be fanciful, can Dick. Put a pint pot in his fist and there's no stopping him. At any rate, he reckons the police are following up a strong lead and that one of these days they'll step in and arrest poor Mrs Blackwood.' Dot's thin face creased up with disbelief. 'I said to him, "Dick, don't be daft! Who's put that idea into your head?" I mean, did you ever hear owt so silly?'

'Strangely enough, I'm afraid it might be true.' Tension in the Falcon was almost palpable; for days now the regulars there had been expecting Superintendent Ford to act. The police had been up a second time to question Ellie. Laura had made two more home visits and had at last persuaded Ellie to cooperate with Luke Altham.

'Well, blow me!' Dot was speechless. 'That pretty little thing? How could she do away with a big, strong man like him?

'I remember once, in 1948 I think it was, there was another terrible murder up at Ravenscar, and that was a case of jealousy between man and wife too. He was a taxi driver from Wingate and when she found out he was carrying on with another woman she poisoned him.'

This was well before Philip's time. 'What did she do with the body?'

'Lord knows how she did it; they say she got him to drive her up to the tarn and poisoned him there. They found arsenic in the sandwiches in the back of the taxi, would you believe? At any rate, she'd picked her spot for this picnic of theirs. He must have keeled over on that same scree slope where Jim Blackwood fell in. All she had to do was get him groggy with the poison and give him a little helping hand into the water. They found him weeks later, weighted down with a big stone tied around him. She even managed to drive the taxi over to Swiredale to throw people off the scent. She'd thought it all out in advance. Premeditated murder, they called it.'

'What happened to her?'

They hung her in the end. In Armley Prison. She ended up admitting it, poor woman. We all said then that jealousy was a terrible thing.'

'It sounds as if I got off relatively lightly.' Philip acknowledged his own misdemeanours with a wry grin. 'Luckily, Juliet isn't the poisoning sort.'

Dot shook her head. 'I'm sorry for your troubles, Dr Maskell, and I hope things work out for you in the long run.'

'I hope so too.'

'And don't be too hard on yourself,' she said quietly, unexpectedly. 'It's not as if you made a habit of it and Mrs Maskell must realise that too.'

He nodded. 'Thanks, Dot.'

'It takes time, that's all, for someone to get over something like that.' Sighing, she got up to show him to the door. 'Both you and Mrs Maskell have always been very good to me.'

'And you to us.' He paused on the doorstep, moved by the fact that Dot had stepped way beyond her customary prim boundaries to offer him sympathy. 'Now all we have to do is to get you through this surgery, eh?'

She waved him away. 'A little bit of new plumbing, that's all I need. I'll soon be up and about, don't you worry.'

But he did worry for Dot as he drove home to Askby, only to be diverted back to Ravenscar within sight of his house. Paul Miller called him on the car phone to go to the aid of a solitary walker he'd found on the Scar. Night was drawing in and the woman had fallen in an inaccessible spot. Philip promised Paul that he would drive straight up and meet him there.

'What was she doing out here by herself?' Philip peered down a deep crevasse in the limestone pavement above Black Gill. Some ten metres down he could make out a huddled shape.

Paul was already fixing up climbing gear to lower himself down the narrow fissure. 'Search me. She lost consciousness soon after I got here. So I knew my best plan was to fetch my ropes from the Hall and give you a ring at the same time.' He was strapped into a harness, testing the rocky ledge for a safe anchor-point. 'Sorry about this, I know you could do without it.'

'How long ago did you find her?'

'About thirty minutes.' He hooked one end of a rope into a swiftly hammered piton. 'Listen, I'll get down there and fix her up with this second harness, OK? See this other rope? Chuck it down when I yell for it. I'm going to stick it through here, see?' Rapidly he fixed another pin into the rock and threaded the second rope through. 'Hang on to this end. Then wait until I shout again and throw it down to me. I'll pull in the slack until I take her weight. This works as a sort of pulley, see? I can hoist her up so you can get to work on her.'

Philip nodded. He thought through the routine and worked on his own role while Paul began the difficult descent. As soon as they got the woman up to ground level, Philip would apply emergency first aid. One problem was having to move the victim before he could examine her, but there was no option. Only a skilled climber like Paul could get anywhere near. 'Did you send for an ambulance?' He crouched and peered down the black crack in the rock; two or three metres wide at the top, but rapidly narrowing.

'It's on its way,' Paul called back. Loose stones peppered down the crevasse, just wide of the unconscious body. 'Hang on, I'm nearly there.' He abseiled into the gap, quick and agile.

'How does she seem?'

'Only just breathing.' He straddled the two rock faces and worked to slide the inert woman's arms into the harness. 'There's a lot of blood, mostly from her leg, I reckon.'

'Let's get her up as quickly as we can.' Philip threw down the hooked end of the second rope. Severe external bleeding could account for loss of consciousness. 'Don't try to tourniquet the wound,' he warned. 'And move the leg as little as possible. Ready? OK, start using your weight!'

Paul steadied himself on the widest foothold he could find. As he heaved on the rope, the woman was winched clear of the ledge where she'd landed. Her body swung upright inside

the harness and began its ascent. It was Paul's turn to avoid
the falling stones down below as she shunted gently against
the rock face, twirling slowly.

'Still OK?' Philip called anxiously. He could see the body
emerging from the deep gloom of the crevasse. It would take
all Paul's strength and weight to pull her clear.

'Yeah, good!' His body took the strain from below as the
pulley system which he'd mocked up worked smoothly.

'Only a couple of metres more!' Philip grabbed the rope and
added his weight. They'd almost made it. He heard Paul swear
as another shower of stones fell on him. 'That's it, I've got
her!'

He seized the harness and dragged the victim clear of the
sheer drop. She hung limp, her face hanging forward; a
woman in her early twenties, well equipped for trekking over
the moor in a good cagoul and tracksuit bottoms. Her short
brown hair was soaked dark red from a head wound but the
main bleeding came from the right leg, as Paul had said.
Philip unhooked the harness and laid her flat on her back.

'I'm coming up!' Paul called. 'I'll only be a couple of
minutes.'

Philip tore one leg of the tracksuit trousers from the ankle
upwards and exposed a deep flesh wound and a messy
fractured tibia. Quickly he rested the leg on a higher ledge of
rock and began to apply pressure to the wound with the pad
of rolled-up trouser material. 'As soon as you get up here, I've
got a job for you!'

'What is it?' Breathless, his face scuffed and scratched, Paul
hauled himself out of the crevasse. He unhooked his rope and
scrambled to join Philip.

'Here, keep pressing until the bleeding stops. Then see if you
can fix the pad in place with bandage from my bag.'

Paul did as he was told.

Meanwhile, Philip tilted the woman's chin back and eased

his forefinger into her mouth. to chech her airway was clear There was no blockage, but he'd checked the pulse in the carotid artery and knew that they were only just in time. The pulse was weak and the breathing so shallow that he could scarcely detect it.

'How are you doing?' he asked Paul.

'Bleeding's stopped.' Expertly he wound the bandage around the leg.

'OK, fetch that blanket. Let's keep her warm.' Gently they settled the woman onto her left side. At least now if she vomited, she wouldn't choke. Philip felt her pulse again. Though still weak, it remained steady. It looked as though they'd managed to pull her back from the brink.

'Good work.' Philip glanced at Paul. 'You saved her life.'

Now, though, they could only wait, keep her sheltered from the wind, and hope that the paramedics would arrive before dark. Temperatures fell below zero quickly at this time of year, and they didn't want to add exposure to the list of the woman's problems. While Paul tucked the blanket around her, Philip checked the head wound; extensive but superficial, he found. 'Do you know who she is?' he asked Paul.

'Haven't a clue. I was just out this way when I happened to hear her shout.'

'Good job you did. I wondered whether she was one of yours from the Hall.'

Paul unclicked his harness. Then he wiped some of the dirt and blood from his face. 'We're out of business at the Hall,' he said with a shrug.

Philip looked up. 'Since when?'

'Since today. We heard the bank won't extend the loan and we've no money coming in. Besides, Ellie's too crook to go on.'

'So you'll have to close down?'

'Yep. I rang and cancelled all the bookings for the summer.'

Philip thought Paul was taking it calmly. 'I guess you thought it might come to this?'

'It's been on the cards since Marianne did her runner. Then there was Jim. Now Ellie. In a way, the news from the bank lets us off the hook. Now we've no choice; we have to close the doors for good.'

Like the others, Philip had seen the outdoor pursuits centre as ill-fated from the start. As the woman began to stir, he rearranged the blanket. 'I'm sorry it didn't work out.'

Paul shrugged again. 'How long did they think we'd last round here? Well, they were right, we didn't even make it past Easter.' He waved as the ambulance Land Rover appeared, blue light flashing, using a tractor track to cross the rough moorland.

For a while it was all action again; stretchers and splints, tubes and monitors. Philip and Paul handed on the details, a paramedic found a driving licence tucked away in the woman's jacket pocket. She lived in Surrey, he said. There was no evidence of why she'd been walking alone on Ravenscar.

'She's probably on holiday up here. We'll phone round for relatives,' the ambulance driver said as they stretchered her into the Land Rover. 'Can you hang on here for the police and tell them we've taken her to Wingate? Thanks. They'll want a few details from you.'

'OK, fine. I'll ring the hospital when I get back home. Will she be in IC?'

The other man nodded. 'They'll hook her up for blood and body fluids. And they'll want to do an ECG. But it looks like you did a pretty good job on her.'

Doors slammed on the patient; a still anonymous woman of twenty-something whose life they had saved. Then the ambulance drove off along the track. It paused beside an approaching police car, then moved on.

'Let's make this quick,' Philip muttered. He was cold, tired and hungry.

Paul hung back. 'There's something about me and policemen right now,' he complained. 'We don't hit it off.'

'It's OK, I know Mike Jackson.' Philip sympathised with what Paul must have been going through lately. 'Let me do the talking.' Whatever the gossip, Paul had proved himself to be the best of co-rescuers; decisive, quick and brave. Now Philip wanted to ease him through this discussion with the police.

'What about the other one? Do you know him?'

Two non-uniformed men were coming towards them, followed by a young constable. Beside Mike Jackson's no-nonsense figure there was a shorter, darker man, stocky and expressionless. Philip shook his head.

'I do,' Paul warned. 'He's the one who's got it in for Ellie.'

It had been a brief, matter-of-fact interview about the young woman's fall. Paul relayed the facts; he'd heard the cry for help at five-thirty and made the phone calls to Philip and the hospital at ten to six.

'Was there anyone else around at the time?' Mike Jackson had asked the questions.

'No.'

'No, well I expect anyone with any sense would steer clear of Ravenscar on a day like this.' As darkness fell, the rain had begun to lash down. 'So what brought you out this way?'

Paul's answer was vague, he'd wanted to clear his head after receiving some bad news.

Philip had noted a marked hostility in the way the police treated Paul; no congratulations for him, but a sniff of suspicion, significant pauses, awkward questions. Paul had been right to anticipate a rough ride, and was obviously relieved when Mike Jackson finally allowed him to go home, while the policemen and Philip drove to the pub.

'What was that all about?' he asked them, once they were ensconced by the fire at the Falcon. Mike had bought the drinks and his superintendent, Martin Ford, had become almost jovial, cracking jokes and pulling hard at his pint of bitter. 'Anyone would think Paul Miller had shoved the woman down the crevasse instead of hauling her out.'

Mike had the grace to look embarrassed. 'Let's just call it tactics.'

'For what reason?' Philip was genuinely angry with them.

But Ford imposed an end to the discussion with one of his hard, unemotional looks. If Mike Jackson came across as the genial local bobby, his superintendent was the rough, tough foil. He looked as if he could handle himself, Philip thought. He wore a layer of solid muscle like armour plating, his shoulders were rugby-player wide and then there was the mask-like face. 'My shout.' He went off to order more drinks, informing Mike that he was driving.

'I take it you have Paul Miller marked down as an all-round good guy?' Mike asked.

'I was impressed by what he did up there today.'

'Would you still think that if I told you there was something going on between him and Mrs Blackwood?' He leaned forward, as if in confidence. 'Would that surprise you?'

Philip flashed back to the glimpse he'd had of them at the funeral. 'Nothing surprises me any more,' he said wearily. 'Not when it comes to sexual entanglements. But that still doesn't mean he deserved to be treated like dirt.' He grew aware of long, hard looks from Brian Lawson. The police presence drew the attention of other customers too. There was a buzz around the place, a build-up to another crisis.

Mike kept one eye on his boss at the bar. 'A bit of pressure does wonders. Turn it up, step back, wait. Move in and turn it up a little bit more. Before long, our killer is falling over himself to confess.'

'Or herself?' Philip noted that Mike pointedly failed to take him up on this. 'Well, you've certainly succeeded in making Ellie Blackwood hysterical, if that's what you intended.'

'Whereas Paul Miller has nerves of steel.' Mike turned down the corners of his mouth. As Martin Ford came back, glasses in hand, he swiftly changed the subject. He leaned back on his stool and smiled at Philip. 'And how's the lovely Juliet? Still giving the best dinner parties in Hawkshead?'

Philip survived the gaffe but it threw him. His mind was off the cruel waiting game being played by the police, and on his own troubles once more, when the emergency tone sounded on his mobile phone. He made his excuses and went out into the entrance passage to answer it. Half-eight on a cold, wet Friday night. Someone somewhere needed him.

'Hello, Philip Maskell here.'

The line buzzed and whined. 'It's Paul Miller.'

'Yes, Paul. What is it?'

'Come to the Hall, quick!'

He recognised the dazed, shocked tone and promised to be there in ten minutes. He drove hard, taking the winding road too fast, grateful that there was nobody equally reckless heading towards him.

He arrived at lonely Ravenscar in a crunch of stones and gravel, slammed the car door and ran for the house.

'Paul?' The front door swung open. Rain blew into the hallway. There were no lights on downstairs.

Paul ran to the top of the stairs and yelled down. 'Jesus, be quick!'

Philip took the stairs two at a time as his eyes grew used to the dark. 'Is it Ellie?'

'In her room. Do something, Philip!' Paul grabbed on to a door jamb for support.

216

'Where's the light?'

'No, leave it!' He wrenched his arm from the switch. 'She's on the bed.'

Philip felt his way past a chest of drawers. A curtain brushed against him. The window was open to the wind and rain. 'It's freezing,' he muttered, sliding the window closed with a grinding, dull thud. His face was rain-spattered as he turned back into the room.

And then he saw Ellie. She lay in a black stain of blood that seeped across the bed sheet and dripped to the floor. The walls were smeared with what must also be blood, as if she'd struggled to pull herself upright. But now she lay still, head hanging over the side, arms outstretched. The wrists were slashed, the veins gaped raw. Her slight body was fully clothed in jeans and T-shirt. These too were stained with blood. On the cabinet nearby lay two open bottles of pills, both tipped over.

'Do something,' Paul begged again.

Quietly Philip drew a pencil-torch from his pocket, bent forward and shone the light into Ellie's wide-open eyes. He listened and watched for breath. Nothing. 'She's dead,' he murmured. 'Dead for some time. I'm sorry, Paul, there's nothing we can do.'

# CHAPTER TWENTY-ONE

Laura arrived at Ravenscar soon after Mike Jackson and Martin Ford. Philip had called her away from an evening at Hawkshead Hall with the news that Ellie Blackwood had committed suicide. The place was crawling with police, surrounded by their white vehicles and cordoned off to prevent the press from encroaching on the work of the forensic team.

'I'm her GP,' she told the sergeant in charge of activity in the grounds.

'There's not much you can do for her now.' He joked to alleviate the horror, keeping Laura talking at the door while a colleague went to find out whether she could be admitted.

'How did she do it?' The cold cut through her thin blouse. She'd driven up without a coat in a state of disbelief. Philip had needed to repeat the news three times on the phone.

'Wrists and pills.'

'How long since it happened?'

'Three or four hours. Mind you, the room was freezing cold, so the body temperature would drop pretty quickly. She did it with the window wide open.'

'Did she leave a note?' Laura struggled to come to terms with each detail. When she'd last seen Ellie on Thursday, she hadn't guessed the depths of her despair. Now she felt that she ought to have done.

'They haven't turned one up so far.' The stolid sergeant made the most of his inside information. He rolled the answers off his tongue, delivered them in a slow, deep voice. 'Maybe she wasn't the note-writing sort.'

Not the note-writing sort. Not the crying sort. Not the sort to pour out her troubles and ask for help. Not the kind of wife who ditched a husband who'd cheated on her. In the end, not a woman who could endure the pressure.

Laura gazed across the hall and up the stairs at the figure of Paul Miller sitting hunched on the top step.

The second policeman came back and nodded that it was OK for her to go up, then went off on other business. She climbed the stairs alone and stopped beside Paul, who stared up at her without speaking. Then she continued on along the landing to a room full of bright lights, blue uniforms, men and women in white surgical overalls.

Philip stood just inside the door. 'I'm sorry to drag you up here, Laura. I thought you'd want to know.'

She nodded. The corpse lay on the bed shrouded by official green covers. Forensic scientists picked over the clues at the bedside like archaeologists piecing together the past. A Stanley knife had been retrieved, labelled and slipped inside a clear plastic envelope. The two empty bottles were taken away for analysis.

'Why?' Laura asked the ultimate, useless question.

'Maybe it was the only way out.'

'But so painful.' She stared at the streaks of blood on the wall where fingers had reached out, for help, perhaps.

Then a note was found after all, by the uniformed go-between who'd let Laura into the house. He came hurrying with it to show his superintendent who stood overseeing the methodical examination of the bed with his blank, expression-less stare. The young policeman gave him an envelope addressed to Paul Miller.

Ford tore it open. 'Confession time,' he said curtly. He raised his eyebrows with a deep sigh. 'Is this her handwriting?' He flicked the note towards Laura.

She read 'Dear Paul', then 'forgive me' in the first line of the short letter. It stated that she had killed Jim and couldn't live with the consequences. It was better to end things instead. No one else had been involved. Ellie had signed it with all her love.

'Well?' Ford grew impatient.

Trembling, Laura handed back the note. 'Yes.'

'It looks like we got a result for the murder,' Ford told Mike Jackson, thrusting the letter into yet another plastic envelope.

'Paul hasn't seen it yet,' Laura reminded them. The envelope had been sealed, ready to be handed over to forensics.

'All in good time.'

'Hang on, you don't think Paul had anything to do with this?' Philip stepped aside as a stretcher was unrolled to carry the corpse away. 'He was out saving a life at the time, remember. I was there with him.'

'True enough.' Ford handed the letter to Mike Jackson. 'Better give him a quick shufty.'

Things were happening with indecent haste, Laura felt, and with a total lack of humanity that only scientists and policemen were capable of. When a patient died, a doctor usually had knowledge of the person and the family; there was never quite this empty efficiency. Here it was body-bags and evidence, measuring this and that, recording details, taking photographs.

'Are you OK?' Philip turned to her.

She exhaled sharply, then shook her head. 'What a mess.'

'At least it would have been quick. It was paracetamol in the bottles, it would have knocked her out nearly straight away.'

'I should have stopped her.' She could have provided twenty-four-hour care, expert counselling. 'I couldn't get her to confide in me, Philip.' There had always been a barrier – something important which Ellie had refused to divulge.

Philip warned against bearing the brunt of responsibility. 'You were only her doctor, remember.'

'No, I was her friend as well.' But not a good enough one. 'She came to me for help and I couldn't give it. I couldn't work out what it was that she really wanted from me. In the end, I let her down.'

Laura's reaction came in slow-motion, one wave after another. She and Philip stayed to talk to Paul after the police had finally left. It was the suddenness of events that distressed him most.

'I was just talking to her. She never let on that it was this bad.' He strode across the hall into the small office and came back out. 'What did I miss?'

'You can't predict something like this. If someone is serious about suicide, they don't drop hints.'

'She must have had it all planned out; the knife, the painkillers . . . and she waited until I was out of the house. The last thing she said to me was not to worry any more. Everything was going to be OK.' He looked startled, as if he could still actually hear Ellie's voice. 'It's not though, is it? She's not here!'

He began to cry, with sobs that were wrenched from deep in his throat. 'How will I go on without her? We were meant to get through this together, we agreed.'

Laura let him weep. 'Even you couldn't be expected to know what she was going through. And imagine what she would have had to go through once the police had arrested her. Prison, a trial, being plastered over the newspapers.'

He raised his head. 'Why couldn't she hang on? It was only

221

Marianne's word against hers.' He looked from Laura to Philip, demanding a reason why Ellie had taken this irreversible step beyond his reach, leaving him behind.

'She said she did it in the note, Paul. You have to accept it,' Philip stated.

But he pulled away from them. 'She's a bloody liar!'

Philip warned Laura not to intervene as Paul knocked things from the desk with a sweep of his forearm. A computer keyboard fell and clattered to the floor, papers drifted down. Paul turned on them, tears still streaming.

'She is, she's a liar! Jesus, Ellie, why did you have to do it?' He yelled at the top of his voice, and left them standing as he rushed across the cold, dark hall out into the windy night. 'Tell the truth, for Christ's sake! Tell them!'

'She can't.' Laura and Philip had to restrain him. 'Come inside.'

In the yard he seemed suddenly to come to his senses and half-collapsed against Laura. Philip helped to steady him, then they led him back into the house.

They talked and looked after him until eventually they felt they could trust him to stay calm. Laura wanted him to leave the Hall and go to stay with friends for at least these first few nights, but Paul resisted. He had a grip now, he said. He would be OK.

'It might be better not to be by yourself at first.'

'No, I want to stay here. I have to get my head around this. Everything's different now. I have to think.'

'But you'll ring us if you need someone?' Philip judged that he could safely be left. His grief was natural, not excessive.

Paul nodded. 'I want to start shutting things down as soon as I can. I'm finished here.'

Philip understood. 'But watch out, the shock could hit you again at any time. If it does, get in touch.'

In the end, they left him and got into their separate cars.

Laura followed Philip out of the yard. For a few moments she turned to look at the outline of the Hall; at its tall chimneys and heavy roofs, its bleak situation on the moortop. There was a light on in the room where Ellie's body had lain, but the rest of the house was already in darkness. She was suddenly unreasonably angry with the place; with its blank walls and narrow windows that gave nothing away. When would Ravenscar give up its secret? Or had Ellie finally taken it with her?

'Such a shock, poor you.' Maisie ministered to Laura in the lounge at Hawkshead Hall.

'You're sure you're OK?' Matthew studied her pale face.

She'd driven here from Ravenscar to explain what had happened, glad not to be alone with her thoughts at Abbey Grange.

'You can see she's not,' Maisie insisted. 'That's the trouble with your job, Laura; you come across appalling situations. It can't be good for your state of mind.' She brought a glass of whisky, easily persuaded her to stay the night. 'You shouldn't be alone,' she insisted.

Laura was grateful. Then she remembered Gerald. 'I should ring him and tell him what's happened.'

'Let Philip do that.'

'Just think!' Maisie figured out the sequence of events on the day Jim Blackwood died. 'It takes a strong nerve to plan that. First she has to give him the overdose without him realising. She has to time it exactly, so that he can leave the house before he suspects there's anything wrong with him. But the tablets have to take effect within minutes after that. Would he realise what was happening?'

Laura nodded. 'He'd feel confused, disorientated. He'd collapse pretty quickly after that; but, yes, he'd know.'

'And she coolly lets him walk out to his death,' Maisie

continued. 'If it hadn't happened by the tarn when it did, it would have been while he was rock-climbing with the students. She waited in the house until one of them brought her news that there'd been an accident. Then she rushed out and played the innocent, so that even Gerald felt sorry for her and rushed through the death certificate.'

'She very nearly got away with it too.' Matthew was also caught up in reconstructing the crime. 'No wonder she went to pieces over the exhumation.'

'Yes, that wasn't part of the original plan.' Maisie pursued her train of thought, though Laura sat silent, staring at her glass. 'Of course, then she knew they'd soon be on to her. Was that when you began to suspect her, Laura?'

Slowly she shook her head. 'I never suspected Ellie, not really.'

Maisie raised her eyebrows. 'That must have more to do with your own generous nature than with her sincerity.'

'But all the time I felt there was something she wasn't telling me.'

'And now we know what.' Matthew took away Laura's empty glass.

'What amazes me is how she could stay quiet.' Maisie rose from her chair. 'Let me go up and fix your bed right now. Take a bath, and sleep in the morning as late as you like. And Matthew, see that she gets straight to bed.' She kissed Laura on the cheek and smiled kindly. 'No long discussions about the meaning of life, OK?'

As soon as she'd left the room, Matthew sat by Laura on the sofa. 'I'm glad you're staying. Don't worry, you'll soon feel better.' He reached to put an arm around her.

'I'm OK, really.' In fact, Matthew's gentleness put her more on edge, she realised.

'Lean this way; that's better.' He began to stroke her hair.

'You did all you could and if anyone's to blame in all this, it must be Gerald for failing to spot foul play.'

She sighed and sat up straight. 'No one's to blame.'

'Not to blame, exactly. Of course not.' He tried to smooth it over. 'I just don't want you to take it on. I know that's what you're likely to do.'

'Meaning what?'

'Only that you do tend to take on other people's problems, you know.'

'It must be the nature of the job,' she said coolly. 'Anyway, I never heard you complain about this so-called tendency before.'

'Laura, don't take things the wrong way.' He stood up and walked round the back of the sofa. 'In fact, let's not talk any more.'

'Now or ever?' With each remark she escalated the argument, knowing that the niggles and misunderstandings masked deeper issues. Like Luke, she thought. Like the fact that she might be falling out of love with Matthew.

'Don't be ridiculous.' It was his turn to flare up. 'What are we talking about here?'

Laura closed her eyes and made a decision to plunge ahead. 'About us.'

'I thought we were talking about your being over-sensitive after a hard day at work. I didn't realise we were discussing our whole future.'

'Matthew.' She stood up to face him. 'We do have to talk.' He was so familiar to her; the clean, clear lines of his face, the deep, quiet voice. She hated to hurt him.

He frowned and shook his head. 'Listen, Laura, I know you're fed up with waiting for me to sort things out with Abigail. But it is a slow process, believe me. And just this last week or so I've felt we've made progress at the therapy sessions. Tim's coming out of his shell, and Sophie's learning

225

not to grab all the attention. They've begun to say how they feel about the divorce and even Abigail is having to listen for once.'

Laura sighed. 'It's not that.'

'It's not still that night when Abigail came and broke up our evening, is it?' Exasperation crept back into his voice. 'How many times do I have to tell you; she messed things up. That's her. Full stop. Stop imagining there was any more to it than that.'

'That's not the problem either.' She must tell him the truth, slowly and deliberately. 'I've been seeing Luke Altham.'

'Yes.' He was puzzled. 'I know. He was in on the Ellie Blackwood thing.'

'More than that. He and I have been out together. I went to his place last weekend.' She waited, watched. Nothing was ever how you imagined it. At first he didn't seem to understand, then gradually it dawned. He gave her a sharp look of betrayal, then the shutters came down.

'Are you going to see him again?'

Always questions from Matthew, never declarations. She realised the pressure of his why, when, how? 'Don't ask me.' There were tears in her eyes.

'OK, OK, I'm sorry.' His voice softened. He came towards her and took her by the arm.

Laura pulled away. 'I need space.'

'And time?'

'Yes.' She was relieved that he seemed to be accepting part of the new situation.

'Take it. Take time, Laura. But don't cut me out yet. That's all I ask.'

She knew she owed him this much, so she nodded. Matthew was part of her life in Hawkshead. 'I only wanted you to know about Luke and to give me space.' A shift, not a break, then.

'Promise me, Laura.'

She heard and saw his self-control begin to break down. It hurt her more than any sarcasm or angry retaliation. 'Don't, Matthew. I haven't made any decision yet. I don't know how I feel any more; everything's in turmoil. But I will try not to hurt you.'

# CHAPTER TWENTY-TWO

'Who said April was the cruellest month?' Philip took Laura to one side before their Monday morning meeting.

'T.S. Eliot. Why?'

'He was right.'

Gerald passed them in the waiting area without glancing up.

'Did you tell him about Ellie?'

'On Saturday. He didn't say much, but it was the look on his face. Janet says she's worried about him. On top of everything, he and Aimee have had a massive blow-up. Aimee's threatening to leave home because of it.'

'What about her exams?'

Philip shrugged.

Just then, Gerald reappeared at the door of his room. 'Do we have a meeting to run, or is it more interesting getting into a huddle to discuss my private affairs?'

They went to join him with Joy and Sheila for a quick resumé of Philip's weekend on duty.

'What's this?' Gerald pointed to a note about a home visit. 'Since when does straightforward achalasia require an emergency call-out?'

'Walter Simons is a heart patient. In him, a developing cough could be significant. He needed reassurance.'

'Hmm. What's this? A middle ear infection, scleral haemorrhage, a rash and another middle ear. Anything on Sarah Jennings at Low Royds?'

Laura listened to the ins and outs, then added her own question. 'What about Paul Miller, Philip? Did he get in touch over the weekend?'

Gerald stiffened. Joy and Sheila looked uncomfortable. Ellie's suicide had brought the usual ghouls and pressmen up to Hawkshead and the village was already heartily sick of them. There was a general desire to bury the incident and let them get on with the business of living.

'Not with me,' Philip said quietly. 'Not that I really expected him to.'

'And since Laura brought it up, you'd better run through the official version of Friday night for our benefit,' Gerald said bluntly.

'It's all logged in the diary.'

'I'm grateful for your tact, Philip, but there's no need to spare my blushes.' Gerald turned to the nurse and receptionist. 'Ellie Blackwood took her own life between five-thirty and seven on Friday evening. She slashed her wrists and bled to death, overcome by guilt for having killed her husband. No wonder she didn't sue me for negligence. There was no need for Philip to inform the police since they were already there, so there was no danger of him repeating my blunder. Naturally there'll be an autopsy, an inquest, the full works.' He spoke drily, in clipped phrases, defying comment. 'Any questions? Right, we can move on. Has the A and E unit sent those X-ray results for Kate Norris?'

'The woman we rescued from the top of Black Gill? Yes, and she's out of intensive care, off all drips and waiting for surgery on the leg,' Philip told them. 'I rang last night.'

Gerald made a note. 'Is that it?' He glanced at his watch.

'Then I suggest we put the events of the weekend behind us and get on with our day's work.'

Relieved that they were back to normal, with Gerald's peremptory manner intact, Philip plunged into the day. He opened and drained an abscess, diagnosed a nut allergy, and treated first-degree burns.

'What can you give me for this pain in my leg?' Harry Braithwaite demanded, planting his sturdy boot in front of Philip. 'It's not half giving me some gyp.'

He examined the leg, gnarled and sturdy as an oak. There was definite swelling around the ankle.

'Aye, roundabout there.'

Philip thought hard. 'Could be deep vein thrombosis, Harry. We'd better get you checked out.'

'Oh heck,' came the reply. 'I don't have to trek over to hospital, do I?'

Then there was a last-minute appointment for Alison Lawson and baby Emma with a case of cradle-cap, before a trip out to Town Head to see Dot, and back to the centre in time for a coffee with Gerald. Their breaks didn't always coincide, but today Philip had made a special effort to plan it this way. As it happened, he walked straight into another of Gerald's tussles with bureaucracy.

'What do you mean, you won't pay our immunisation fees? Don't be bloody silly. We sent you the documents. I've checked. Yes, of course we got them in on time.'

Sheila shook her head as Philip paused at her desk. Behind her, Gerald bellowed down the phone. Philip went to make the coffee. 'Is Laura around?' he whispered to Sheila, loath to interrupt.

'No, she's out at Waite. How's Dot?'

'Fine. Can't wait to get her op over and done with now.' He poured and stirred. The immunisation fee would only come through to the practice if they met their target and completed the documentation.

'What do you take us for? Of course we kept a copy. Hold on, here it is.' As he checked it over, Gerald stopped abruptly. 'I see. Yes, got that. My signature? Will do.'

He dropped the phone with a disgusted snort. 'Red tape, signatures. Where's Laura? Isn't she supposed to oversee that side?'

'Senior partner must sign.' Philip handed him his coffee while Sheila vanished tactfully into Joy's room. 'You know that as well as I do, so leave Laura out of it.'

'And you let her fight her own battles,' Gerald countered. He sat down with a weary sigh. 'That's the problem these days.'

'What is?' Philip could easily ride Gerald's waves of irritation, but he worried about these lapses into tired non-sequitur.

'Everything's an uphill battle. Not just the money business, though that's bad enough.'

'Oh dear, I hope this isn't going to be another of your lamentations.' He would deal with it in his usual way; acknowledging Gerald's point but keeping things light.

'I'm serious, Philip.' The mannerisms dropped away and there was a sense of purpose in his tone. 'What we have here is a good, solid practice. Good name, strong on primary care, getting better at managing the dratted new system; agreed?'

Philip nodded. 'Largely due in the first instance to your personal touch and sense of continuity, as I've said before.'

'It's a reputation we'd be sorry to lose. We want people to look up to us, not to be the subject of bar-room tittle-tattle.'

'If you mean the Blackwood business . . .'

'*And* the psychogeriatric business. *And* the immunisation fees.' He recalled recent minor blunders.

'No one needs to know about that, Gerald.'

'*I* know. *You* know. Laura, Sheila and Joy know.'

'But think of your value to the practice over and above these one or two hitches.'

'You call missing a murder a hitch?' He waited while Philip failed to find a way past this one. 'The implications are vast. Bad publicity, erosion of confidence in the practice as a whole.'

'Let us worry about that when it happens,' Philip advised. 'We all know that what you bring far outweighs the recent problem. You're exaggerating its importance, as usual.'

Gerald bit his bottom lip. 'I'm over sixty, Philip. I trained in the mid 1950s. That's prehistoric in terms of medical advances.' As he talked on, he seemed to grow calmer, more reflective. 'You remember that scene in *Alice Through the Looking Glass* where the Red Queen describes what it's like to live in a world that constantly runs on ahead of you? She says you must do all the running you can, just to stay in one place. Well, that's what it's been like for me these last few years. I'm tired, out of puff, and the world won't stop and wait for me to catch my breath.'

'We all feel that way sometimes.'

'But for me it's true.' Gerald stood and tipped his coffee dregs down the sink. 'It's taken me long enough to accept it, but when my daughter confronts me with it, even I, thick-skinned and self-opinionated as I am, have to accept what she's telling me, poor girl. And no, Philip, this isn't a temporary loss of confidence. This is reality.'

Philip protested. They had years of working together behind them. Gerald was a tradition in Hawkshead, a fixture, a figurehead.

'Time to go,' Gerald said quietly. He'd spent the weekend convincing himself.

'Think about it.'

'I already have. I've discussed it with Janet, and she agrees.'

232

He lifted his head. 'Mind you, she probably sees Mediterranean cruises and Scottish golfing holidays beckoning.'

Philip refused to let him get away with being flippant. 'It's a big decision, Gerald. Take more time to think it through. You know how much we'd miss you here.'

For a moment, Gerald stood with head bowed. 'Thanks for that, Philip.' Then he pulled himself up and went to the door. 'But no man's indispensable, you know.'

The seasons were turning. Evenings had grown longer since the clocks had moved forward into summer time. Temperatures lagged behind, however. Philip had gone out into his patch of back garden with its rough grass and tall lap-fence to see the river and listen to the birds. After a day like today his spirits needed something to lift them.

The sky was clear, there would be an overnight frost. He tried the gate at the bottom of the garden, hoping for a direct route to the water's edge. This was the first time since moving into the house that he'd come out this way.

Gerald had told Laura the news immediately after evening surgery. He had been less open with her, probably due to the deep-seated chauvinism that prevented him from admitting his vulnerability to a woman.

Laura took it quietly. 'Big decisions need plenty of thought. We won't accept your resignation straight off, will we, Philip?' She persuaded Gerald they should wait a month before they made any moves whatsoever.

He'd grumbled about the delay, but Philip could see he was gratified. He could read him like a book, the old phoney. But the underlying decision to leave the practice was genuine enough.

Where did it leave them? Philip picked his way down to the river bank where an area of flat rock overlooked the mill race. He stared down at the powerful current, the whorls of clear green water and white foam. They brought to mind Gerald's image about running with all your might just to stay in one place.

'Philip?'

The voice startled him; not by its unexpectedness but by its soft familiarity. Juliet must have followed him through the open gate and found him standing at the very edge of the rocks.

'Janet rang me about Gerald. I knew you'd be upset.'

'I think it's a lousy way for him to end, feeling that he can't keep up.'

'It must be so common. But I agree. I think it's very sad.' She stood quietly beside him, watching the water.

It was like Juliet to seek him out when he was at his lowest ebb. 'This Ravenscar tragedy is only the final straw, you know. I've known that it's been coming for some time.' He described Gerald's struggles over funding, capitation, retraining, spreadsheets, costs and profits. 'It's foreign territory for all of us, but Gerald hates change for change's sake. And Hawkshead is a brilliant example of the old-style practice; something really to be proud of.'

'And that's what people will remember him for,' Juliet reminded him. 'As a rock-solid, knowledgeable doctor who was good at his job. They appreciate that in this dale.'

Philip smiled at her. 'So he needn't bother about going down in their estimation because of the Blackwoods?'

'They didn't take to the Blackwoods, you know. From what they've heard since, their first impressions have turned out to be accurate. Wife-swapping, poisoning, all kinds of skullduggery. Gerald can only come out of it as their innocent victim. Who would have suspected that Ellie Blackwood was capable of doing what they say she did?'

For a moment his attention was diverted. 'Don't you believe it's true?'

234

'I can't say. I didn't know her.'

'So Gerald comes out smelling of roses?' He laughed. 'He'll like that. Not that it will change his mind.'

Juliet poked the toe of her shoe into a small indentation in the rock. 'Does that mean you'll be senior partner?'

'I suppose so.'

'Congratulations.'

'It feels pretty hollow just now.' He began to walk upstream towards the old mill building. 'All of it. Since we split up, I'm struggling to make sense of anything at all.'

Instead of trying to change the subject, she followed him quietly.

'I know you don't want to hear this,' he continued, 'but I never knew it was possible to be so miserable. I have to remind myself to eat to keep body and soul together. I know I deserve it all, and worse. But it is strange; like living at a slight remove from myself all the time, watching myself shave, telling myself to answer the phone when it rings, the simplest things.'

'How about work?' She watched him, buttoned up in her dark green jacket, hands in pockets. Daylight was fading, and shadows from overhanging trees threw her face into darkness.

'That's OK, luckily. I can use it as an escape.' He turned again, waited for her to join him. 'Are you sure it has to be like this?'

'Between us? For now, yes.' It was her turn to walk ahead. On the still pool above the race, two ducks swam in quiet circles.

'But you came to see me. You could have stayed away.'

'I've been thinking about you a lot lately.' Juliet's soft, slow voice allowed for long, thoughtful pauses. 'No, that sounds odd. I've always thought about you, trying to work things out, to put my finger on one good reason.' She drew her hands from her pockets and spread them, palms upwards.

'Yes, I know, it's futile. And painful. There was a time when I couldn't bear it, when I was so angry I literally could have killed you. Never mind the consequences, there were certain moments when I could have done it.'

They both stopped to draw the parallel with Ellie Blackwood.

'I couldn't help imagining you two in bed together.'

'Juliet, don't.'

'It was a kind of obsession. Sexual infidelity – it sounds so formal. It's what lies behind the words that I couldn't get out of my head. Two bodies making love; one of them you, the other not me.'

He couldn't listen any more. He'd hardly thought of Mary these last few months.

'Well, I'm over that now,' Juliet told him. 'It has taken me some time, but I've got it under control. I can even be quite dispassionate about it.'

He wasn't sure where this was leading. As it grew dark he waited to show her the way across a ditch, heading for the path where it would be safer to walk.

'But I'm left feeling empty. At least when I was angry, I knew what it was.'

They came along the path, back towards the small development of restored mill cottages where Philip lived. He invited her in for a drink, and she accepted.

But she quickly grew uncomfortable. 'This doesn't feel right.' She glanced round the anonymous room, so carelessly made habitable by him.

'I know. I don't expect I'll stay here long.' He thought she meant the depressing modernity, the contrast with their own Bridge House.

'I meant me being here. I feel like an intruder.'

She was curious, though, to see how he lived. He watched her eyes light on certain objects; the new, cheap music system he'd bought to make the house less silent, a tablecloth he'd brought from home. When he handed her a drink and kept his hand round hers, she didn't object.

'I'm determined not to feel sorry for you,' she warned with tears in her eyes. 'It would make me act for all the wrong reasons. I want to be strong.'

He was overwhelmed by the fact that she was here, that they could communicate honestly once more. He took a deep breath, withdrew his hand and reached for his drink. 'I'm just glad, that's all. I thought you'd cut me out for good.'

# CHAPTER TWENTY-THREE

Aimee's excuses to herself for not going back to school after the Easter break varied from day to day. Yesterday it had been because she needed time to catch up with her sociology notes. Today, as she stared at her reflection in her bedroom mirror, it was that all exams were a waste of time. She believed neither reason.

Only one thing in her life meant anything now, and that was Sean. It was his face in her dreams, his voice she listened to when she needed answers to her questions: how could she go on living at home now that her parents refused to speak to her? And why bother studying when her father's scorn for her achievements burned deep into her psyche?

Sean was everything; her lover, her confessor, her friend. But did he feel the same way? He said he did, but ... Frowning, she flicked her hair behind her shoulder and turned away from the mirror.

Downstairs, a key turned in the lock. Realising that it must be her mother back early from an auction in Merton, Aimee decided to brazen it out. She went out on to the landing. 'Yes, I'm still here,' she said defiantly. 'And no, I'm not at school because sociology lessons are useless and I'm better off revising at home.'

Janet looked up and sighed. Carefully she put down her keys and took off her fawn jacket.

Aimee was taken aback. 'Don't you feel well?' She went downstairs to see.

'I'm all right, Aimee. I just don't feel like arguing with you, that's all.' She'd had what seemed like a lifetime of writing notes about colds, flu and measles, going to parents' evenings, keeping her two children on track for good jobs, status and contentment. 'It's up to you what you do with your life.'

Aimee's resentment flared and she flounced into the kitchen to make coffee. With Nick, she noticed, it had been different. They'd kept up the pressure on him until the bitter end.

'For heaven's sake, Aimee, do you have to slop coffee all over the place?' Janet mopped up after her. 'And don't take it up to your room in that state. Look, it's dripping everywhere!'

'Anyone would think it was a major crime – Daughter Spills Coffee on Stairs!' Aimee turned, bumped into a drawer and spilled the lot.

'Oh!' Janet looked stricken. 'Oh, you stupid girl! Why can't you ever do as you're told?'

To Aimee's surprise, her mother burst into tears.

'Leave it.' Aimee tried to push Janet away from the cupboard where she kept the dishcloth. 'I'll do it.'

'Stupid, stupid girl.'

'Mum, leave it!' Coffee dripped from the work surface on to the floor.

'Haven't you done enough damage already?' Janet wrenched at the door while Aimee tried to stop her. 'Isn't it enough?' she cried, her face twisted with anger, her voice cracked.

'What are you talking about?' Aimee watched her mother stoop for the cloth, tears still falling.

'You and this stupid feud with your father. Day in, day out, week after week. How long is it going to go on?'

For the first time in ages, Aimee realised how tough it must be for her mother. 'Why not ask him?' she asked.

Speechless, Janet stared at Aimee. Then she swung her arm in a wild attempt to slap her face. Aimee dodged out of the way.

'Say you're sorry!' Janet demanded. Her face was drained, her hands trembling.

'What for? Sorry that you just tried to hit me? Sorry that my father's a shit who never even notices I exist?' Aimee felt herself tip out of control.

This time Janet seized Aimee by both arms and shook her violently. 'It's you. You provoke him. Look at you!' She dragged her to the table and sat her down. 'Everything about you – your hair, your make-up, the way you dress – is an affront to your father, and you know it.'

'You've got it wrong. He treats me like a six year old, and makes me look small. What does he want? Another little mouse like you running around after him; yes, sir, no, sir, three bags full, sir!' She was yelling, gasping out the words.

'No.' Janet pulled herself upright. 'He wants your respect. Only, you're so wrapped up in yourself, so sure you're right about everything that you can't see him for what he really is.'

'Don't stick up for him, Mum. It makes me sick. Haven't you seen him poncing around with his glasses perched on the end of his nose, humming and hahing, curing the sick and working miracles!'

'Aimee!'

'It's true. He thinks he's Jesus Christ, but he's a sham. He's years out of date, Mother. And he tries to make up for it by pretending he knows it all. If it wasn't so pathetic, it'd be hilarious!' Instead of laughing, she cried.

'You're cruel,' Janet said, shocked.

'Well, don't expect me to apologise.' Aimee moved towards the door.

'That would be too much to hope for.'

'What have *I* got to say sorry about?' Aimee demanded. 'Apart from being born?'

'For taking away his dream.'

Aimee stopped short. The force of the row had stunned her. Her mother was rarely angry and even now Aimee could scarcely see what it had been about.

'His dream,' Janet repeated. 'Of being good at his job, of being appreciated warts and all. You couldn't bear to leave him that, could you? You had to tell him he was past it and that it was time for him to pack it all in. You forced him to face a huge fact instead of letting him edge gently towards it in his own good time. After all these years in Hawkshead, it was the least he deserved.'

Aimee turned slowly. 'What are you saying?'

'That anyone with a grain of maturity would have forgiven your father his weaknesses. It takes someone like you to be cruel enough to confront him.'

'What's happened? What have I done?'

Janet shook her head. 'He's decided to retire, Aimee. He's admitted defeat.'

Aimee sat on the bus for the long, slow journey out of the dale. They drove at a near-crawl behind a heavy wagon, round endless bends, through small villages, stopping to collect fresh passengers and reaching Merton at about lunchtime.

She'd packed a bag without any real plan. Her mother hadn't tried to stop her; another example of things not working out how Aimee expected. She'd pictured tearful pleas for her to stay, to sort things out with her father. Instead, Aimee had looked back at the tall, blank house and been forced to go through with her grand gesture.

Her one clear idea was to see Sean. She'd rung his house from Merton. His mother had told her he was at college until four, then from five onwards he would be working at the hotel. Aimee decided to meet him there.

She had an afternoon to kill so she wandered through Leeds city centre and sat outside the general hospital amongst beds of daffodils and tulips, alongside pigeons and the homeless. Had she left home for good? If so, where would she stay? She hitched her bag over her shoulder and walked up the hill to the university. It was only four; still an hour to go before Sean was due at work.

There were the wide, white steps opposite the Ridgeway. Students hung around here chatting in small groups, waiting for buses. Aimee merged with the crowd. She sat on a low wall with a good view of Sean's approach, impatient for him to arrive.

She soon grew cold. Traffic roared by. Everyone passing had a goal, it seemed. Their lives were so much more straightforward. Time on her hands gave Aimee the opportunity to wonder whether or not Sean would be pleased to see her. They'd sworn always to help each other but she couldn't see him agreeing that she should chuck it all in at Hawkshead and come to live with him. It wasn't practical for a start; not so long as he stayed at home. And even she thought he shouldn't uproot just for her, not with his 'A'-levels coming up. She pulled her jacket tight around her and sat staring through the cars and lorries at the polished glass hotel entrance.

People came and went. The doors revolved. The blue interior with its sparkling lights invited guests to enter.

Then a figure startled Aimee out of her speculation. It was a youngish woman dressed in a pale green jacket and matching skirt, with trim black shoes, shiny bag and medium length hair. A woman on business or coming away from an interview. It was Marianne Miller.

She crossed the road towards Aimee, walking quickly away

242

from the hotel, hardly noticing the heavy traffic. Aimee got to her feet and ran towards her.

'Marianne, it's me, Aimee Scott.'

The woman brushed her away and made as if to carry on towards the city.

'Sean Armstrong's girlfriend.'

Marianne paused.

'What are you doing here? I thought you'd left your job?'

'I did. Now I want it back.' She glanced at Aimee. 'I have to earn a crust somehow.'

'What did they say? Did you explain about Ravenscar?' Aimee found herself breaking into an undignified trot to keep up.

Marianne's hair swung across her face as she turned away. 'I tried. They didn't want to know.'

'Stop a minute. Come in here for a coffee.' Aimee pointed to a small, dim café close to the pedestrian crossing where they stood. She could see that Marianne was upset by the hotel manager's rejection.

She allowed Aimee to lead the way. 'They said I'd let them down once and they weren't prepared to risk it again.' She sank into a seat in the corner.

'Did you tell them your life was in danger?' Aimee's sense of injustice was quick to ignite.

'No. I told them it was family problems.' Marianne pulled a cigarette from her bag and lit it, inhaling deeply. 'You can't go round telling your employers stuff like that. They wouldn't touch me with a barge-pole if they thought I was mixed up in a murder inquiry.' She paused to stare at Aimee. 'Anyway, that's all cleared up now, from what I hear.'

'Ellie left a note.'

'Saying she'd done it?' The smooth, immaculately made-up face wrinkled into a scornful frown. 'And they believed it?'

Aimee's own expression changed from earnest to puzzled. 'Why shouldn't they?'

Marianne tilted her head back and blew smoke at the ceiling. 'You didn't know Ellie, did you?'

Aimee shook her head. 'But I know she had a motive to kill him.'

'Trust the police to go for what's easiest.' Marianne drank from her newly served cup. 'Nice and neat, complete with suicide note. Now I expect they'll close the case and Paul will walk away scot-free.'

Aimee drew a deep breath. It wasn't so much what Marianne was saying as the way she was saying it. She'd known these people yet she spoke coldly of a friend who'd killed herself and her ex-husband who was caught up in a murder. What Aimee had taken as poise and sincerity during their first meeting now came across as definite callousness.

'Still, life goes on.' She stubbed out her cigarette. 'If that was Ellie's choice, so be it.'

'What do you mean, Ellie's choice?'

'To write the note and do the deed. Pretty messily, from what I hear. After all, no one can interrogate a corpse.'

Aimee felt her flesh begin to crawl. The café was cold and dark, its spartan decor miserable. But it was Marianne who gave her the creeps. 'What did she have to hide, exactly?'

The other woman finished her coffee. 'Poor Ellie, she was tough in some ways, but too soft in others. I couldn't have trained to run all those races to save my life; I don't have the self-discipline. She was good at self-denial and, when she set herself a goal, she could go for it. But she couldn't stand up to outside pressure.'

'Pressure to do what?' Aimee felt the whole story unravel around her.

'Look, she was covering up for him.' Marianne looked pointedly at Aimee. 'For Paul. The police must have known that. All they had to do was to wait for her to crack and tell them the truth.'

'Why would she do that?' It was like the Lady of Shalott in the poem when she looked directly at the river; the web flew wide and everything in her safe world unravelled.

'Because she loved him,' Marianne said simply.

Aimee abandoned her plan to meet up with Sean. Instead, she ran for the station. Her chance meeting with Marianne seemed to Aimee to have cast a new light over things. She must tell someone.

There was the train to catch back to Merton and the bus at rush-hour. The more she thought about it, the more likely Marianne's version seemed. In her newly fledged romantic heart, Aimee could well believe that a woman like Ellie would sacrifice herself for the man she loved. Besides, there was additional proof; the fact that Ellie had been so shocked when Sean first took her the news of Jim's death and the fact that Aimee's own father had believed in her innocence.

She let her thoughts spin on. The road ahead wound on up the narrowing dale, the limestone escarpment of Ravensdale pale on the misty horizon. What if her father had been right about Ellie all along? And Laura had never believed that Ellie was guilty either. In fact, Laura was the person Aimee should turn to now with the new theory. Her heart beat fast as the bus crawled along past the Abbey and St Michael's church-yard into the village square.

Once off the bus, Aimee ran for the health centre. Laura's big, four-wheel drive car was still there, though it was past six o'clock. The main door was open and Philip was on his way out. He stopped when he caught sight of Aimee.

'Hey, what are you doing here?' he stood in her path.

'I have to see Laura,' she pleaded.

'I thought you'd packed your bag and gone for good?' He

struck a balance between teasing and seriousness. 'That's what your mother rang Gerald to tell him.'

'Did they send out a search party?' She peered over his shoulder, shrugging it off.

'No, but they were obviously worried. Your father went home early.'

'I'll go home and grovel as soon as I've seen Laura. Please, Philip. This has got to do with Ellie Blackwood.'

He grabbed her by the arm. 'Listen, Ellie Blackwood is dead. Show some respect, can't you?'

'But I've found something out and I have to tell Laura.' Exasperated, she pulled free, then squeezed past into the waiting area. She saw Laura come out of her room to check what the noise was.

'I'll sort it out,' Laura told Philip, prompt and firm. 'Come in, Aimee.'

Aimee ran towards her before Philip could intervene again. She went into Laura's room and closed the door behind her.

'Take your time. I don't have to go anywhere.' Unlike Philip, Laura didn't try to offer advice. 'I hear you left home?'

'Yes, but it's not that. It's Marianne Miller. I've just seen her in Leeds.' She described how they'd met in a disjointed, breathless jumble.

'Has she heard about Ellie?' Laura took everything in. Her face was sombre, her voice quiet.

'Yes, and she says it was a cover-up. Ellie did it to protect Paul. Can you believe it? She actually committed suicide to save him!'

Laura leaned forward, elbows on her desk. 'That's serious, Aimee. What proof does Marianne have?'

'She says they were lovers; Ellie and Paul. Ellie was like the rest of us, like the police at first; she thought that Paul had committed the murder. That's why she confessed and then killed herself.'

'Listen, Aimee, the police knew what they were doing. They had reason to suspect Ellie. They seem to be satisfied now that they've got to the bottom of it.'

Disappointed, Aimee sat back. 'You don't believe me?'

'It's Marianne Miller that I'm inclined not to believe. I've never met her, but every time she appears, dropping seeds of doubt, it stirs up the whole thing again. I don't trust her.' Laura stood to gaze out at Ravenscar. 'You're sure she wasn't intending to mislead you?'

'Do you think I'm that gullible?' Aimee's protest was met with silence. 'Do you?'

Laura turned. 'I think Marianne must be a clever woman. And she obviously hates Paul.'

'What should we do?'

For a while Laura didn't answer. She seemed to turn things over as she stared through the window. Then she reached out to snap the blind shut. '*You* shouldn't do anything, Aimee, except perhaps go home and tell your parents where you are.'

This wasn't the answer Aimee had hoped for. 'What about you?' She felt herself being shepherded out of Laura's room towards the main exit.

Laura switched off lights, locked doors and followed her into the car park. 'I'm going to drive up to Ravenscar Hall,' she told her. 'Paul Miller leaves for good at the weekend, and I want to talk to him before he goes.'

247

# CHAPTER TWENTY-FOUR

Laura knew that a building alone couldn't create an air of mystery. It was the eye of the beholder that found secrets in the shadows, menace in the bolted windows and doors. Yet Ravenscar had always invited such wild imaginings. It stood isolated, bearing the brunt of the moorland winds, unsoftened by surrounding gardens, lacking the shelter of trees. It was stark and bare, lonely.

So, though the spring evening cast a pinkish light over the heather and the still water of the tarn, though the whistles and wheezy cries of birds soaring overhead and the steady grazing of sheep softened the picture, nevertheless Laura approached the house with a sense that its stones and slates were in some way responsible for the recent disasters and that they had gathered secrets in their grainy millstone crevices, along with the moss and damp accumulated over years.

She shook off the superstitions as she knocked at the closed front door. She needed to gather her wits, plan what she would say to Paul. Still, the memory of her last visit here haunted her; the scene of Ellie's desperate death, blood on the walls, and her neat, precise handwriting in the note that claimed guilt for Jim's murder.

She knocked again though it was obvious that she would get no reply. The house was shut up and had already reverted to an uninhabited air. But Paul's car stood in the yard to one side of the Hall and, as Laura peered in through the windows of his living quarters, she could see signs that he wasn't far away; a half-full coffee mug on the kitchen table, indoor shoes kicked off and lying by the door.

She imagined his state of mind, alone in the house now that the police had removed all signs of their presence. The funeral was over; few mourners, a great many curious onlookers and Paul himself standing totally isolated. Suicide had never been in doubt. Even the Jeremiahs at the Falcon had been unable to whip up any enthusiasm for yet another murder theory.

So Paul was left in . . . Laura almost thought 'peace', but the word was grotesquely inappropriate. He was left in pain, no doubt, and God knew what state of fear and confusion. She could hardly contemplate what he must be going through now and this didn't depend on whose theory about the murder was the correct one. Innocent or guilty, Paul Miller was a man to be pitied.

The evening light was strikingly clear on top of the Scar. The sky was flushed by sunset, the horizon darkly silhouetted. But closer to, Laura could make out the trees by the tarn; each individual branch, and the rocks jutting out into the water. Dusk pressed them strangely flat, took away their depth and made them look like paper cut-outs. There was very little movement and only the sounds of birds crying and the soft lapping of water against the shore.

Laura was drawn towards the water. If Paul wasn't at home, no doubt he would soon be back. The alarm she'd felt at Aimee's revelations had settled. Instead of being frightened by a possible confrontation with Paul, of putting herself in danger by pressing him for the truth, she began to view her visit as an opening of doors, a shedding of light. She had to trust her instinct that whatever Paul's role had been in all this, he was not naturally a violent man. Driven, cornered, trapped; all these might apply. But unless she had him completely wrong, she didn't see him as likely to do her harm.

She was glad when she spotted him at the far side of the tarn returning from the direction of Joan's Foss. She identified with his need to be out in the open, seeking the beautiful spots and the solace to be found there. Waiting quietly for him to see her, she sat on a low wall and studied his approach.

Gone was the solid dependability she'd first seen in Paul. He walked slowly, unobservant of his surroundings. There was no energy in his step, no sureness. His head was down, his face in shadow. No sunset could rouse him from his misery; there was no consolation in a warm spring evening after a hard, cold winter.

'Paul?' Laura had to step across his path to make him notice her.

He glanced up bleakly, unable to give her a context and not even bothering to try.

'It's me, Laura.' She slipped into step beside him, felt the heather tug at her feet as they trudged towards the house. 'Have you spoken to anyone since the funeral?'

He shook his head; an animal-like gesture as if ridding himself of a small nuisance.

'Have you been taking care of yourself?' She was shocked by the void in him. It seemed that trying to get a response would be like digging into sand on the shore, watching the hole fill as the waves swirled over it. He walked on, locked in his own thoughts.

Laura followed him through the gates of the Hall into the yard. He left the door open as he went inside; a sign that he didn't positively object to her presence. She decided to organise a hot drink for them both.

She made coffee and followed Paul into the lounge. A sleeping-bag on the sofa made it plain that this was where he had chosen to hole up since Ellie's death. Laura moved it to one side and watched him slump automatically into the space. He took the cup without comment.

There were signs of Ellie everywhere; a photograph on the slate mantelpiece, a magazine lying open on the coffee table. 'Paul, I'm so terribly sorry . . .' She crouched beside him and touched his hand.

He clenched his jaw, but tears began to trickle down. His hand shook uncontrollably. 'If she could have done it any way but that!'

'I know.'

'When I went in and saw her lying there, I couldn't believe that she'd done it; not Ellie.'

'It doesn't mean she didn't love you,' Laura explained. She tried to imagine his loneliness. 'In fact, it probably means she loved you more than anything else.'

'She didn't. How could she? She wouldn't have left me like this.'

His was the egotism of the bereaved, the anger against the lost one, all the more severe when it was suicide. There was blame mixed with guilt that he hadn't been able to prevent it.

He began to sob. 'She was my life, you know that? She meant everything. I'd have done anything for her.'

'It was the same with Ellie,' Laura insisted gently.

'She told you that?' He grasped at Laura's hands, implored her.

'I think that's why she killed herself. She did it to save you.'

He stood up, and walked away from Laura towards the window. 'How do you mean, save me?'

'She confessed to killing Jim because she thought you were the one who'd done it.' Laura held her breath.

'Me? She was protecting me?' He leaned on the windowsill, arms braced, head hanging.

'Remember the Glyclozide tablets, Paul?' She watched his every movement; the flicker of awareness behind his half-

251

closed eyelids, the strained shoulder muscles. 'The ones that sent Jim into the coma? Well, Ellie came to me with a different version of the story before she handed them over to the police. She told me that it was you who'd given them to her, that you'd found them amongst Jim's effects. But the official story was that she'd found them herself. Which was it really?'

'What does it matter now?' he groaned.

'If it was you and Ellie lied to the police, she was already covering up for you.'

Paul seemed to undergo a huge struggle. 'It was me. I found them,' he said at last.

'Where?'

'Underneath Jim's bed.'

Laura wondered which way to go next. 'And did you know what they were?'

'I guessed.'

'So what did you think when you found the half-empty packet?'

'Not much at the time. We were all too cut up by his death.'

A new thought struck Laura. 'Did Jim and Ellie still sleep together?'

'No. They had separate rooms after Marianne left.' He sighed and shook his head. 'I guess I did wonder what they were doing there. I didn't look too hard for the answer, though. I just handed them over to Ellie.'

'And she came to me later and told me you'd found them in a file drawer. Then she told the police *she'd* found them.' Laura was still puzzled. 'So what you're saying is that deep down you thought that Ellie might have used them to kill Jim, and I'm saying that she was afraid *you* had!'

He nodded.

'Why didn't you two talk about it? Didn't you trust each other?'

Paul frowned. 'You've got to understand what it was like up

here after they dug up the body. Everything was unreal. Ellie went to pieces overnight. She must have thought they were going to bang me up for killing Jim.'

'Weren't you scared?' Laura recalled the nastiness of Superintendent Ford, the eyes of suspicion firmly focused on Paul.

'The only thing worrying me right then was looking after Ellie. Plus trying to stop Marianne from poking her nose in.'

Paul's ex-wife lurched into the frame once more. 'Did you think she was?'

'I knew she was. Once Jim was dead there was no stopping her. No way would Marianne stand by and watch me and Ellie get together!'

'Jealous?'

'As hell.'

'Even though she'd broken your marriage up in the first place?'

Paul looked down. 'I got involved with Ellie before Marianne and Jim had their thing,' he confessed.

Laura stared. This was the secret that Ellie had clung on to.

He gave an empty laugh. 'Marianne couldn't stand me being happy after that.'


One question above all stood out for Laura as she walked from the Hall to her car. Not the one that everyone else would still be asking, that would turn heads from Ellie to Paul and back again, like spectators at a tennis match: who did kill Jim Blackwood? For Laura the turmoil came from a different direction, involving her professional ethics and almost flattening her with the force of its implications. As she got in the car, switched on her lights and drove down Hawk Fell into the black valley, she asked herself again and again, 'Could I have saved Ellie Blackwood? Who might I have told about the

Glyclozide and her conflicting stories? The police? Philip or Gerald? Luke?'

If Luke had known that Ellie had changed her mind, and if he had used that knowledge to persuade her to tell the truth, would the outcome have been any different? Laura was convinced that it would. Ellie's subterfuge would have broken down and she and Paul would have had to talk.

She drove through Hawkshead, almost blind to where she was, along the Merton road and straight to Luke's house.

She found him working at the desk in his front room. The lights were on and the curtains open, so she saw him look up at the sound of her car. He came to the door to meet her, took one look and put his arms around her.

'Someone's dead who could be alive!' She was furious with herself for putting patient confidentiality above all else. 'I knew Ellie was lying one way or another. If I'd told you, you could have straightened it out with her.'

'How?' Luke waited for the storm to die down.

'You could have cut through the rubbish and given the police a clear run. If they'd known that Ellie was unreliable, they wouldn't have been thrown off the track.'

'Who says they were?'

'She as good as incriminated herself!'

He held on to her and she didn't resist. Luke didn't make light of her troubles but neither did he view them tragically.

'Laura, listen.' He stroked her cheek with his thumb. 'Stop giving yourself a hard time. I keep reminding you, we're doing a job here. Ethics are part of it and saving lives is part of it too – sometimes. Other times, there just isn't anything we can do.'

'I wish I could believe that.' Such a waste, she thought; such a tangled waste.

'Suppose I said I knew what Ellie was up to all along?'

Startled, Laura looked up at him.

'Nothing felt quite right. I talked to Mike Jackson about it and he agreed. Some things, like Marianne Miller's evidence about the row between Paul and Jim, pointed one way, while the Glyclozide evidence pointed another. In the end, they decided to sit back and wait for Ellie or Paul to make a decisive move.'

'So my silence made no difference?'

He shook his head. 'You're off the hook, Dr Grant.'

Laura rested her head against him. 'All these tiny threads,' she sighed. 'I can't get them to shape up into any pattern. Until I went up to see Paul, I was pretty well convinced by Aimee's story that he was guilty. Then when I saw him and listened to him, I could have sworn he was telling the truth.'

'The whole truth and nothing but the truth?'

'I wouldn't go so far as to say that.' She turned her head and put her arms around Luke's neck. 'Thanks.'

He smiled back. 'Relax. It's out of your hands.'

'Are you saying you wouldn't have felt the way I do?' Boundaries between professional and personal responsibility were always blurred.

'No, I'd probably have got myself into the same sort of mess.'

Reflecting on the shock waves still widening and rippling, Laura was glad to rest for a while. She stayed at Luke's house, talking and listening, feeling that this was exactly where she wanted to be. There was no pressure; rather, an unravelling of a tangled thread and a feeling that she would, sooner or later, be able to straighten out her confusions.

She left the house at midnight, knowing without putting into words what she must do. See Matthew. Talk. How it would turn out she still had absolutely no idea.

# CHAPTER TWENTY-FIVE

During meetings, or driving to call-outs, part of Philip's mind was always on Juliet. Whereas at first he'd been numb with the shock of their separation, hammered into apathy by the hopelessness of the situation, now he saw glimmers of changes for the better. They'd talked, at long last, and they saw eye to eye over Gerald. They shared a concern for Dot.

Town Head was on his list that Thursday morning. Despite Dot's serious condition, he looked forward to his unscheduled visit. He would be made welcome, he would check her blood pressure, discuss practical arrangements for surgery the following week and then they would move on to tea, cake and chat.

The doorbell's two-note chime sounded loud and clear. He peered through the letterbox down the polished corridor. But there was no answer to his ring.

Philip glanced at his watch; ten-thirty. He had other calls; to an eighty-year-old patient still living independently in a remote farmhouse beyond Ginnersby. Then on to Swiredale to check on a possible ectopic pregnancy, with a probable referral to hospital to follow. He decided to go on with his round and to come back to Dot at the end of the morning.

Juliet had offered to take Dot into Wingate next Thursday morning. Since she planned to go shopping there in any case, she would drop Dot off at her daughter's house to save Valerie the bother of a drive out to Hawkshead. Typical Juliet. Philip tapped the steering-wheel in time to the cello concerto playing on tape. Dot had graciously accepted her offer, relieved to avoid the drama of an ambulance driving up the steep cobbled street to collect her.

'I don't want a fuss,' she'd insisted. 'And I'll leave everything in order, just in case. I don't want Valerie finding lots of loose ends to tie up if it should turn out that way.'

Philip was half way up Hawk Fell, within sight of the empty farm at Oxtop, when he decided to turn around. It meant pulling into a gateway, shunting the car across the narrow road to point downhill and driving back to Hawkshead. He would be late for his other appointments but that didn't seem as important as the sudden urge to check on Dot.

'Stupid,' he told himself, dipping down into the valley. 'You should have double-checked. Where would she be at this time on a Thursday?' There was no market, her son and daughter were both at work and few of Dot's friends had cars to drive her out on a spring jaunt. She lived a life of routine, especially now that she was ill.

A couple of heads turned as his car made its way back to the house. A neighbour made a point of coming to the kerbside for a word.

'Is it about Mrs Wilson? There's been no sign of her this morning. Normally she'd pull back the front bedroom curtains, see.'

Philip craned his neck to look. Now he was even more angry with himself for not keeping his mind fully on the job.

'We would have rung you by dinnertime anyhow,' the woman told him. 'It's not like her to let things slip.'

He nodded, considering how to get into the house. The door was locked but not bolted, he guessed. 'Does Dot leave a spare key with anyone?'

'No. She keeps one under the pot there, though.' She

pointed to a large earthernware flower-pot full of winter pansies.

Philip fumbled underneath with his fingertips. Sure enough, the key was there. Thanking the neighbour, he went on into the house alone.

A clock ticked in the narrow hallway, the old-fashioned telephone sat shiny and silent on a small glass table. He glanced into the empty sitting room and kitchen and called her name. The work surfaces were pristine, the kettle stone-cold.

He went upstairs. The double bed in the front bedroom was empty. The boards creaked beneath his feet. Curtains were closed in the second bedroom where Laura had once lodged, and in the third. It was to this room that Dot had retreated from the bed where she'd slept all her married life.

He would never know why she'd chosen to sleep here on the night she died. The spare bedroom had a temporary feel; second-best bedspread, bare dressing table. Dot had lain down on top of the covers. She was in her nightdress, with her slippers neatly by the bed. Her face looked peaceful.

Philip sat by the bed listening and watching for breath. There was no pulse, no heartbeat. The body was cold.


'Every last item is in order,' he told Juliet, who came to Town Head when he returned with Valerie that evening. 'Dot's bills are all paid, building society books set out inside the bureau.'

'All these tins are empty,' Valerie told them from the kitchen.

Philip and Juliet stood together in the hall. The undertakers had moved in at midday and done their smooth, tactful business. The neighbours had stood on the street to watch as they drove the coffin to the chapel of rest.

Valerie came out to show them the containers. 'Not a single

258

biscuit or cake left in the house. That's not like Mum.' Her lip trembled; she shook her head.

'She must have been getting ready for going into hospital,' Juliet said. 'She wouldn't have known exactly how long she'd be away.'

Valerie's willpower gave way. 'I think she knew she was never coming back!'

Philip said Dot would have died quickly and that it had happened in the early hours without a struggle.

'She did look calm,' Valerie agreed. 'Poor Mum.'

The son, John, took over the few practical arrangements necessary to close up the house. He turned off water and electricity, rang to disconnect the phone. Philip and Juliet only waited to make sure that Valerie had recovered. There was nothing they could say that would show their affection for the woman whose heart and soul belonged to the dale.

Juliet hugged Valerie and Philip shook John by the hand. They walked out of the house, away from the village up towards the moor. The view of hawthorn trees in bud, pale limestone walls, ridged green hills and the long horizon would stand as Dot's testament.

'In a way it's what she would have wanted,' Juliet said. The evening threatened rain. Banks of purplish cloud rode towards them on a high wind. She sighed and turned away from Philip to take the path down to the Foss. 'And she would have hated to be an invalid if the operation hadn't worked.'

He followed more slowly. 'There's never been a single time in all my years of tending to the sick that I haven't thought that dying isn't the most lonely thing on this planet.' He recalled the deep, throbbing notes of the cello playing on his tape and was silent.

Juliet took his hand. 'It certainly puts other things into perspective.'

They walked on until the steep, narrow path to the waterfall forced them to break hands.

'"The grave's a fine and private place, But none I think do there embrace." Do you believe that?' he asked.

'I've never had to think about it,' she confessed. Then she shook her head. 'No, that makes it sound like the end. That's not what I envisage. I don't mind if you tell me that believing in life after death is like buying insurance; if we don't get it right now, then there's always a second chance later on. But I just can't accept that death is all there is.' She spread her hands at the tumbling water, the green fern shoots, the mossy stones.

'Sometimes I think that's enough.' He felt moved beyond his fear that he and Juliet would never be reconciled into a quiet acceptance. He looked up from the water and smiled at her.

'It is beautiful,' she agreed. 'It's time I was grateful again!' Briskly she stepped on between the rocks, only stopping when she reached the Foss. 'Aren't words extraordinary?'

'Which words?' He was bemused.

'"Grateful." "Full of thanks." And "resentment": literally, feeling again; rerunning the tape and grinding yourself into the ground. That's what I've been doing. I just realised that as I sat on this rock.'

'And?'

'It's unhealthy. I never used to run things through again and again. I just got on and *did*. That's what I was good at. Now I think too much.'

'Can't you do both; think and act?'

'No. The first gets in the way of the second. Most things are too complicated for me to come out with a clear answer. That's why I have to run them through again. Why did you fall in love with Mary? When did you decide to deceive me? Where did I go wrong? And then I'm back, deep in the throes, hating everyone all over again.' Her voice rose and fell as the various emotions took over.

He recognised the pattern. 'So what do you do when it hits you? I generally reach for the bottle.'

'I probably get out the Hoover and pulverise you in my fantasies. You don't know how many dust-bags you've been thrown out with during these last few months.'

She glanced up through the tree branches. 'Thank you, Dot. What's an ounce or two of infidelity weighed in the grand scale of things? Will it matter in the next life? Or even in this one at this time next year?'

Philip was swept along, unsure where the current would take them. Raindrops began to spatter on to the stones and splash into the deep green pool. Then the heavens opened.

'Shall we run for it?' he suggested.

Juliet shook her head. 'I like the rain.'. They walked out of the woods and across the field towards the village. They passed Matthew Aire's car parked next to Laura's outside Abbey Grange and tramped up the lane through quickly forming puddles, heading for the shelter of Bridge House. By the time they arrived, they were soaked to the skin and shivering with cold.

'Shall I come in?' He stood on the doorstep, rain dripping from his jacket, his shoes sodden.

'I can't turn you out in this!' She stared out at the downpour.

He stepped inside, feeling awkward. She fetched him a towel from the bathroom, then went back upstairs to change. He stood in the hall to take off his jacket and shoes. For several minutes he hovered like a stranger.

Then he went up. He found Juliet in tears in the bedroom. She stood up when she heard him come in and resisted as he put his arms around her.

'It's the shock over Dot. I thought she'd go on for ever.'

'Not even Dot,' he said gently.

'I'll miss her, Philip.'

He noticed that, like him, she still wore her wedding ring. 'Can't we go back to how it was?' She was here, he was holding her; it seemed possible.

'Philip, no. Believe me, we can't!' She was afraid.

'Then can't we move on? We could sell this house, buy something smaller, put it all behind us.' His plans sounded mundane, his heart swelled to bursting point.

'Don't. Please, don't.'

'Juliet, if I can't be with you again, I might as well pack it in. I don't mean I'll do anything stupid. It's just that I'm drifting, I can't get a hold on anything. It's as if I've been hollowed out.' He struck his chest. 'My fault, not yours. And if you decide I've got to pay the price, I won't argue . . .' He stumbled to a halt, letting her fall to the bed as his arms gave way.

'I'm not your judge,' she sobbed. 'I don't want to be.'

'What do you want?' To save his life he couldn't have kept his distance now. He sat beside her, urging her to look up. 'Tell me.'

'I want not to be lonely.'

'There's no need,' he whispered.

She looked at him, her eyes blurred with tears.

He knew each line and contour, had watched her face change over the years. Now he thought she was more beautiful, more dignified than ever.

And as they lay together, there was the old closeness and a strangeness. The disbelief at being here, the sweetly remembered feel and scent of her skin. He breathed her in, held her to him. These were the exact curves and proportions; this was his wife.

# CHAPTER TWENTY-SIX

'As it happens, I don't feel a thing.' Sean looked out over Ravenscar tarn for the first time since the day of Jim Blackwood's death. He'd come up here on a soft spring Saturday morning, very different from the sleeting, bitter conditions of early February. The silvery surface of the tarn, the light white clouds scudding overhead transformed the scene lodged in his memory of ice and black depths. 'I expected to feel spooked, but it's like it's not the same place.'

They'd come to lay a few ghosts; Aimee's idea. Though Sean rarely talked of his part in the failed rescue attempt, she knew that it preyed on his mind. Every time there was a new twist in the tale he seemed to suffer again from a feeling that he should have done more to save Jim's life. The tarn featured in his nightmares; he described himself as a small figure trying to find his way through a maze to a lake at the centre and every turning he made was a dead-end. 'Around here is where it must have happened.' She stood quietly at the base of the scree slope.

'Over there.' Sean pointed to the rocky ledge where they'd tried to haul out the body. 'I know it doesn't make sense, but I expected it to be more like it was then. It's really weird.' He gazed round with relief at the new growth of reeds at the water's edge, the green hills. 'We came over from Black Gill across the top there, heading towards the house.'

Aimee watched him relive the scene, completely taken up by past events.

'Steve and me, we had to cut across these rocks by the edge of the water. I was swearing to myself and wondering where the hell he was. Jim was the one who laid into us if we were even a minute late. Anyhow, we're running across here in the freezing rain and I see what I think is a bit of tree trunk sticking out of the water, like there's a branch poking up through the ice, but most of it's under the surface. Then I find out it's not a branch, it's an arm. I knew straight off who it was.'

'What did you do?'

'We had to try and get him out, didn't we?'

'No, you could have gone straight for help.'

'The poor sod might still have been alive; just. I hadn't a clue how long he'd been in there. So I said we should give it a go. I got down on to my hands and knees to grab his hand.' Sean shuddered, pointing to the spot. 'It was freezing cold but not stiff, like they're supposed to be if they're dead. So I'm pulling and Steve is standing behind me yelling at me to watch it, but the rest of the body is jammed under the ice and it's beginning to crack. That's what I still hear – sharp, jaggedy cracks as the ice broke up. And the body's wedged fast in something under the water; I can't see what. If more ice breaks loose, we're not going to be able to stay close enough to pull him clear. We need help. That's when I run for the house.'

'To find Ellie?'

He nodded. 'She just looked at me. I said I wasn't sure but I thought it was Jim. She started yelling for Paul to come and help, but he'd just gone out with another group of kids. So we had to head back here, just the two of us. Ellie rang for your dad to come up. She was cool about that. I never even thought about it, but she had it in her head; we needed someone up here straight away. As it happens,' he went on, 'by the time he got here, it didn't make any difference.'

Aimee sat down on the ledge of rock. 'You did everything you could.' These last few weeks had changed her life. If this hadn't happened up here on that horrible day, she would never have noticed Sean sitting by himself in the pub that night; never have got to know him and fallen in love with him. Now she unlaced her boots and took them off, sticking her bare feet into the icy water.

'You're mad.' He came over and sat beside her, legs crooked, arms dangling over his knees.

'So you keep saying.'

He picked up a smooth stone and flung it far out into the water.

'It's lovely and warm,' she insisted.

'Liar.'

'It is. I'm going for a swim.' Glancing round, she stripped off her top and trousers, and plunged from the ledge.

'Nuts!' Sean stood up with a yell as she splashed out at him.

'No, it's brilliant.' She thrashed waist-high into the water. It was, if only she would admit it, so cold it took her breath away. She turned, waded out and dived under the surface, coming up in time to see Sean run in, minus his top but still dressed in his jeans and trainers. He jumped and crashed into the water.

'It's bloody, bloody freezing!' He made a huge noise, whooped and yelled, and frightened the birdlife for miles around. He swam after her, threatening to duck her, but she swam for the shore. Soon they both staggered out, laughing and shivering.

'Better?' Aimee challenged. She grabbed her clothes away from him as he dripped all over them.

He wouldn't say so, but she'd broken him free of the grip of memory. 'Lend me your T-shirt. I want to dry myself with it.'

'No chance.' She ran off, struggling to pull it over her head. 'Look out, someone's coming.'

A gaggle of middle-aged walkers came from the direction of the gill, appearing in the distance in sturdy walking boots, anoraks and woolly hats. They headed their way.

Aimee fled, clutching her jeans and boots. Sean squelched after her. They ran for cover, chilled to the bone, exorcised.

'Come back with me and meet my parents,' she offered, still laughing. They hid behind a wall, huddled together for warmth, until the walking party had passed.

'Like this?' His hair was dripping, his jeans wringing wet, he was blue with cold.

'Why not? I want to ask my dad something.' She'd pulled her clothes on and was on her feet, heading for home.

'I thought that was down to me,' he protested. '"Sir, may I have your permission" . . . blah, blah!'

'No, you idiot. I want him to give you a categorical, medical-type answer on whether you and Steve could possibly have been in time to save Jim Blackwood's life.'

There was a scene which Aimee had studied at the end of *Othello*, where the fallen hero asks the Venetian consul to listen to the reasons for his misguided actions: 'I have done the state some service, And they know it.'

That was how her father had been behaving during these last few days; broken but dignified, a man bemused by the villainies of the reformed NHS and betrayed by those closest to him. Her mother had stood by her man, however. This very afternoon they were due to go off to Scotland for a few days' break, before the practice got together to set about replacing their senior partner. Meanwhile he was in retrospective mood, remembering the good old days of look-in visits to old farmers on the fells; men who were sparrow-like in build but had the stamina of carthorses.

'High pain threshold, those old boys,' he told them as they sat in the conservatory at the back of the house. Sean's jeans steamed gently in the warmth. 'In the winter they were in bed by six-thirty and up again at five in the morning; always on the go.' Gerald accepted a cup of tea from Janet. 'Do you remember old Geoff Maynard up at Ginnersby?' he asked her. 'He was well into his eighties and still managing fine until he fell and broke his arm. His wife brought me up there and he was very put out by it. Called her and me all the names under the sun, tried to tell us "it'd mend on its own"!'

'Wasn't he a Home Guard captain in the last war?' Janet asked him.

Aimee raised her eyebrows at Sean. 'Sean's dad was in the army,' she told her father.

Gerald coughed sceptically. 'Which regiment?'

'The Paras. He's always going on about how tough the training was.' His coffee cup rattled in the saucer. To Sean, Gerald was the archetypal strict father. His only first-hand knowledge of him came from the day by the tarn that they all preferred to forget.

'Sean, would you like . . . ?' Janet began to offer him a dry pair of jeans from Nick's drawer.

'Dad, we wanted to ask . . . '

'I was a navy man myself.' Gerald's voice overrode Janet's and Aimee's. 'What was that?' He turned towards his daughter.

Aimee was stunned. This was the first time he'd spoken to her since their giant row. The house had been a war zone ever since though her mother had tried to make it up to her on several occasions. 'We've just been up to Ravenscar,' she told him, 'and Sean was describing exactly what went on that day.'

Janet hovered in the kitchen doorway. Gerald bristled and

267

grew defensive. 'It's all written down plain and clear in the inquest report.'

Sean came in quickly. 'It's not the official stuff that bothers me. I was telling Aimee, the worst bit for me is not knowing if I could have saved him. Say we'd been able to pull him out straight away, would it have made any difference?' He spoke earnestly, his thin face flushed, leaning forward in his chair.

The question caught Gerald off-guard. His own obsession had been with the manner of Blackwood's death, not the timing of it.

'I can't help feeling we did the wrong thing running for help. It was like I panicked and if I'd kept my head he'd still be alive.'

Gerald looked him full in the face for the first time. Until this moment he'd only seen Sean as Aimee's appendage, part and parcel of her adolescent stage. 'You saw how long it took four of us to get him out, let alone two.'

'Maybe if I'd jumped in and pulled him free on the far side?'

'And died of hypothermia in the process?' Gerald grunted. 'Anyway, it's just as well you didn't indulge in unnecessary heroics. They would have been futile.' He paused to stare out across the garden. 'In my *expert* opinion, he'd been dead a good hour before we pulled him out.'

'That would make it thirty-five, forty minutes before Steve and I first found him.' Sean did the arithmetic and drew a deep breath. 'Definitely an hour?' he checked.

'At least.' Gerald glanced at Aimee. 'Whose idea was it to revisit the scene of the crime; yours?'

She nodded. 'We went for a swim.'

'So I see. Was there anything else you wanted to know?' He got up abruptly, but he was looking from one to the other with new curiosity. 'Your mother and I want to be away soon after lunch.'

'No.' Aimee smiled at Sean. 'Thanks, Dad.'

Janet came forward with the offer of the dry jeans. 'You're pretty much the same size as Nick, so these should fit.'

Embarrassed, Sean took them.

'I'll show you the bathroom,' Janet suggested, leading him off.

Aimee blushed as Gerald continued to stare. Their battles seemed suddenly to have fallen away. All her life she'd striven for his attention and now she'd secured it without even trying. 'What do you think?' she ventured, gesturing after Sean as his footsteps receded.

There was a long pause, a series of clicks and grunts in his throat. 'From what I can see, he seems a decent sort,' Gerald conceded slowly.


'You're a decent sort.' Aimee spoke in curt, clipped army tones. They were in her bed, in the middle of the afternoon. Her mother and father were somewhere on the A1 north.

'Now I feel like a real shit,' Sean admitted. His decency didn't stretch so far as to resist the temptation of Aimee all to himself in an empty house.

'No, they like you!' She curled up close.

'They probably trusted me not to take advantage.' He twisted strands of her hair around his forefinger.

'You didn't; I did.'

'True,' he sighed.

They'd put the answer-machine on and luxuriated in the freedom and comfort of the house.

'Anyway, don't take Dad at face value. He's not as straight-laced as he looks.'

'Watch it.' He smiled down at her. 'You'll be saying something nice about him again if you're not careful.'

'I could tell he was pleased when you asked his advice. It probably means a lot to him.'

'He did everything he could that day, and more. In fact, he

269

was brilliant with Ellie afterwards.' Sean could recall those details without distress.

'Tell him,' she whispered, reaching up to stroke the back of his head. 'He'd like to know that.'

When the phone rang yet again and they realised that they'd spent the whole afternoon in bed, they finally managed to prise themselves apart.

'Too late!' Aimee ran to the phone in the hall.

'Play the messages.' Sean came down barefoot in Nick's jeans.

She pressed the Play button. There was one message from Philip reminding Gerald and Janet that Dot's funeral was planned for Wednesday and one from a friend of Janet's who didn't realise she'd gone away. They let the different voices and machine noises flow over them. But the third message brought them back into the hall from the kitchen.

'Play that one again,' Sean said.

She rewound and repeated the message.

'Dr Scott, this is Marianne Miller. I need to talk to you urgently about Jim Blackwood's death. It's to do with my ex-husband's involvement in the murder. I've tried everyone else and I know you were the doctor on the scene. The police say they'll probably close the case. I don't want to let that happen, so will you talk to me, please? I'm on my way out to Hawkshead now.'

Aimee flicked off the machine. 'What time was it when she left that?'

'I don't know, but let's get out of here quick.'

'Where to? What shall we do?'

'Go and tell someone.'

Aimee agreed it was best to find help. 'Who? I know, Laura!'

They rushed to get properly dressed and out of the house before Paul's wife showed up.

'I reckon she'll be driving here.' Sean followed Aimee up the drive on to the road. 'God knows what she'll do if she finds there's no one in.'

'There's a phone box.' Sean pointed to the one opposite the Falcon. 'Let's ring from there.'

Luckily Laura was at home, and when they described the problem, she agreed to step in. 'You stay where you are. I'll drive over and pick you up, then we can go back to your place together. I've never met her, so it'll be easier if you two come along.'

Aimee told Laura that Marianne had sounded out of control.

'Don't worry, I'll be there.'

'Thanks, Laura.' She put down the phone and stepped outside the booth to wait. It was one thing saying don't worry, quite another to act on the advice.

Their meeting went according to plan five minutes later. But their timing was bad. When the three of them drove to the Scott's house, there was no sign of Marianne. A neighbour, busy in her garden, had noticed a strange car, a small white Fiat, draw up a few minutes earlier, she told them. And, yes, the driver was a well-dressed young woman with shoulder-length light brown hair. She'd rung the bell several times, then driven off at furious speed.

'Which way did she head?'

'Back into the village.' The woman, who was used to strange comings and goings outside the doctor's house, hadn't paid too much attention.

They thanked her and retraced their steps, on the lookout for Marianne's white car. They imagined her frustration at not finding Gerald at home and tried to guess what she would do next.

'What's the betting she heads up to Ravenscar now she's here? It sounds like she's squaring up for a big confrontation.'

'Is Paul still there?' Sean had heard that he was packed up ready to go.

'He's supposed to leave today or tomorrow.' Laura had kept in touch by phone since Wednesday, when she'd last seen him. He'd seemed calmer, more able to accept Ellie's suicide.

'He'll go mad if she shows up there, won't he?' Aimee saw it as a potential flashpoint.

'Let's go and see,' Laura suggested. Hawkshead was so near to Ravenscar Hall; she too doubted whether Marianne would have the willpower to turn round and drive away.

'We'd better warn Paul that she's around,' Aimee said.

'You make her sound dangerous.' Sean held tight as Laura swung her car up the steep hill.

They drove the last stretch and pulled up outside the house, hoping in many ways that they were too late, that Paul had already closed up and left. But his car was in the yard and the front doors of the Hall stood open. They went inside and called his name, saw that boxes stood half-packed in the big reception area, and that personal possessions were still scattered about the living quarters. If he intended to be gone by the end of the weekend, he would have his work cut out.

Aimee felt uneasy. She didn't like poking around other people's things. She turned her back on the photograph of Ellie still standing on the mantelpiece.

'I'll take another look outside,' Sean offered. He went and then quickly returned. 'I think Marianne's car is round the side.'

A small white Fiat was parked roughly and out of sight.

'So where is she?' Aimee's exasperation broke through.

Laura peered into the car; a woman's handbag lay on the passenger seat, some high-heeled shoes had been kicked off on the driver's side. 'Do you think they heard us arrive?' It occurred to her that one or the other might be hiding from them.

'Sound carries a long way up here,' Sean confirmed. He remembered Ellie's cry for Gerald to save Jim. 'But there was no one out by the tarn; we'd have seen them when we drove past.' There were no trees to block their view except those at the top of the steep scree.

'Let's try the house again,' Laura said slowly. She looked up at its tall, plain frontage. 'We didn't look upstairs in the bedrooms.'

Reluctantly Aimee followed the others back inside and up the main stairs. Without school parties to fill its high rooms and corridors, the Hall had quickly regained its unlived-in, anachronistic air of bedrooms that were too large to heat, corners that remained shadowy no matter how many lights were installed. The bare floors echoed to their footsteps and every closed door seemed to contain a secret.

Then they heard voices beyond a locked door at the end of the landing. Laura stood back to try to work out where they were coming from.

'We'll have to go downstairs, through the sitting rooms and up the narrow staircase at the back of the house,' she explained. 'I think they're in what used to be Ellie's bedroom.'

'Why not shout from here?' Aimee didn't want to creep up on Marianne and Paul. 'Then they could unlock this door.'

But Laura shook her head. She showed them how to back-track, through the Blackwoods' and Millers' private quarters and up the second staircase. She raised her hand, warning Aimee and Sean to stay quiet.

The woman's voice was barely above a whisper. The man stumbled over his words, which amounted to no more than short questions.

'Isn't this enough?' It was Paul, standing out of sight inside the room where Ellie's body had been found.

'Let go. You can't blame me. She must have been half crazy in the first place.'

Marianne seemed to struggle. Someone fell against a heavy piece of furniture. Instinctively Sean moved forward, but Laura put out her arm to stop him. 'What do you mean, not blame you?' Paul's shadow fell across the doorway. 'It's all down to you. Everything you did, every lie you told is down to you.'

They heard Marianne gasp as he grabbed hold of her.

'Every single drop of blood on that wall is there because of what you did. And you couldn't resist coming here to gloat in the end, could you? Look at it, don't turn away. That's Ellie's blood, see!'

'Leave me alone, Paul.'

They heard another struggle, shoes scraping over the floor, a frightened cry from Marianne. Laura listened and held her nerve, while Aimee hid her face against Sean's shoulder.

'No, I haven't finished yet. Look at it, feel it. There. Think of Ellie!'

'Don't. Don't!' She sobbed and fought back. 'Oh God, it wasn't my fault!'

'Tell her that. Go on. She's still here in this room, waiting to hear that it's not your fault. You never went to the police with that shit story about some phone call that never happened, did you? That wasn't you, it was someone else. You didn't want to get your own back on us. Go on, tell her; Ellie's listening!'

Aimee put her hand over her mouth, Sean held on to her. Laura stood and listened.

'Jim did make the phone call,' Marianne pleaded. 'It was itemised. The police could check the number for themselves.'

'And what did he say when he rang you? Tell her, she's listening!' Paul's voice was savage. His back came into view, blocking the doorway.

Aimee broke away from Sean and ran towards Paul, wanting to put an end to what was going on inside the room.

Laura tried to catch hold of her but Paul swung round and saw them. His face, like his voice, seemed to belong to a stranger.

'You listen to this!' he ordered, pulling Aimee into the room. 'She likes an audience, don't you, Marianne?'

They saw her curled in a corner beside the bed which was stripped of its mattress and headboard. On the wall above were the trails of dried blood, a picture knocked out of true, its glass cracked.

Laura slid past Paul to pull Marianne to her feet. 'She won't say anything else until you've calmed down,' she warned him. She stood Marianne in a corner by the window and spoke quietly to her. 'It's time to tell the truth.'

'Jim rang me,' she insisted. She was shaking as if she could really feel Ellie in the room, as if her body was still sprawled on the bed.

'But there was no row going on in the background with Paul, was there?'

Marianne pulled away from Laura's protective hold. She shook her head and cried. 'No.'

'No mention of Paul at all during that last phone call?'

'No.' The sigh turned into a moan. She was shaking her head over and over. 'I just made it up, I don't know why. It came to me that it could have happened that way. I heard Paul threatening Jim later, inside my head, after I heard Jim had died. But I never really heard it.'

Paul turned and slumped against the wall.

'No threats?' Laura repeated.

Aimee stared at the pattern of bloodstains on the wall. 'No.'

'So what did Jim say?' Laura knew this was Ravenscar's last secret; the one that had driven Ellie to her death.

Marianne looked wildly through her tears from Laura to Paul. 'I don't remember!'

'Try,' Laura insisted. 'Tell us exactly what he said.'

'That he'd had enough,' Marianne whispered. 'That he'd had bad news about his blood pressure and kept having these pains in his chest. He knew what it meant.'

'More tests,' Laura prompted. 'Confirmation that his heart was failing?'

Marianne nodded.

Aimee stared incredulously. 'You told us the complete opposite! You said Jim didn't have a history of heart problems.'

'But they drove him to it!' Marianne flashed back in self-justification. 'He couldn't bear it when he found out about Ellie and Paul. It drove him past his limit.'

'So you stepped in to comfort him,' Laura said flatly. She held on to her. 'Listen, none of that matters any more. What did Jim mean when he said he'd had enough?'

'He didn't want to be an invalid. If he couldn't live the life he wanted, out climbing mountains or teaching others to climb, he didn't want to go on.' She hung her head and sobbed bitterly.

'How did he plan to do it?' Laura dredged the last dregs of information from her.

'He told me he had some tablets. He'd been saving them up for ages, knowing they would do the trick when the time came.'

It had come then, after his visit to Philip's surgery had confirmed the worst. It had come on a bitterly cold February morning when the warning pains had gripped his chest and spread down his arms to his fingertips. He'd signalled his intentions and left them in no doubt that this was the way he'd planned it.

Laura stood back from Marianne and stared at her. 'He rang you to say goodbye,' she whispered.

# CHAPTER TWENTY-SEVEN

Winter hadn't yet released its grip. A clear evening meant a heavy frost on the morning of Dot's funeral. April, the month of contradictions, was going out on a bleak white note until the sun rose over the hill behind the Abbey to melt the slopes and cliffs of Ravenscar into sweet greens and gentle browns. The valley was still in shadow, however, when they carried Dot's coffin to the family graveside in the Abbey grounds and committed her to rest.

The packed church had swelled with song. All was fitting; the ceremony and the sorrow, the bank of flowers in the hearse, the mourning children and grandchildren.

'She would have been proud,' Laura told Valerie after the final prayers.

'We did it properly for her. I chose her favourite hymns.'

'And everyone came.'

People were beginning to disperse; some making for the W.I. hall where there was to be a brief gathering, others less closely connected to the family drifting back to work and homes. Dot had been a key figure in Hawkshead for many years; another of those they were sad to lose.

Gerald and Janet came up to Valerie and John to shake hands. Laura made her way under the lychgate to join Matthew and Maisie, who stood waiting in the road. They spent a few minutes with Philip and Juliet, talking quietly about Dot's life, her love of method and order, her kind heart and decided opinions.

'It was the way she used to look at you.' Juliet smiled at the memory. 'She rarely said anything openly disapproving but she would purse her lips and concentrate on her dusting, and you knew as clear as day what it was she was thinking.'

'And when she did open her mouth, you had to pay attention,' Philip added.

'I was terrified of her at the start.' Laura recalled how she had arrived at Town Head for the first time to be greeted by apple-pie order and Dot's penetrating gaze. 'But that didn't last long. I thought she was really lovely. If I'd been born into her era, Dot was exactly the sort of woman I'd want to have been.'

'And on that note, it's back to work.' Gerald came up briskly from behind. 'We can't leave poor Sheila to hold the fort any longer. I'm due over in Wingate at one-thirty. Who's on call-out?'

Laura saw they were among the last to leave the subdued scene. 'I'm on my way, Gerald.' He'd come back refreshed from his trip to Scotland, doubly determined to quit as soon as was practicable. Meanwhile, it was back to his old management style.

She said a quick goodbye to Matthew, who was ready to drive Maisie home.

'See you this evening?' he asked.

She nodded. 'But not for dinner. I have to catch up on some paperwork later tonight.' Instead, she arranged to call in after surgery for a flying visit.

The dale was at its best as she drove up Hawk Fell; light, lively, full of promise. Laura felt the regrets that had clustered around Dot's funeral begin to lift. She stopped at the top of the hill, got out of the car and took a long look back at Hawkshead.

She breathed deeply. The crises of the past few weeks were already fading. Ravenscar Hall was shut up. Though it would quickly be put up for sale to satisfy creditors, Laura guessed that it might be months, even years before another bold spirit would take it on as a business enterprise. In years to come she imagined a hotel there, a management training centre or a retreat for some obscure sect . . . Meanwhile, the wind would blow, leaves would gather in corners, curious bypassers would approach and peer through a window. They would wonder about its history, its present disuse.

Paul Miller had gone earlier in the week, leaving the Hall as it was on the Sunday when Marianne had descended on him and confessed everything. He hadn't had the heart to pack Ellie's belongings, so Laura had promised to sort through and pass them on to charity shops. All he had taken with him was the photograph from the mantelpiece. He was going home, he said. In New Zealand he would attempt to put the past behind him.

Marianne had quickly regained control after her terrified confession. Recriminations resurfaced: none of this would have happened if Ellie and Paul hadn't sliced through the arrangement by starting their affair. Marianne wasn't sorry she'd gone to the police with a perfectly plausible story about Paul's involvement.

Laura had felt nothing for her but contempt. She realised that Marianne was not the guilt-tormented sort. But it was a brittle woman who'd left the Hall without looking back, slipped her feet into her high-heels and checked her hair in the driver's mirror. Laura had disagreed with Aimee's protest that Marianne was getting away with what amounted to murder. 'Not in the long run,' she insisted.

Now, as she gazed on the distant village, she felt a sense of endings and new beginnings all intermingled. There was to be a major change when Gerald left the practice. Regrets and anticipation; another new partner following on so soon after Laura's own arrival. They would want someone energetic and on top of the NHS reforms, yet someone not too intimidatingly progressive for their more old-fashioned patients. Another woman perhaps?

Then there was Gerald, Janet and Aimee. There was peace at home at last. Likewise between Philip and Juliet. Laura had rejoiced for them when she saw them together at the funeral. Since the weekend, Philip hadn't stated anything openly, but given her to understand that they were rebuilding. 'Wish us luck,' he said. 'I think there may be a chance for Juliet and me.'

Laura recognised the need for caution, recalling how she and Tom had been reconciled, only to be disappointed and torn apart. She even realised that the fact that Philip and Juliet were both 'nice' people was no guarantee. 'What's nice got to do with it?' was one of Tom's frequent sayings and Laura had come to agree.

She drew strength from the fresh wind tugging at her hair, the solidity of the stone wall she leaned against and the space all around. She knew now what she would say to Matthew that night.


'I won't give up without a fight,' Matthew warned. She'd told him that they must finish. 'You can't walk away; I must mean more to you than that.'

'I'm not walking away.' It was early evening after a day spent on call-outs and afternoon surgery and they were standing in the lounge at Hawkshead Hall. 'I'm finding my way as we talk. I only know I don't want to go on as we are.'

'If I knew what you wanted, I'd be able to do something.'

Laura's confusion worsened. 'Oh, Matthew, if you can't see without having it explained, what can I do?' In the end, he was too hesitant, too cautious. He was afraid.

He grasped the most obvious straw. 'You want me to stop seeing Abigail? I can arrange it. We can do the hand-overs for Sophie and Tim through a third party. I won't need to talk to her, if that's what you want. And we can go to different therapy sessions, take it in turns to avoid me having any contact with her. Is that better?'

'Matthew, don't, please!'

'I can understand it. She makes you feel insecure. But I promise there's nothing left between us. You can trust me.'

'That isn't the point.' She struggled to free her hand from his. 'How can I set up those kinds of conditions for us to continue? I'd hate myself for making you stick to them. It's not Abigail; it's us.'

'You said you loved me.' He stood back, sounding hurt.

She stopped him from coming near again. 'I know how it feels; I'm letting you down. That's one reason why it's been so hard.' It wasn't in her nature to take away support. 'But now it feels as if I'd be letting you down if we stayed together too. Unless I'm wholehearted, I can't do it. It's the doubts and conditions I can't stand; if this works out in such and such a way, if Abigail backs off, if the children begin to accept me. Every day more ifs and buts and it feels like I'm helpless to do anything about them. And you, Matthew, I don't think you're going to find any solutions either.'

She felt cruel as she spoke, but this time it was for her own survival. She had to leave. She couldn't be there to take the brunt.

'I won't give you up.' He was stubborn, murmuring the words. It was as if he knew the power of his voice over her; the deep, gentle tone that would caress her into staying. 'Laura, if you leave me, what will I do?'

'I'm not leaving you, it just can't be the same.' These black and white choices made no sense yet they were what people lived by. 'I'll still be around.'

'Don't tell me you'll still be my friend.'

She took another quick step backwards and looked at him without speaking.

'I'm sorry. I just don't think I can switch from one thing to another. I can't make you mean less to me.'

Pulled in different directions, Laura began to shake with tension.

'And I can't watch you be with someone else.' He hung his head. 'It's Luke Altham, that's who we're talking about here.'

She couldn't deny it. If there was one simple reason, it was Luke.

He watched her nod, stared at her for a few moments longer and then turned away.

Laura raised her hand to comfort him, then let it drop. She left the room, walked out of the house and down the wide steps to her car. She didn't look round as she drove away, not wanting to know if Matthew had tried to follow her, certain in her own mind that they'd made the painful final break, one heart from another, to spend the rest of their lives apart.